ORIGINAL SECRETS

A Whispering Pines Mystery, Book Three

Shawn McGuire

D1522696

OTHER BOOKS BY SHAWN MCGUIRE

WHISPERING PINES mystery series
Missing & Gone, prequel short story
Family Secrets, book 1
Kept Secrets, book 2
Original Secrets, book 3
Hidden Secrets, book 4

Gemi Kittredge mysteries
One of Her Own
Out of Her League
Over Her Head

THE WISH MAKERS fantasy series
Sticks and Stones, book 1
Break My Bones, book 2
Never Hurt Me, book 3
Had a Great Fall, book 4
Back Together Again, book 5

Short Stories
The Door
Escaping the Veil

ORIGINAL SECRETS
A Whispering Pines Mystery, Book Three

Shawn McGuire

Brown Bag Books

Copyright © 2018 Shawn McGuire
Published by Brown Bag Books
ISBN-13: 978-1987706208
ISBN-10: 198770620X

For information visit:
www.Shawn-McGuire.com

Cover Design by Steven Novak
www.novakillustration.com

First Edition/First Printing April 2018

For everyone different enough to belong.

Chapter 1

MEEKA SAT AND WATCHED ME, HER head cocked curiously, as I sat on the edge of the pier and placed my feet into the well of the kayak. The last thing I wanted to do was to have to haul myself back out of the boat after managing to get into it, so before making another move, I went through the mental checklist in my head: *Dry bag with cargo shorts, T-shirt, and uniform shirt, check. Hiking shoes and socks, check. Keys for the station, check. Notebook and pencil, small flashlight, pepper spray, handcuffs with keys, check. Holster with Glock, check.*

Funny, if someone didn't know I was

the sheriff, they'd wonder what exactly I was planning to do with all that.

"Okay. I think I've got it all," I told my dog. "If I forgot anything, you get to come back for it."

She yawned and turned away, my threats having no impact on her.

Using my feet, I held the orange and yellow kayak tight against the piling then lowered myself down onto the seat with shaking arms. I really needed to get back to doing the upper body workouts I used to do, pushups and triceps dips in particular. My heart raced, sure the boat would tip as soon as I released my white-knuckled grip on the edge of the pier. This fear was not unfounded; it had happened before. Three times. Today, no problem. I was securely on the seat, my feet resting comfortably on the foot pegs. Cheers went off in my head for the accomplishment. Then I realized I'd forgotten one item not on my sheriff list.

"Meeka, can you push the paddle over to me?"

The little West Highland White Terrier looked from my pointing finger to the double-bladed paddle sitting about six inches out of my reach. She snorted, a mocking sound that said she wondered just what she had done to deserve me as her owner. Using her nose, she pushed the paddle one inch, and then another inch, then looked at me and wagged her tail as though expecting a reward.

"Good, girl. Keep going." I stretched my arm and wiggled my fingers. "I can't reach it yet."

She repeated the process until I could finally hook my fingertips around the shaft.

"Success! I knew we could do it. What a team."

"Jayne, you could've called for help."

I spun to look over my right shoulder, causing the kayak to tip precariously to the left. Friend, business partner, and man hoping for more than friendship, Tripp Bennett was standing thirty feet away with his arms crossed over his lean, muscular chest.

"How long have you been there?" I asked.

"Here?" He pointed at the ground near

his feet. "A few seconds. I did, however, enjoy the entire show from the far side of the boathouse."

"You were spying on me?"

"I wouldn't call it spying. More like ensuring your safety in case you tipped. Again."

"I do have on a life jacket." I hooked my right thumb into the armhole of my yellow vest.

"That's true," Tripp said. "Then maybe I was spying. Either way, you got into the boat with far fewer gymnastics today. Good job. Anything else you need while I'm here and able to help?

He was such a brat. "Nope. We're good to go."

"Is this really how you're planning to get to work today?"

"We live in northern Wisconsin. We have to take advantage of the warm weather while it's here. I figure in about six months, I'll be able to cross-country ski across the bay and through the village to the station." I reconsidered this. "Maybe snowshoe. I don't know how to ski cross-country. Or downhill for that matter."

He shook his head, amused by my babbling. "You do realize that when you're able to cross-country ski or snowshoe it will most likely be below zero? A balmy twenty-something if you're lucky."

"What's your point?"

"I've seen you turn on the deck heater when the temperature drops below seventy at night."

He knew me too well. "Shouldn't you be getting to work?"

"Yep. The crew will be here any minute. So unless you want to have an even bigger audience . . ."

I signaled for Meeka to get into the kayak. Cautiously, she stepped her front paws on to my left leg, crossed one and then the other over to my right leg, and then stepped down with her back paws. Once she had settled herself into the well between my legs, Tripp came over and gave us a gentle push away from the pier.

"Have a good day at work." He flipped his shoulder-length blonde curls out of his face. "I hope it's slow and boring."

I started paddling and once I had my rhythm down, Meeka stood on her back legs, front paws braced on the side of the kayak, and tried to catch the drops of water that came off the paddle.

Mornings on the lake were the perfect way to start the day. Sometimes that meant simply standing on the sundeck with a cup of coffee, watching the early-riser fishermen trying to catch their limit before the tourists hit the water with their speedboats, jet skis, and wakeboards. Other times, like today, it meant going for a paddle.

The thumb of land holding my house, garage, and boathouse jutted out into the lake and formed a circular bay between it and the village. Directly across the bay from my pier, the marina marked the entrance to the village commons from the lake. The three- or four-hundred-yard trip was easy. One I could make in a few minutes, but I wasn't quite ready to head to work yet. Meeka looked at me, confused, as I headed south instead of east.

"We have time," I told her. "Let's go

for a little ride first."

She wagged her tail and pranced her paws, happy for this side trip.

In the distance, one of the half-dozen or so fishermen was just heading in. Normally, the old guy, who reminded me of my grandfather with his white goatee, would have gone in a half hour ago.

"You're usually in by now," I called out to him. "Did you catch anything?"

"Perfect morning on the water," he called back. "Hit my limit fifteen minutes ago. Just been sitting out here enjoying the peace."

"Good plan. It's supposed to get humid again today."

"No doubt. We just can't catch a break from it this summer. Have a good day, Sheriff." He gave me a salute and headed into shore.

A second or two later, gentle waves from his outboard motor rocked the kayak, exciting Meeka enough that she hung her head over the side of the boat and snapped at the waves. I knew what was coming next.

"Don't do it," I cautioned. "You're

going to smell like wet dog all day."

I had no sooner said the words than she dove in and dog-paddled around the kayak in big, lazy circles.

We went another fifty yards or so away from the village, following the shoreline into a little cove, when I heard someone calling for help.

"Where are you?" I shouted while scanning the water's surface left and right. "I hear you. I can't see you."

"Here!" He made big splashes in the water. "Help me!"

Meeka swam ahead, looked back, and barked, alerting me to the proper direction.

"Meeka, come." I didn't want her near the struggling man. He'd likely grab onto anything that came close to him, and I didn't want that something to be my dog.

She paddled over to me, staying next to the boat on my left. The man splashed and called out again, sounding more frantic. He was struggling in a cluster of water weeds not far from us. I grabbed onto Meeka's harness, hauled her into the kayak, and set her down in the well between my legs.

"Meeka, down," I ordered. She immediately dropped to her belly. "Stay. No moving. The boat might get a little tippy."

She froze, as though she were a little Westie statue. Good girl.

Getting close enough to offer the man comfort, but far enough away that he couldn't grab the boat, I took off my life jacket. "Can you hear me?"

"Help me!"

"I'm going to throw my life jacket to you."

"Throw it already."

The jacket landed two feet in front of him, too far for him to reach easily, so I got closer and pushed it with the paddle.

"It's right in front of you. Reach out. Hug it to your chest and try to catch your breath."

His head went underwater before he got a good grip on the jacket, and I was afraid he wasn't going to come back up. Finally, he wrapped both arms around the life preserver, leaned back in the water, and gasped for breath.

"Are you okay?" I asked.

"I'm stuck. My legs are tangled in the weeds. I'm okay right now, but I can't get out."

"I have some rope in the cargo area. I'm going to toss it out to you and tow you out with the kayak. Do you understand me?"

"I understand." He sounded much calmer now, nowhere near as panicked, but dangerously tired.

Using slow, cautious motions, I turned and unhooked the bungee straps keeping the lid on the kayak's cargo well. There was a small emergency pack in there, one that either Gran or Gramps had added long ago. I retrieved the small skein of paracord from the pack, dropped the little bag back into the cargo area, and reattached the lid. Then, I secured one end of the cord to the handle of the cargo lid and turned back to find that the man had managed to put on the life jacket. He was still breathing hard, but at least he was bobbing in the water now. Good, this just got significantly easier.

I tossed the free end of the paracord

out to the man. "Wrap this around your wrist a couple of times. Make sure you've got a good grip so it doesn't slip out of your hands."

Floating on his back, he wrapped the cord around his right wrist two or three times and then around his palm twice more. He clutched the rope tightly in his fist and gave me a thumbs up.

"Okay," I said, "now relax and let me do the work. I'm going to start paddling slowly at first. Hopefully that will pull you free from the weeds. Don't kick your feet, if you feel like the weeds are tightening around your legs, tell me and I'll paddle harder. Just don't kick. You'll only get wrapped up even more. Ready?"

"Ready."

Using firm but slow strokes, I aimed for the middle of the lake. Weeds grew in the shallower spots all around the lake, where the water was warmer. Once we'd gotten out of the cove and away from these weeds, I'd tow him to the marina. Gil, the marina owner, hired a crew to go through the bay every day and clear away the weeds to ensure that they didn't get wound up in boat propellers.

After a minute of paddling, the man called out to me that his legs were free.

"See that pontoon in the distance?" He pointed past me to a spot on the lake near the public swimming area.

"I see it."

"Those are my friends. Would you drag me over to them?"

Questions immediately filled my head. These people were his friends? Did they know he had swum so far away from them? If they did, were any of them looking for him? If they weren't, what kind of friends were they?

It took another two minutes of steady paddling to get to the pontoon. When we were thirty or forty yards away, one of the women on board spotted us.

"Barry?" she called out. "Oh, thank God."

The other eight or ten people on board the pontoon gathered near the woman and looked our direction as well, shouting and waving.

I came to a stop at the stern and hung onto the pontoon's swimming platform to help keep the kayak steady. One of the men pulled Barry onto the platform and unwound the paracord from his hand. The exhausted man lay on his back, his chest heaving, his arms limp at his side. I gave him a minute to catch his breath and then called out to him.

"Barry?"

He sat up, and I pointed at the life jacket.

"Oh, yeah, you probably want this back." He sat with his legs dangling in the water, unzipped the jacket, and handed it to me.

Feeling instantly better to have the jacket on again, I asked if he was all right.

"I will be now. I can't thank you enough. You saved my life. I couldn't get out of those weeds. The more I struggled, the tighter they wrapped around my legs. If you hadn't come when you did, I would've drowned for sure."

A few bits of black slimy-looking weeds stuck to his legs and just that fast, I recalled a vision that Lily Grace, the village's youngest fortune teller, had a few weeks earlier. She claimed to see "a lady in the water with black stuff on her." Obviously, Barry wasn't a lady, but he did have black stuff on him. Lily Grace's visions were spot on, even if the details weren't exactly accurate. Perhaps this was the event she had seen.

"I'm glad I was there for you, Barry. Are you sure you're okay?"

He coughed and nodded his head. "Swallowed some water, and I'm a little winded, but I think I'll be okay."

"Whispering Pines has a clinic of sorts," I told him. "It's called the healing center. Straight across from the public beach is the library. You'll find the entrance for the Fairy Path right in front of the building. There are plenty of signs along the path that will lead you to the center."

"I'm okay," Barry repeated. "Thanks, though."

I motioned for him to lean closer to me. "You came with these people?"

"Yeah, we rented two of the cottages for six weeks. Everyone's been here off and on since the middle of June." He pointed north across the lake to the area where the guest cottages were scattered throughout the woods. "This is the first weekend we've all been here together."

"Did they know you went out swimming?" I asked.

"We've been out all night. Partying on the party barge, so to speak. We were getting ready to head in and get some sleep, when Angel decided we should have a swimming contest."

"A swimming contest?" After being awake all night and probably still somewhat inebriated?

"I'm not saying it was a good idea, but that's what we decided to do. We were to swim to that point, the one just before the cove where you found me, and back to the pontoon. Three of us went out at the same time. I wasn't paying attention to how far I'd gone." He gave a sheepish shrug. "I wanted to win and just focused on swimming fast. When I turned to go back, I realized I'd gone too far. That's when I got tangled up in those weeds."

"You're telling me that three of you went out, two returned, and no one came to look for you?"

His face paled at that revelation. "I hadn't been gone that long." He looked away from me. "I know what you're thinking, and you're wrong. They wouldn't have let anything happen to me."

"But they did let something happen to you. You said that if I wouldn't have been there, you would have drowned."

Uncomfortable with my accusation, Barry pulled his legs out of the water and prepared to join his friends.

I held my hand out to him. "I'm Sheriff Jayne O'Shea. I'm glad you're safe and sound. If there's anything else I can do for you, come to the station."

He hesitated before nodding his agreement and shaking my hand and wholeheartedly thanked me again for saving his life.

As we paddled toward the marina, I couldn't help but wonder again if there was some kind of ill will between Barry and his supposed friends. Why the sudden need to race? From where the pontoon was anchored, there was no way they could have seen him in that cove.

Had they even tried to look for him?

As I closed in on the shore, I made a mental note to find out which cottages Barry and his friends were staying in and go check on him before going home tonight. Then I told myself to stop being so suspicious of everyone. Not every accident was an attempted murder.

Chapter 2

THE WHISPERING PINES MARINA had four piers, each with five or six boat slips per side. Larger boats could moor in the bay and one of the marina employees would motor out and bring the passengers ashore. The piers were too tall for someone in a kayak, so I aimed for the small beach area near the cottage that served as the marina's office. When I was about ten feet from the shore, a tall and lean teenage boy came out to greet me.

"Good morning, Sheriff."

"Good morning, Oren. I swear, that hair of yours gets bigger every time I see you."

He laughed and patted the Afro that was easily twice the size of his head. "We've been so busy this summer, I haven't had time to get a haircut. It's driving Lily Grace crazy. She keeps threatening to bring over a pair of clippers and shave it all off right here on the beach."

I frowned and shook my head. "Don't let her do that. I kind of like the 'fro."

Oren stepped into the water, took hold of the front of my kayak, and pulled us onto the rough sand. As soon as we were on land, Meeka leapt out of the boat and back into the water.

"You heading to work?" Oren shook his head when I said I was, his hair bouncing in the opposite direction of each shake. "You're gonna be smelling wet dog all day."

He took a wide stance and held out his arm to help me stand. Like a little girl hanging on her father's strong arm, I pulled myself up.

"Tell me about it." I sighed, watching Meeka snapping at the foam on the little whitecaps floating past her. "Can you keep an eye on my kayak for me today?"

"Sure. I'll put it on the rack inside. Otherwise, someone might assume it's available for rent."

"Perfect. Give me a minute before you take it, I need to change clothes."

I unlatched the cover of the cargo well, took a minute to rewind and return the paracord I used to tow Barry, then pulled out my dry bag and whistled for Meeka. She took four or five steps onto the beach and shook wildly, spraying water everywhere. She trotted over to me, and I removed her harness so both she and it could dry. The moment she was free of it, she shook again, this time spraying Oren and me.

"Sorry. I should've known she'd do that."

"No worries." Oren pointed at his soggy and now sand-covered feet. "I spend half the day wet anyway."

On one side of the building were two changing huts, too small for me to stretch my arms out wide but big enough to change in. I stepped inside one of them to take off my athletic shorts and tank top and put on my uniform. A couple weeks ago, I got a box from my mother that was filled with beauty supplies from her salon in Madison. Honestly, I couldn't care less about the beauty supplies, but she insisted on sending them. What I did care about were my tactical cargo pants and shorts that were also in the box.

The roomy, pocket-covered shorts were much more comfortable and practical than jeans. The best thing was, I could carry everything I needed for the day in the pockets. A loaded Sam Browne belt weighed in at ten pounds or more. It got heavy and was always in my way and my arms got chafed within ten seconds of putting it on. One of the best things about moving from patrol officer to detective when I worked for the Madison Police Department was not having to wear that belt. Now, the only thing strapped to my body was a shoulder holster with my station issued 9mm Glock on my left side and a pouch big enough for two extra magazines on my right. I only carried one extra magazine and even that seemed excessive in Whispering Pines.

"All set," I told Oren as I placed the dry bag and my water shoes back into the cargo well of the kayak next to the life jacket.

"We're open until seven," Oren reminded me. "Do you think you'll be back by then? If not, I'll give you the combo for the lock."

"I'd love to say that I'll be back by seven, but I should plan ahead. I wouldn't want to bother you or your dad. What's the combination?"

Oren showed me how to operate the high-tech keypad lock on the cottage door. "We change the combo every day, so if you don't pick up your ride tonight, it'll be different tomorrow."

I jotted down the combination in the notetaking app on my phone and thanked him for the help. "Hopefully we'll both have non-crazy days and will see each other again well before seven."

From the marina, Meeka and I headed northwest toward the village commons. The quaint, part Renaissance, part medieval England village had a quiet, sleepy feel to it this morning. At this time of day, there were primarily older couples and the occasional toddler leading a parent in a game of chase around the pentacle garden. The garden, as the name implied, was shaped like a giant pentacle, encompassing the equivalent of a standard city block. Pea gravel pathways made up the lines of the pentacle while dozens of varieties of flowers and plants, herbs and vegetables filled the triangular sections. At the very center was a gleaming white marble well, which the villagers called the negativity well. Instead of wishes, you threw in negative thoughts and feelings in the hopes they would leave you alone.

"Good morning, Sheriff," a grandfatherly man greeted, his voice shaking with age. "We going to have a good day?"

An innocent question, but his tone implied he was hoping for something more . . . exciting. Word had spread that the quirky little Wiccan village of Whispering Pines, Wisconsin, had murderers running around the woods. As far as I knew, that wasn't true, but a trickle of thrill seekers had made the pilgrimage to the Northwoods in hopes of being able to "help" or simply be here for the excitement.

"Isn't it always a good day here?" I joked, dismissing his vigilante dreams.

"Meh. We'll be here for another day or two." He indicated the woman next to him. Wife? Sister? Fellow ambulance chaser?

What, were they expecting I'd stage a murder for them to solve if a body didn't show up soon? Actually, murder mystery dinner theater type events at the B&B might be something fun for Tripp and I to plan.

Meeka and I wished the couple a good day and continued our trek around the garden, greeting shopkeepers who were getting ready for the crowds. Without even having to lead her, Meeka headed straight toward Ye Olde Bean Grinder, the village coffee shop. Inside, we found that all the café tables and each of the four cozy lounge chairs surrounding the unlit stone fireplace were full.

"Looks like people are getting their fill

of hot drinks while the weather is still cool," I told Basil, the man behind the counter.

"Iced beverages will be in demand in a couple hours." Basil had been focused on a sleeve of paper cups and looked at me then. His face lit up with a cheerful smile. "Ah, good morning, Sheriff. Your regular today?"

"Yes, please."

"Jayne's here?" a woman's voice floated out of the back room. Five-foot-tall Violet, the shop owner, appeared and made a beeline to my side. She took my hand, pulled me down so my ear was close to her mouth, and said, "What happened at the lake?"

How did she know these things? Both Violet and Basil were green witches, meaning they had special skills with plants. In Violet's case, her plant of choice was coffee. The woman could blend beans like no one else on the planet. As talented as the violet-eyed woman was with her witchy ways, she seemed to be part psychic as well. If you believed in that sort of thing. Which I didn't.

"Everything's fine." I looked pointedly at the customers in the sitting area. Another death or near-death of any kind wasn't what the village needed right now. "A man was struggling in a weedy patch, but I was able to help him. He's okay."

"Thank the Goddess." Violet sniffed, made a face, and looked down at Meeka. "Someone's been swimming in the lake this morning, hasn't she?"

"Sorry, I forgot. Meeka, outside." I pointed to the open door and the little Westie slunk away. "I told you not to swim, didn't I?" I turned back to Violet, expecting her to grill me more about what had happened with Barry, but she had slipped away to clean off the tables and collect empty mugs.

"Extra-large mocha, double-pump vanilla, and extra whip," Basil called.

As always, along with my drink, a small waxed paper bag filled with biscuits for Meeka waited for me at the counter. Good thing she was such a hyper little dog or she'd weigh fifty pounds by now. Every shop we went to had biscuits for her.

"Thanks, Basil. I'll see you later."

Looking like a traditional Bavarian beer girl, but holding coffee cups instead of steins, Violet scooted past me with four mugs in each hand and a towel over her arm. "Have a great day, Sheriff."

Out on the shop's front porch, I found Meeka sitting facing the corner. Apparently, she had put herself in timeout.

I knelt down next to her and offered her a biscuit. "I'm sorry you had to come outside, but nobody wants to smell wet dog, especially when they're eating or drinking."

She licked my hand before taking the biscuit, and we continued along the red brick pathway around the pentacle garden.

Outside Shoppe Mystique, the little cottage next door, a woman dressed in a short black A-line tank dress and strappy black platform sandals was tending the mass of flowers overflowing the pots on the porch. No one in the village had flowers like Morgan Barlow.

"Blessed be, Jayne." It took half a

second for her to add, "What's the matter? What happened?"

Morgan was not only the most powerful green witch in Whispering Pines, rumor had it she was the most powerful in the entire Midwest. Possibly in all of North America. Probably the world.

She had quickly become my best friend. I met her the day after arriving in the village. Well, technically, that was the day I re-met her. My sister Rosalyn and I met Morgan when we were little girls, here visiting Gran and Gramps. Every time we came into the village, we found Morgan in the pentacle garden, talking to the plants. Or maybe she was talking to the fairies that she claimed lived among the plants. At the time, we thought she was a weird little girl. Honestly, when I re-met her two months ago, my first thought was that she was a weird woman. Now, she was like a sister. Better even. Rosalyn was a pain in my backside.

In answer to her question, I told her what had happened with Barry.

She descended the porch stairs and

came to my side. "Is he all right?"

I nodded. "If I would've come straight to the village—"

"But you didn't, thank the Goddess. The universe guides us sometimes, and it seems that this morning you were listening. You saved his life?"

"I did. He would have drowned otherwise."

She wrapped me in a hug and scratched her long matte-black nails over my back. The sensation was comforting and reminded me of when I was little, and Rosalyn and I would take turns scratching each other's backs before going to sleep at night. I guess Rozzie hadn't always been a pain.

Once Morgan released me, I said, "I stopped by for a reason other than to say hi. Would you happen to have anything to wash a smelly dog with?" I looked down at the guilty terrier. "Someone decided to swim into work today. She's going to stink up the station if I don't do something about it."

"One moment, I have just the thing."

A few minutes later, we met Morgan

behind the shop where she handed me a small apothecary bottle filled with purple liquid.

"Let me guess, it's your own special blend?"

"Indeed, it is," she confirmed. "A combination of castile soap, coconut oil, and lavender and lemongrass essential oils. Not only will your pup be squeaky clean and moisturized, the lemongrass will keep fleas away while the lavender relaxes her."

I cast a skeptical look at her. "Relax her? You have met Meeka, right?"

I handed Morgan my mocha and Meeka's treat bag in exchange for the bottle of doggie shampoo.

"You may want to stand back," I cautioned. "She gets water everywhere, and I don't think you want to start out your day soggy. With as humid as it's been, you'll be lucky to dry by quitting time."

Morgan smiled down at Meeka. "You won't splash me, will you?"

Meeka gave a small, agreeable *ruff* and moved to a patch of grass ten feet away.

"What, did you put some kind of hex on her?"

"I would never put a hex on an animal." Morgan winked while taking a sip of my coffee.

A few minutes later, my squeaky clean, fresh smelling dog and I said goodbye to Morgan and followed the Fairy Path until it came to a Y with the sheriff's station straight ahead. Inside, I went right to work while Meeka crawled beneath a cot bolted to the wall in one of the two holding cells. She liked curling up in the corner on the cool concrete. In a few months, when the winter winds blew through, she'd surely change her mind. I'd have to bring in a doggie cushion for her.

Telephone interviews with potential deputy candidates kept me busy all morning. Unfortunately, none of them were going to work out. One was far too military and wouldn't be a good fit for laid-back Whispering Pines. One was interested in the position, but only if I provided housing and nearly double the salary I was willing to pay. The third would have been a perfect fit, but her husband wasn't interested in moving somewhere so remote. They also had little kids so Whispering Pines' ever-growing reputation as being a hotspot for murderers didn't help.

At the end of my list with no prospects, I picked up the phone and dialed the number for my former captain at the Madison PD.

"Sheriff O'Shea," Captain Russ Grier said in lieu of a more formal greeting. "Did you get the list I sent you?"

"That's why I'm calling, sir. I spoke with four of them yesterday and three this morning and none of them will work. Well, one of them would be perfect, but she declined for family reasons."

"This surprises you? You're up there in the middle of nowhere, Jayne. How long has it been since you experienced a Northwoods winter?"

I had to laugh at that. "Never. My family only came in the summer."

"Think there might be a reason for that?"

He was right. Gran used to tell me

about the howling winds and bone-chilling below-zero temperatures. Guess it did take an especially hardy constitution to live here. Tripp and I were already contemplating flannel sheets and electric blankets on every bed in the B&B. Honestly, though, I was excited for the experience.

"There's one guy I talked to two days ago. He was promising, but I haven't heard back from him. I'm assuming he's a no. That means I'm out of candidates. Do you have anyone else I could talk to?"

We spent the next ten or fifteen minutes discussing not only a few people from his current crew but also a few trainees that could be ready for assignment in a month or two. That was too long.

Shortly after I had agreed to take on the responsibilities of sheriff of Whispering Pines, my mother informed Tripp and I that we could go ahead with our plans to open Pine Time, our bed-and-breakfast. Tripp was skeptical about me being able to pull off both sheriff and B&B responsibilities, even though I insisted I'd be fine. Of course, I'd been counting on a deputy's assistance. I survived my first three weeks in office, but that meant putting in twelve hours during the day to keep the station staffed and then being on call at night. Fortunately, the tourists had been behaving themselves for the most part, but I didn't have much time to dedicate to the house renovations. I couldn't keep up this pace for long, I needed somebody in the deputy position sooner than later.

"Tell you what," Captain Grier said, "I'll expand my search. I've got some contacts over in Milwaukee. I'll see if they have anyone who might be interested in reassignment."

My hopes sunk. What I'd likely end up doing was lowering my standards to get someone in the position. Something I had passionately criticized former Sheriff Karl Brighton for doing. Lesson learned. Until having worked someone's job, criticism, constructive or otherwise, couldn't be offered.

The man on duty when I first got here, Martin Reed, had been a subpar deputy.

He had the desire, but nowhere near the skill. His mother, Flavia, told me every chance she got that he was ready to come back to work. At least with him I wouldn't have to give a tour of the station.

"Let me know if you come up with anyone, Captain, but I have an idea. Thanks again for your help."

I was debating the positives and negatives of bringing Reed back on staff when a woman burst through the station's front door.

"Are you the Sheriff? I need help."

I studied the woman for a second; she looked familiar. *Five foot four, short dark-blonde ponytail, squared shoulders.*

"I recognize you. You were on the pontoon, right? What's going on?

"It's Barry. You remember Barry? You saved him this morning? He's dead."

Chapter 3

THE WOMAN LOOKED AT ME LIKE I was insane when I asked how she knew that Barry really was dead. A seemingly unnecessary question, but when I left the pontoon this morning, everyone on it seemed to be either still inebriated or heavily hungover from the partying they'd done all night. Before I called the medical examiner to drive an hour to look at another body in Whispering Pines, I wanted to be sure that Barry wasn't simply passed out.

"I was the designated driver," she explained. "Since it was my responsibility to drive the boat, I had one hard cider at the beginning of the night and nothing but iced tea or Mountain Dew after that. I'm not drunk now and wasn't at any time during the night." She shrugged. "You get to watch the show and learn things when you're the sober one."

Very true. "What's your name?"

"Lori Ashley."

"I'm sure you can understand why I might assume otherwise, Ms. Ashley." I capped my gel pen and shut off my desk lamp, preparing to leave the station. Whatever had happened to Barry, I was going to have to go check it out.

"I understand," Lori assured, "but I checked Barry myself. I was a nursing student for two semesters." She shivered as an apparent memory struck her. "Body fluids are way more disgusting than I thought they'd be. Anyway, I know how to check vitals. I didn't feel a pulse, and he wasn't breathing. I figured that was a pretty good indication. And there's his eyes."

"What's wrong with his eyes?"

"They're stuck half open." She placed her index fingers to her eyelids and dragged them downward, manually closing them.

"Some people sleep that way, with their eyes partially open," I informed. "It's a condition called *nocturnal lagophthalmos.*"

She looked at me like I was a freak. "How do you know that?"

"Because one night when I was on patrol, a woman called 9-1-1 hysterical, convinced her boyfriend was dead in bed. I responded to the call. Turned out they'd only been dating a few weeks, so this was the first time she'd witnessed his odd way of sleeping."

Lori blinked.

"So, you couldn't get a pulse on Barry. Did you do CPR?"

"I did. Never dreamt I'd need to put that skill to use in everyday life." She stared into the distance for a moment. "I'm going to renew my certification when I get home."

"All right. Give me a minute to call the medical examiner."

I couldn't wrap my head around the fact that there was another death in the village. I'd been in Whispering Pines for almost two months and in that time three people had been murdered, one had killed himself in front of me, and now Barry. It was little wonder the village had developed such a dark reputation.

There were also the circumstances around my grandmother's death. No matter how many ways Tripp and I had tried to piece together the details of how she died, according to the letter my family had received from the sheriff, we couldn't make it fit. The only way I'd be able to figure out the truth was from her autopsy report, which was missing from her police file. I'd ordered a replacement, but who knew when that would arrive.

"To Whispering Pines again?" Dr. Bundy's assistant asked. "Are you serious?"

My thoughts exactly. "I'm serious. We have another dead body. I haven't investigated yet; I'm on my way to the scene now. I don't know what the situation is, but the witness says he's not breathing. She performed CPR and couldn't get a pulse."

"Sounds like a stiff."

I turned to Lori. "You guys are staying over at the rental cottages? That's where Barry is?"

She confirmed the location, which I passed on to the woman on the phone.

"Okie dokie, Sheriff, I'll tell Dr. B to get over there."

I whistled for Meeka, who crawled halfway out of her napping spot.

"Come on. We've got a scene to check out."

She didn't move.

"Meeka, working."

The command put her into K-9 mode and she sprang out of her hidey hole and made it to the back door before I did.

That's when I realized the problem with kayaking to work. I had no vehicle. I dug through my desk to find the extra set of keys for the station's van parked in the small lot behind the building. It had never occurred to me that I would need to use the vehicle, so I had no idea what was inside. It should have everything I'd need for an investigation, but I'd have to take a full inventory sooner than later.

The inside of the old Chevy cargo van, with "Whispering Pines Sheriff" in big bold black-and-gold letters on the side, smelled a lot like the prior deputy. My nose was assaulted by the combination of body odor, motor oil, and the salty-sweet aroma of trail mix. I'd never seen the man without a bag of the stuff. Meeka refused to get in until I opened the passenger's side window to let in fresh air.

Once we were situated, I called to Lori as she backed her older model Explorer out of the lot. "Okay, lead the way."

The southeast section of Whispering Pines' two thousand acres held a cluster of rental cottages. I'd been past the spot numerous times on my way to Sundry, the general store, but I'd never gone into the area. Lori led me to the very farthest end of the grounds, to the point where the narrow gravel drive started to circle back toward the entrance. There, I found two small A-frame cottages, one close to the road, the other set back behind it.

"We're renting both of these cottages," she explained.

"Barry mentioned that. How many of

you are there?"

"Twelve."

"How many bedrooms per cottage?"

She looked away and quietly said, "Two in the first. Two plus a sleeping loft in the other."

"What's the maximum capacity per cottage?"

She didn't answer that question. They were way over capacity, but that wasn't what I was here for.

In the back of the van, I was happy to find a camera case. The batteries in the 35mm camera were dead, but there were extras in the case. I could use my cell phone to take pictures, but then I risked my phone getting confiscated for the evidence inside it, so I only used it in an emergency.

"Which one is Barry in?" Taking the camera bag and the well-stocked investigation kit, I followed Lori to the cottage at the back, Meeka at my side.

This second structure was slightly bigger than the one closer to the drive, so I assumed it must be the one with the sleeping loft. And if things went the way they normally did in situations like this, Barry's body would be up in that loft.

Lori opened the front door and stepped aside so I could enter first. There, I found ten people—seven men and three women, all in their mid- to late-twenties—gathered in a living area big enough to hold only a loveseat, a lounge chair, and a small round kitchen table with four dining chairs. Half of the people were crying; the other half wore shocked expressions. As soon as they saw me, everyone pointed upstairs.

"Barry is up in the loft," Lori said.

I knew it. "Have any of you been up there?"

"I was," Lori said. "Like I told you, I tried CPR on him. Rochelle and Blake went up there, too."

Two people, presumably Rochelle and Blake, stood.

"Did either of you touch anything up there?" I asked as I slid a pair of latex gloves out of one of my cargo pockets and snapped them on. "Anything at all?"

"There are two twin size beds up there," reported Blake, a pale blonde guy who looked like he spent too much time watching Netflix or playing video games. "Barry was using one of them, I took the other. So yeah, I touched a lot of stuff up there."

"I only touched the ladder to climb up," said Rochelle, an average sized redhead, hair twisted into a bun that wobbled precariously on top of her head. "And Barry's shoulder. I was the first one up there. I went up to check on him and tried to shake him awake. I got Lori, because she's the only one of us who knows CPR." She covered her face with her hands for a second. "I can't believe he's dead."

I scanned the group as the three spoke, watching body language for both appropriate and inappropriate reactions. The only one that stood out to me was a dark-haired stocky guy sitting alone at the kitchen table. He looked angry; an uncommon initial reaction to a death. Normally, I saw shock and tears. Disbelief. Sometimes hysteria. But not anger.

"How did this happen?" one of them

asked.

"I'll do my best to figure that out," I promised. "Right now, I'm going to investigate the area. I want to talk to all of you later, so stay here. As in, stay in the area. I need you all to leave the cottage so nothing else gets disturbed. Lori, Rochelle, and Blake, I'll want to talk with you three first."

The other eight people stood, popping up randomly like the critters in a Whac-A-Mole game, and left the small cottage in silence. Lori, Rochelle, and Blake were ready to start telling me their versions of the events, and I held up a hand.

"Not yet. I want to see the scene upstairs first without any prior knowledge. When I'm done, we'll talk. Why don't you three wait for me right out front?"

I was about to tell them not to talk with each other about what had happened, but if the group was going to create a story, they would have done that before Lori came to get me.

A trained cadaver dog, Meeka had indicated that she scented a corpse in the loft the moment we entered the cottage. Currently, she was standing at attention, her gaze locked on the loft.

"Good, girl," I told her with a scratch behind the ears. "At ease, partner. I've got it from here."

With the crime scene kit over one shoulder and the camera bag over my other, I climbed the simple wooden ladder to the small, steeply-peaked sleeping loft. From the top of the ladder, I immediately noticed the body on the bed, but before looking more closely at him, I took in the condition of the room. It looked and smelled like a typical guys' dorm room. Clothing was scattered all around, piles shoved under each bed. The empty bed was unmade with the white sheets crumpled in a heap at the foot. Pillows were scattered across the bed, one on the floor. Despite the lack of reception in Whispering Pines, cell phones were charging on the nightstand between the two beds.

I scanned from the right side of the room to the left as I stepped off the ladder onto the floor. Tucked between the bed with Barry's body and the nightstand was a violin case. Partially visible beneath the bed was what looked like a bicycle tire. Finally, my gaze came to a rest on the body. He had seemed familiar to me out on the pontoon, but I'd been more concerned about his safety at that time than to figure out why. Now I knew.

"You're the Speedo-wearing violin-playing unicyclist."

Chapter 4

THE SPEEDO-WEARING VIOLIN-playing unicyclist had become popular around the village as he followed the local nun on a bicycle. They were a strange pair, but they seemed to fit together, and everyone, tourists and villagers alike, would stop, watch, and wave as they went past. Did they know each other, or were they simply riding buddies?

Dark-haired Barry was lying on his back, and as Lori had reported, his partially opened eyes were staring up at the peaked ceiling. With gloved hands, I pressed my fingers to his carotid artery even though it was obvious there wouldn't be a pulse. There wasn't.

Other than to check for a pulse, I wasn't supposed to touch him, so I did a thorough visual search of his body. There were no signs of trauma, nothing out of the ordinary. Except . . .

I leaned in a little closer and saw what looked like fine white fibers around his nose and mouth. His skin had a slight blue tint, which told me that at some point he had suffered from a lack of oxygen.

The bed on the other side of the small room had three pillows—two at the head and one lying three-quarters of the way to the foot of the mattress. The pillow on the floor lay at the bed's foot. All of them had pillowcases that matched the white sheets. Had one of the pillows been used to suffocate him? Was that what the white fibers around his nose and mouth were? Bits of pillowcase?

Using a small penlight, I looked as closely as I could into his partially opened eyes. Suffocation often created petechial hemorrhaging, tiny dots of blood in the whites of the eye. His eyes weren't open wide enough for me to tell, but even if petechia was evident, it wasn't a guarantee of anything nefarious. Coughing could cause blood vessels to burst and create the dots.

I backed as far away as I could, to the top of the ladder, and tried to visualize events through Barry's perspective.

I'm exhausted from struggling to stay above water in the lake. It's taking all my remaining energy to climb this ladder and fall into my bed. I lay down . . .

And then what? An image of Lori at Barry's side filled my vision next.

I can't feel a pulse, and he's not breathing. I have to do CPR. First, I have to lay him flat . . .

At that point she would have tossed the pillows aside. That would explain why they were all on the other side of the room. My mind had immediately gone to murder, but I had no reason to believe that was true. The village's murder rate was making me paranoid. I had to stop creating a story and gather the facts to uncover the truth.

Since I couldn't do any more with the

body, Dr. Bundy would take care of Barry when he arrived, I did what I was able to do. I took pictures from every possible angle in the small space, including multiple shots of the body, and all the items in the room including those beneath both beds. Then, I climbed down the ladder, ready to interview witnesses. Meeka, surely bombarded by the smell of the body upstairs, was sitting in the fresh air of the open front doorway waiting for me.

"There's a violin and unicycle in the loft," I told the trio waiting for me outside. "Barry's the guy who's been riding around wearing the Speedo and following the nun, right?"

They laughed at this.

"Yeah, that was Barry," Lori offered with a fond smile. "He could be a goofball at times. Stuff like that was his way of blowing off stress."

"I first saw him a few weeks ago." I smiled with them, then got back to business. "This morning, he mentioned that you all have been coming and going for the last few weeks. Has he been up here all this time?"

"Pretty much," Lori confirmed.

"As long as the internet connection held," Blake said, "a few of us can work remotely. Barry could."

I jotted that in my notebook. "That's what caused his stress? His job?"

"He worked in finance. High stress." Blake paused, considering something. "He was so excited when he got the okay to work from here."

"How was he acting?" I asked. "After his trouble in the lake this morning, I mean."

"He seemed tired," Rochelle said, "which was understandable, I guess." She tapped her chest. "He had this cough, but otherwise he was okay."

"He did seem tired," Lori agreed, "but fine while we were out there, joking around with everyone and stuff. We stayed out on the pontoon for maybe another hour after you dropped him off."

"That's when he started getting crabby," Blake added. "The cough was bugging him, so we figured it was best to come in. I asked him if he wanted to go to that health place you mentioned."

"You mean the healing center?" I asked. "Did you feel he should go?"

"I didn't see any harm in just running over there," Blake said. "He kept insisting he was fine, though, and that he just wanted to take a nap."

"Is that what he did? Took a nap?"

"Yeah," Lori said. "He went right upstairs to bed when we got back."

I jotted more notes, calculating the approximate time they had returned here, and then asked, "Do any of you have any reason to believe that anyone from your group could have harmed him?

"Why would you ask that?" Lori wanted to know, angry at the accusation.

Blake and Rochelle glanced nervously at each other.

"Something you two want to tell me?" I asked the pair.

"It's probably nothing," Blake said. "Barry had this thing for Marissa."

"She's one of the women staying with you here?"

"Right," Blake said.

"Is there a problem with him having a

thing for Marissa?"

"Only because," Lori began, "Angel has been after her, too."

"Hang on." I thought back to my conversation with Barry. "Angel arranged the swimming race, right?"

The three agreed that he had.

"What's the issue with Angel?" I asked.

"Angel is a hothead," Rochelle said with her own fiery anger. "He and Barry are always going at it. They don't want to be in the same car with each other. Then they don't want Marissa to be in a car with the other guy. It's so juvenile."

"If we'd go somewhere as a group," Lori continued, seemingly as annoyed with the guys' behavior as Rochelle, "we'd have to take multiple cars to keep the two of them from killing each other." Her eyes went wide. "Wait, I didn't mean that literally." She objected more when I wrote this in my notebook. "I mean, sure, Angel has a temper, but he would never hurt anyone."

"How did Marissa feel about this attention?" I asked.

"She's sick of it." Rochelle shook her

head, disgusted, the wobbly bun on top popping loose in places. "She was kind of flattered at first, but it was getting stupid."

"Was Marissa interested in Barry?" I asked.

"No," Rochelle said. "Not Angel either."

"You sound pretty sure of that."

Rochelle and Lori exchanged a look.

I gestured between them with my pen. "What's that look for?"

Lori gave an encouraging nod.

"Marissa and I have been together for four months," Rochelle admitted.

She seemed confident in her relationship status, but that didn't mean Marissa wasn't playing around. Maybe she'd been more flattered by the guys' attention than Rochelle knew.

I turned to Blake. "Do you think Angel could have done something to Barry?"

"Doubt it," he said. "Angel and Barry have known each other for a long time. They just get into it sometimes. Arguing mostly, pushing each other's buttons. We did our best to keep them separated whenever the group was together."

"It wouldn't take long to sneak up there and do something." I pointed toward the upper floor of the cottage. "You're saying someone was at Angel's side every moment since you got back from the pontoon?"

None of them had a response for that.

"You resort to taking three cars," I said, "but there are only two cottages. Barry told me this is the first time the whole group has been together. How did you handle them up here? I assume they couldn't be in a cottage together, so one was in a cottage with Marissa. That had to cause problems."

"Yeah," Blake said, "that was a problem. Since this is the bigger cottage, it's been the four women in the two rooms downstairs, with me and Barry upstairs."

"Angel couldn't be very happy about that," I noted.

"That's an understatement," Rochelle muttered. "Honestly, I'm not sure Barry really even liked Marissa that much. I think it's just that he didn't want Angel around her."

I knew a guy in high school like that. He'd be really interested in going out with me if I was dating someone else. Soon as I was single, nothing.

"Interesting dynamic you all have going on here," I told the threesome. My nice way of saying that as a group, they were a disaster. A disaster waiting to happen? Had a death been inevitable? "The medical examiner will be here soon. Once he's doing his thing, I'm going to talk to everyone else. I might have more questions for you afterwards. In the meantime, I'll need your contact information in case I have follow-up questions."

While waiting for the ME, Meeka and I inspected the area around both cottages. The ground beneath all the pine trees was bare, which meant there was nothing for evidence to hide beneath. The rental office ground crew kept the area clear of debris. That was for both aesthetic and fire safety reasons. Dead pine needles could ignite in a flash from a blown campfire ember or carelessly discarded cigarette butt. We found nothing during our search, not that I expected we would, and were waiting by the Cherokee when Dr. Bundy and an ambulance pulled into the driveway.

"I'm starting to think I should move my office closer to Whispering Pines," Dr. Bundy said while tugging on a pair of gloves. "I'm here more than anywhere else."

"Just make sure to pad out your gasoline budget," I suggested.

"What have we got this time?"

I led him into the cottage and over to the ladder, explaining that the body was upstairs, and offering what information I had gathered.

"Climb a ladder. Great." He put his hand to his lower back and groaned. "Can I ask you to look away? You laughing at me would be a real blow to my ego."

"I need to interview a few more people while you're doing your thing anyway. Your ego is safe."

Inside the smaller of the two cabins, I found the other eight people quietly gathered in the living area. I pulled them outside one-by-one and asked them the same questions I asked Lori, Rochelle, and Blake. Their reports closely echoed what the first three had told me. Marissa, my second to last interviewee, corroborated Rochelle's claim that the two of them were together and that the guys had been driving her crazy.

Five foot one, pug nose, medium-brown skin, straightened dark-brown hair half twisted in a bun, half hanging past her shoulders.

"I never once said I was interested in either of them," Marissa insisted. "Barry was a nice guy, successful, fun to be around, but he wouldn't leave me alone. It was like an obsession of some kind. Angel can be super-sweet, but he also has a temper. The two of them kept poking at each other." She let out an exhausted exhale. "We were all super sick of the competition thing going on between them. Guess we won't have to worry about that anymore."

I purposely saved Angel for last. I stuck my head in to the cabin and called him outside.

Five foot four, bodybuilder physique, hair shaved to about a quarter inch, olive complexion, black-brown eyes.

"Tell me your full name and give me your contact information, please," I started.

"Angel Delgado." He gave me his address and phone number, but before I could ask anything else, he asked, "So, he's really dead?"

"Would that be a good thing or a bad thing if he is?"

This took him by surprise. "What's that supposed to mean?"

"I heard from your friends that you and Barry had issues with each other. Care to comment on that?"

"Guess that's a nice way to put it. He knew how much I wanted to go out with Marissa. He kept asking her out anyway, didn't matter how much I told him I liked her or how many other women he could have."

This supported what Lori, Rochelle, and Blake told me. "Barry was a ladies' man?"

"I guess. You saw him. He's like Mr.

Perfect. Stinking rich, good looking, party guy. Every girl he ever talked to wanted to go out with him."

"Except for Marissa. She told me she wasn't interested."

Angel smiled at that comment but didn't respond verbally.

"How long had you and Barry known each other?"

"We were roommates in college."

My turn to be surprised. "You guys were roommates even though you seemed to hate each other?"

"Didn't hate each other then. We only roomed together for two years. I dropped out after that. Not because of him. I got an opportunity to open a gym and jumped at it. Barry went on to get a degree in finance or whatever. Ended up making a ton of money in the stock market. Anyway, stuff started between us during our freshman year."

"What kind of stuff?"

"Like, he'd jump ahead of me in the cafeteria line and take the last piece of peanut butter pie even though he hated that pie and knew how much I liked it. Or he'd turn on a football game in our room, but never the teams I liked. And even though he hated football, he'd insist on watching the game just so I couldn't watch my team. Stupid stuff like that, you know?"

I got the feeling that Angel told this story to anyone who would listen. Probably even a few who weren't listening. Right now, he was making my job easy. All I had to do was stand there and take notes. Still, I couldn't help but ask, "That was just the first year?"

"Yeah."

"And you roomed with him again after all that?"

"I figured it was easier to deal with what I knew than to figure out someone else. I stopped telling him about what I liked. That way he didn't know what to go after. Then I screwed up."

"How did you screw up?"

Angel shook his head as though reliving whatever had happened. "There was this girl on the floor beneath us. Damn, she was hot. Really nice too. She and I had lunch together every day for like two weeks. One night I told Barry I was gonna ask her out. The next day she tells me that she's going to the movies with him that weekend."

It sounded like sibling scuffles, like Rosalyn *accidentally* deleting the television shows I recorded. Once was an accident. Five times? No.

"Sounds like you have a lot of anger toward Barry."

Angel shrugged a muscular shoulder. "I guess."

"Barry told me that he got off-track during the swimming race this morning. That race was your idea, right?"

His expression shifted from annoyed sibling to one I'd seen on determined athletes. Jaw set, arms stiff at his side, hands clenched.

"It was my idea."

"Why? You're the better athlete, right?"

"I'm way better, and he knew it."

"Then why challenge him?"

Angel looked off into the pine trees. "Because he was going after Marissa again. He wouldn't leave her alone."

"You wanted to take him down a notch. Best him at something before Mr. Perfect got his way again."

He considered this. "I guess."

"Did you know he'd swum too far?"

He laughed, a derisive little snort. "We were just supposed to go to the point and back. It was like, what, fifty yards? Maybe seventy-five. Wasn't my job to tell him to turn back. Not my fault if he can't follow directions."

"Nobody went to look for him? None of you were concerned when he didn't return with you and the other guy?"

"Look," Angel defended, "it hadn't been that long. We were getting ready to pull up anchor and go to look for him when Lori saw you coming."

"Angel, did you do something to Barry?"

It took a second for my full meaning to hit him. "He got stuck in those weeds. How could I make that happen?"

"I mean after you got back here."

"After we got back here?" His forehead wrinkled with confusion. "I wasn't anywhere near him. I wanted to stay out on the pontoon, but he wanted to come back and take a nap like a little baby. Dude shoulda worked out more, focused on his stamina. Everyone else felt bad for him, so we ditched the pontoon. He took a nap, I went for a walk to blow off steam."

His voice trailed off, as though the reality of everything was finally hitting him. Since I had no proof anything had been done to Barry, and I got no indication from Angel that he was lying, I ended the interview.

"How much longer do you expect to be here?" I asked.

"I don't know. We've got the cottages for another week or whatever, but no one's gonna want to stay in that one. Not after a dead body's been in there. Everyone's probably gonna want to just leave now."

"I've got your contact information. I'll call if I have more questions."

Angel wandered into the woods, and I found Dr. Bundy waiting for me outside Barry's cottage.

"I don't have anything preliminary to

report," he said. "I'm not going to make any guesses about what could've happened to him because I've got nothing to go on at this point."

"What about the white stuff around his nose and mouth and the blue tint to his skin?" I asked in a hushed tone.

"I'll analyze the white substance and figure out the cause of the blueness, but like I said, I don't want to speculate."

We widened the gap between us a few feet as the EMTs came out of the cottage with Barry's body on a stretcher. I watched somberly as they steered him to the waiting ambulance.

"Just so you know," Dr. Bundy informed, "I'm backed up right now. It might be a day or two before I get to the autopsy."

"Why so busy?" I asked.

"Partly staffing issues due to budget cuts and summer vacations. Partly people being foolish. Car accidents, drownings, head injuries because people won't wear helmets when they mountain bike. If they saw what I saw . . ."

"Speaking of drowning," I said, "it's

been a few weeks since I ordered my grandmother's autopsy report. Any chance you could check on that for me?"

"A few weeks?" He put a hand to his belly and laughed. "You make that sound like a long time. I'll look into it, see if I can put a rush on it for you."

Chapter 5

WE LEFT THE RENTAL COTTAGE area and were about halfway to the station when it occurred to me that I was driving the van. As in, I wasn't driving the Cherokee because I kayaked into work this morning and now it was well past dark. It was only a few hundred yards across the bay from the marina to my house, but there was no way I would do that in the dark. If I had a bigger boat? Sure, no problem. The creatures that lived in the lake couldn't tip a bigger boat. At least that's what my twelve-year-old brain told me. Twelve-year-old Jayne believed that there was a Loch Ness type monster living in the lake that would attack small vessels and swallow the passengers.

I paused at the station and grabbed my laptop—there was paperwork to do for Barry's case and I could do that at home— and then debated about grabbing some dinner from Grapes, Grains, and Grub. The village pub served amazing bar food, which sounded really good right then, but I was too tired to eat at the pub tonight, and takeout would be cold by the time I got it home. Hopefully Tripp made something for dinner. The guests who stayed at Pine Time B&B were never going to want to leave. Not after indulging in one of Tripp's breakfasts. He was an amazing cook.

I continued west for a short distance along the two-lane highway that bisected the village—the shopping and business district, so to speak, was south of the highway near the lake, and the residential district was north—and took a left at the campground. At the end of the quarter-mile-long driveway, I spotted Tripp sitting outside his popup trailer in the front yard, his portable gas fire pit lighting up his space next to the tree line. The fire had to be for ambiance because he couldn't possibly need heat. It was still 80-some degrees and humid.

I pulled to a stop in front of the detached garage and the second I open the driver's door, Meeka launched herself out of the smelly van and darted to the backyard to chase fireflies and yap at shadows.

"What are you doing over there?" I called out to Tripp. Our normal routine had been to meet for dinner on the boathouse sundeck and then hang out and talk and take in nature—the lake, the loons, the pine trees. It had been a week ... no, two weeks since we'd last done that.

"Wasn't sure you were coming home tonight," Tripp called back.

Sometimes, Tripp got a little pouty when I had to work late. His vision of us running the bed-and-breakfast was exactly that, us running the B&B with nothing else taking time away from it. That had been the plan, then the village council offered me the sheriff position.

Those responsibilities would ease at the end of the busy summer tourist season, and I'd be here with him much more often. Hiring a deputy would help. Then again, when it was no longer the busy summer tourist season, we wouldn't have many visitors at the B&B. We had to come up with an incentive during the winter months to lure people up to Wisconsin's Northwoods, or we'd be sitting here looking at each other.

I crossed the yard to Tripp. "What do you think of staging dinner-theater murder mysteries?"

"In general or . . . ?"

I laughed as I dropped onto his second lawn chair. My tired body instantly slumped. "I was thinking of ways to get people up north in the winter. We could get a couple snowmobiles and rent those out. There's also cross-country skis and snowshoes. People love winter sports on a frozen lake. Oh, ice fishing, of course."

Not that I would ever sit out on a frozen lake. Hours of watching a bobber in a hole? No thanks.

"There could be something there. We'll

add it to the list." He ruffled Meeka's ears when she stopped to greet him, and then she was off again. "Were there problems in the village today? Is that why you're home so late?"

"Not in the village exactly." I told him about coming across Barry this morning and what had happened to him a number of hours later.

"Don't tell me there's been another murder." Tripp let his head drop back and stared at the sky as though scolding the universe.

"I'm not sure what happened. I don't have reason to believe it was murder, but he seemed okay when I left him this morning. There are a few more people in the village I can speak with, our resident bicycling nun to start with, but otherwise, there's not much I can do until Dr. Bundy gets back to me with the autopsy results."

"You interviewed all of the people he was here with?" My detective skills were wearing off on him. Tripp knew the process almost as well as I did.

"I interviewed them all, and other than one guy, I don't think any of them are guilty of anything. Even the one guy is iffy."

"This is going to bother you now, isn't it?"

"Of course it is. A person I rescued this morning has died, and I want to know why. What if I missed a sign? He almost drowned; maybe I should have insisted that he get checked out at the healing center." I tugged my uniform shirt free of my cargo shorts. "Right now, I'm starving. Do you know if there's anything in the refrigerator?"

"No leftovers. I just hung it up for the day not too long ago so didn't make anything. I had a sub sandwich. Would you like one?"

"That sounds fast, which translates to perfect."

"I'll make one for you."

I could make myself a sandwich, but his always seemed better. "Thanks. I'm going to run up and change clothes. Meet you in the house?"

"Roger Wilco." He stood and gave a crisp salute.

I wandered across the backyard to the

boathouse built on the edge of the lake. A small sliver of the building was on land, but most of the boathouse was over the water. The area above the boat garage was a cozy little apartment I shared with Meeka. It was the perfect size for us with a sleeping area facing the backyard, a small kitchenette and bathroom in the center, and a living area overlooking the lake. I pulled off my uniform shirt and shorts and pulled on a pair of sweatpants cut off at the knee and an oversized T-shirt. I looked like a complete slob but couldn't have been more comfortable and that's all I cared about at that moment.

I had just placed my Glock into its case in my nightstand when I heard Meeka's claws clacking on the hardwood floor.

"Ready for dinner?"

She wagged her tail, turned in a circle, and crossed the floor to stand by her dishes. After putting a scoop of kibble in one bowl and filling the other with fresh water, I stepped out onto the sundeck.

"I'm going to the house to eat."

I said this like the little white dog understood every word. She gave a soft *ruff* and dropped her face into her dish.

I left one of the house's patio doors open a crack, so Meeka could come in if she wanted, and found Tripp in the kitchen. He was just placing my sandwich on a plate along with some baby carrots.

"Ham, turkey, and roast beef on a 9-grain sub bun." He presented the plate like a gift to a queen—resting on his outstretched hands, head bowed—then set it on the counter in my usual spot. "A swipe of seedy mustard, Muenster, tomato, lettuce, and pickles."

"You say the nicest things to me." I filled a glass from a pitcher of lemonade in the refrigerator and climbed onto my barstool. Before stuffing the sandwich into my mouth, I asked, "How was your day?"

"We got a lot done today." He looked proud of this fact. Getting the B&B up and running was almost a bigger goal for him than it was for me. "I'm happy to report that the main level is completely done, with the exception of re-staining the floors and filling it with furniture."

"Now that is something to celebrate. I

should have grabbed a beer instead of lemonade."

Tripp opened one of the kitchen cupboards, pulled out a small bottle of vodka, added a generous shot to my lemonade, and then prepared one for himself. He sat on the stool next to me and held out his glass to clink against mine.

"Here's to progress being made," I said.

He gave me that look. The one that told me that the "progress" he was thinking about had nothing to do with the house. Over the last two months, Tripp and I had become very close. He didn't hesitate to let me know that he wanted to take our relationship further. My problem was that I had ended a seven-year relationship with Jonah, my ex-fiancé, shortly before coming to Whispering Pines. While the pain of that breakup had dulled to the point that I was pretty much over it, I wasn't quite ready to step back in to another relationship. I cared too much about Tripp to rush things between us. If I was being honest, and I couldn't say it out loud yet, I wanted the same thing he did. Just the thought filled me with terror, though. I wanted Tripp to be in my life for a very long time and was scared that if we took things to the next level, something bad would happen and he'd leave.

"To progress," he said with a husky voice and a wink.

Without realizing I'd done it, I had chugged down half my glass of vodka lemonade. To absorb a little of that, I took another huge bite of my sandwich.

"This is really good," I mumbled around my mouthful.

He gave a nod that said he knew I wanted to take the conversation in a different direction. "Would you like to see what we did today?"

"Absolutely."

Leaving my drink on the breakfast bar, I followed Tripp around the main level with my plate in hand, munching my sandwich and baby carrots as we wandered. The dining room was the first room we completed. We had painted every other room on the main level a light blue that perfectly coordinated with the lake, but for the dining room walls we chose a light blue-gray with just a touch of green.

The only room we hadn't done anything to on the first floor was my grandfather's den at the front right corner. We'd re-stain the floor in there along with the rest, but that room would be the bed-and-breakfast office so there was no rush. Maybe we'd leave it in its original state. It made me feel like Gramps was there with me when I sat at his beautiful roll top desk. I liked that.

The last room Tripp had to finish on the main level was a nice size bedroom next to the kitchen. Also nice was the fact we didn't have to do anything to the bathroom in there. Every other bathroom in the house needed refurbishing.

"If they would've used the same tile they used in here upstairs," I said of the simple, classic white tiles, "we'd be almost ready to open."

"Possibly. You'll be happy to know that all of the dreaded peachy-pink tile upstairs is gone."

"Oh my god, really?" I nearly choked on a baby carrot. "Show me."

We left the only bedroom on the main floor, one we thought would be perfect for any visitors who couldn't manage the stairs, and went to the second floor. By this time, Meeka had found us, raced ahead, and was sitting at the top of the stairs looking smug that she beat us.

To the right of the stairs was my grandmother's bedroom suite.

"Where's the bathtub?" I asked.

"We took it out," Tripp explained. "I didn't want anything to happen to it during renovation, and it was in the way. We put it in the garage and will reinstall it once everything else is done."

I had mixed feelings about Gran's prized antique clawfoot bathtub. While it was a beautiful piece that I knew she loved and used every single night before going to bed, it was where she had died five months earlier. The police report stated she had fallen, struck her head, and drowned when she fell into the already-filled tub. I could barely wait to get my hands on that autopsy report. I was sure someone had removed the original report from her file, which meant someone was hiding something. Hopefully Dr. Bundy could push that along for me.

Since Gran's bedroom was the largest and grandest in the house, we were going to go above and beyond with the bathroom as well. Marble tiles would be installed on the floor and halfway up the wall. Mr. Powell, the owner of The Busted Knuckle, the village maintenance construction repair you-name-it business, had shown up one day with a beautiful, petitely proportioned crystal chandelier that he thought would look perfect hanging over that tub. He was right. I could hardly wait to see it there. When done, this bathroom would rival even my mother's day spa, Melt Your Cares, in Madison.

"It's kind of a disaster in here." I slid some tiny peach shards of tile aside with my foot. The walls were down to the studs in places, the floors bare, and dust was everywhere. "But it actually looks better than it did before you removed the tile."

I grinned at Tripp and took another big bite of my sandwich.

"You really hated the peach, didn't you?"

"I can't even express how much."

Walking down the hall, our footsteps echoed since they had also removed all the ancient carpeting and padding today. We paused at each of the other five bedrooms so I could see the destruction in each bathroom.

"You're right," I said. "You guys did get a lot done today."

"Destruction is the easy part. And the fun part. Nothing like hitting stuff with a sledgehammer."

"I'm glad you brought on Mr. Powell's men to help. This would've taken you a year to complete by yourself."

"Or more," Tripp agreed. "Tomorrow, we'll address any questionable plumbing or electrical issues, reinsulate, and then get it ready for the new tile."

"I can hardly wait. What's your best guess? When will we be ready to let in guests?"

"A few weeks if everything goes

smoothly. We should pad that out and plan on at least a month and a half."

That long? I was anxious to open. "The website is ready, with the exception of pictures. Once we have those, all I have to do is hit publish. I've also got flyers ready to hand out around the village and post on the village bulletin board. I also have ads ready to run on vacation rental websites."

"Impressive. You've been busy, too."

"And you thought all I did was sheriff stuff." I stared down the hallway, pondering. "No reason we can't start taking reservations, though, right? Six weeks?"

"These things never go the way you think they will. Might be best to wait a little while longer."

I nodded, but felt like I should start planning. Having the grand opening in six weeks put us toward the end of the summer season. For most, that meant Labor Day weekend, but Whispering Pines followed a Wiccan calendar. "End of summer" here meant the autumnal equinox on or about September 22. If we opened in six weeks, we'd still have three or four weeks of prime tourist time left.

Done with the tour, Tripp was ready to head back downstairs, but I paused outside the door that led to the attic on the third floor. On normal nights, when I made it home in time to have dinner with Tripp, I spent time going through Gran's things up there. Mostly, it was furniture and boxes of holiday decorations. Some of it we'd be able to use in the B&B, some of it could be taken to the resale shop near the pentacle garden, and the rest was getting deposited into the ever-present dumpster in front of the house.

"It's late, Jayne. You can skip the attic for one night."

He was right, I could. The thing was, I was hoping to come across something that could tell me about the history of Whispering Pines. A few of the villagers had told me that if I wanted to know the truth behind my grandmother's death, I had to look back to the village's inception. I was positive there were records of some kind somewhere in the house that would help me with that. It was almost becoming an obsession. So while the research wasn't urgent, especially considering everything else we had going on, part of me was saying, *but tonight could be the night everything starts falling together.*

Tripp placed a hand on my lower back, sending shivers through my body, and steered me away from the attic door.

"Let's go relax for a while," he said. "We'll sit by the fire until we're ready for bed."

"I've got paperwork to do," I said with a groan. "I was too tired and hungry to do it at the station, so I brought the computer home to work on it here."

"How about," he suggested, still steering, "you work on that by the fire? I promise I won't bother you."

A yawn snuck up on me. "We can give that a try."

I put my sandwich plate in the dishwasher and grabbed my beverage from the counter, topping it off with more lemonade. I grabbed the laptop from my apartment while Tripp re-started the fire in his portable fire pit. I got myself situated in the yard chair, opened the laptop, and immediately forgot what I was about to do.

"Jayne? Are you with me?"

I looked at him and blinked. "Hmm?"

He stood and took the computer from me. "We're going to set this aside. You can work on it tomorrow. I'm pretty sure anything you typed up tonight would just get deleted in the morning anyway."

He was right. Why was I pushing myself so hard?

I sank into the chair and took in the night noises—the water sloshing against the dock, the chirping of crickets, and the mournful cry of a wolf far in the distance. The wolf was probably one of the animals up at the Whispering Pines circus, but Meeka went on high alert for predators just in case. There was also the whispering of the trees. When the wind blew through the pines, the branches waved back and forth and rubbed together, making it sound like the trees were talking.

"What are they telling you?" Tripp asked. I had expected him to think I was nuts the first time I told him they spoke, but he said that he could hear it, too.

"Nothing tonight."

"You're more tired than you look. And you look exhausted. Why don't you go to bed? Everything will be waiting for you in the morning."

He stood, walked behind me, and put his hands on my shoulders. He squeezed my tight, sore neck muscles for a few minutes, relaxing me to the point that I almost fell asleep right there in the chair. I felt him kiss the top of my head, then he pulled me to my feet and walked me home.

"Good night, Jayne." His voice held that husky, sexy quality that made me shiver again. Not for the first time, I thought about what it would be like if he were to just come inside with me, slip into my bed, and hold me all night. Then I gave myself a mental head slap, knowing darn well it wouldn't stop at just holding.

"Good night, Tripp. Thanks for everything today."

Less than a minute later, I was in bed, my body getting heavier by the moment but my mind thinking about the attic and Whispering Pines' history. How had these two thousand acres gone from the three O'Sheas to hundreds of villagers? And what could have happened way back then that resulted in Gran's death five months ago?

Chapter 6

MY CELL PHONE WOKE ME TO THE sound of chirping songbirds at five o'clock the next morning. Not because I preferred to get up at this ungodly hour, or because I had to type up the paperwork for yesterday's investigation, which I did, but because this morning was the regular bi-weekly village council meeting. I had completely forgotten. Tripp, however, knew my schedule better than I did and was waiting for me on the patio below the boathouse sundeck.

"You forgot, didn't you? I knew you'd forget today." He pointed at a steaming mug of coffee sitting on a table then to the chair next to him. "Sit a while before you go."

All the attention he paid to me and my needs confused me at first. Now, I realized that Tripp wanted someone to take care of and to create the family life he never had as a kid. His mother left him with his aunt and uncle when he was thirteen years old, and he never saw her again. His aunt and uncle loved him dearly but living with them was unsettled and far from the hearth-and-home vision in his head. I think he was trying to create that vision with us.

Many women would consider this a blessing, and I was beyond grateful for every effort he made. Meeting me with coffee in the morning and having dinner ready for me almost every day was very sweet, but at times I felt almost smothered by the attention and could barely breathe. Maybe it was because here was another man trying to fit me into his version of home life. I needed to get past this. But what if this was all an act to hook me? Would this attention stick around, or would it disappear if I let a relationship happen?

Good lord. What was wrong with me?

"Strawberries and blackberries, too." I snagged a couple berries from the bowl on the table. "Why are you up so early this morning?"

"I've been getting up this early for the last week or so. It's a big relief to have the crew here to help with the renovations, but you know me; I'm not used to having people around all the time. So, I get up early, have some coffee, and spend a few minutes with the lake before they get here. You'd know this if you got up before seven-thirty."

"Why should I do that? Nothing happens around the village until later in the afternoon, mid-morning at the earliest. Getting to the station by eight or eight-thirty is fine. Besides, if I got up that early, I'd interfere with your alone time."

"I think I could handle being alone with you."

There was that sexy, husky voice again. As usual, I stepped right into it.

I took a sip from my mug, let out a

coffee sigh, and then popped another strawberry into my mouth. The morning was slightly overcast, but it didn't look like it would rain. That was both a blessing and a curse. Tourists tended to stay inside when it rained, which meant the local businesses wouldn't get as much traffic. However, the greenery around the village looked like it was struggling a bit.

"What's on the docket for this morning's meeting?" Tripp wanted to know.

Before I could respond, three pickup trucks loaded with ten crew members between them pulled up to the house.

Tripp's shoulders dropped. "They're over an hour early. I told them they didn't have to be here until seven."

"Pine time. You know folks here work on their own clocks."

He stood, waved, and called out, "Go on in, I'll be there in a minute." Then to me, "I could handle fifteen minutes early. Not an hour and fifteen, though."

Even this early in the morning, the guys were loud, cracking jokes and laughing. Since this was how they were every time I saw them, I had to assume this was how they were all day long.

"We're used to it being quiet here," I said. "It'll be nice when this is done and it's just us again."

I did it again. Fortunately, he let the "us" comment slide this time.

"Once the work is done, the house will be full of visitors," he reminded me. "Especially during the summer. There won't be a lot of quiet here anymore."

"The blessing and the curse of getting what you ask for." I took another long sip of coffee. "Thank you for this and the berries. I hope you have another productive day."

He held my gaze for a second, and I swear he was about to lean in and give me a goodbye kiss. At that moment, Meeka charged across the yard, breaking the spell with her *intruder alert* bark.

"You know who they are," Tripp told her. "They help me here while you're off being a K-9."

It was funny how he had taken to talking to her the way I did.

Meeka looked up at Tripp, ran to the

middle of the yard, and tilted her head as though trying to place the trucks. She gave another soft bark, one that sounded like *right*, and returned to patrolling the yard.

"Time to get to that meeting." I swallowed the last of my coffee and handed him the mug. "I'll do my best to be home in time for dinner tonight."

"Then I'll do my best to have something ready."

I ran upstairs to get Meeka's harness and leash, loaded my cargo pockets with the items I carried around with me all day, and shrugged into my Glock holster. When Meeka and I rounded the corner of the garage, we both paused, momentarily confused by the station's van sitting there.

"We have to remember to pick up the kayak tonight."

She sneezed in agreement.

Twenty minutes later, after dropping the van off at the station, Meeka and I were approaching The Inn. Effie and Cybil, fortune tellers and two of the thirteen council members, were just entering the building. Since no one else was outside, I assumed we were the last to arrive.

Echoing its exterior, the inside of The Inn had the appearance of being at least two hundred years old. The ceilings were short, the floors crooked, the atmosphere cozy and inviting. The lobby was empty except for an older couple sitting near the large stone fireplace reading a newspaper, probably waiting for the restaurant to open for breakfast, and the pock-faced young man behind the registration desk.

"Good morning, Emery. How are the plans coming along?"

He sat tall and proud. "I finally have enough to put a down payment on my land. I was worried someone would snatch it from me. Now I can start with the blueprints and putting together a supply list with Mr. Powell."

"Congratulations. Where exactly are you planning to build this dream cottage?"

"About half a mile north and a little east of the Meditation Circle." His grin was huge. "It's got a little pond."

I bit my lip as I crossed behind the registration desk to the doorway to the conference room. I didn't want to tell him that the pond would probably turn into a mosquito pit in the summer. Which was likely why no one snatched his land. Maybe Morgan or one of the other green witches in town could come up with a mosquito solution for him.

"I'm happy for you, Emery. Keep up the hard work." I slipped into the conference room, and as I figured, everyone else had arrived.

"Finally." Flavia, the village's self-appointed mayor, sniffed at me.

This was how she greeted me at every single meeting whether I was the last to arrive or not. I responded with my own standard greeting of ignoring her.

"What kind of scones do we have today?" I asked Honey, co-owner of Treat Me Sweetly, as I peeked in the box on the chrome and glass conference table.

"The wild raspberries are perfect for picking right now," she explained. "There are a ton of them, so we have raspberry-almond buttermilk today."

My stomach rumbled, always a good sign. I chose a scone, filled a paper cup with the coffee Violet had brought over from Ye Olde Bean Grinder, and took my seat at the far end of the table across from Flavia.

"We have three items on the schedule for today." Flavia turned her head slightly to the two people on my left. "Creed and Janessa—"

"Credence," Janessa announced and tilted her head toward the woman sitting next to her.

The fact that Credence, the transgender ringmaster for the Whispering Pines circus, was with us today instead of Creed told me they had something emotional to talk about. Credence was more nurturing than Creed.

Annoyed with the correction, Flavia cleared her throat. "Janessa and *Credence* requested to speak with us. Second, Effie's granddaughter, Jola, has officially started at the healing center and has some items regarding that to tell us about. Finally, Sheriff O'Shea will give us her blotter update of the last two weeks."

She held out a hand to Janessa and Credence. "You have the floor."

Janessa, who suffered from a birth defect called phocomelia which meant her arms extended only six or eight inches from her shoulders, struggled slightly as she pushed away from the table to stand. I'd never seen her struggle with anything. What was going on?

"There's no point dragging this out." Janessa's voice broke.

Credence took over for her. "Janessa would like to step down from the council."

"Why?" Laurel, Maeve, and Morgan asked in unison.

Janessa cleared her throat. "Everything around here is growing. As more and more tourists come to visit us each season, the businesses are becoming busier. Litha and Lughnasad are almost blending right into Mabon."

Litha was summer solstice, Mabon the autumnal equinox. I had no clue what the third was. Morgan lifted a hand in a tell-you-later gesture.

Janessa continued, "As much as I have

appreciated having a voice in the goings-on around the village, it doesn't feel right for the circus to have two representatives."

"We've talked about this extensively," Credence added, "and we've decided that since I have more contact with the carnies, I will stay on as the voice for them. Janessa will step down, and we think another business owner in the village should take her seat."

"Sounds reasonable to me," Donovan said. "Never made sense that the circus and the fortune tellers took up four of the seats. In fact, it seems reasonable that either Effie or Cybil step down as well."

"Not going to happen," Cybil snapped at him. "We are Originals. Originals have first choice at being on the council and can bump off a non-original at any point to hold a seat. We just can't have more than thirteen members. It's in the bylaws. Read them."

Donovan, village resident of seven months and owner of Quin's clothing shop, turned a bright, angry red. "As an Original myself, I am quite familiar with the bylaws. I thought perhaps one of the two of you might see the importance of having more voices from business owners."

"I think this is a lovely gesture from Janessa," Morgan interrupted the escalating tension. "We will miss you greatly, Janessa, but I'm sure Credence, or Creed, will keep you up-to-date with our discussions as well as pass along any ideas you may have for us."

"I have an idea for the business owners," Mr. Powell began.

He stood and promptly became entangled with the legs of his chair, resulting in him sprawling out on the conference table and sending the box of scones flying. Fortunately, I caught the box before it landed on the floor, losing only a single scone in the process. Meeka, delighted by this minor mishap, snatched up the scone and ran to a corner to enjoy it.

"Are you okay?" I asked the world's klutziest man.

"A-Okay." Mr. Powell brushed off his accidents like dust. "What if the local business owners, myself included, have separate meetings and then those of us on the council share their concerns here?"

"That sounds like a perfect plan to me," Laurel said. "I recently acquired a few of the guest cottages. The other cottage owners and I get together once a month to discuss any issues over there. I'd be happy to sit on a business council as well."

She ran The Inn, The Inn's restaurant, and now guest cottages? Whenever I started feeling overwhelmed by the amount of work I had to do, I just needed to think of Laurel.

"I call for a vote," Flavia said.

"Seconded," Donovan said.

She scowled at his interruption. "The vote being, shall we accept Janessa's resignation from village council immediately or have her resignation become effective as soon as we find a replacement?"

The half-hearted vote was for her immediate resignation, leaving us with an even number of members. That meant, in the event of a tie, Flavia got two votes.

Janessa bowed her head and sniffled. "I'll miss seeing you all."

"You're not leaving Whispering Pines, are you?" Morgan asked.

"No," Janessa assured. "This is my home, I'm not going anywhere."

"Thank the Goddess for that," Morgan smiled warmly. "You leaving would be unacceptable."

"I'm going to go get some tea in the restaurant," Janessa told Credence. "I'll meet you there after the meeting."

"Janessa," Flavia said, "Jola should be out in the lobby. Would you ask her to come in now, please?"

A minute later, a woman—*five foot five, slender, glowing medium-brown skin, close-cropped Afro*—entered the conference room and took the seat next to Credence.

"I just wanted to introduce myself to the council," Jola said, "and to thank you all for agreeing to let me work at the healing center."

One of those bylaws Cybil had mentioned was that the council needed to approve new people moving to and working in the village. If the person was a member of one of the Original families, one of the first families to move here fifty years ago, they were in without question. Otherwise, the council got to decide if a person was worthy. The acceptable list included people who were ostracized because of their religion like the Wiccans, or looked at as unusual like the fortune tellers, or had a decreased quality of life due to a physical disability like many of the carnies at the circus.

I understood the rule, sort of, but it felt like reverse discrimination to me. Jola was in because her grandmother, Effie, was an Original. Tripp, for example, "could fit in anywhere," as Morgan once explained so the only job he could get was working with me. No one was going to say no to me. I owned the land they lived on, after all.

"We're happy to have you here," Maeve, proprietress of Grapes, Grains, and Grub, told Jola.

"What did you need to tell us?" Flavia asked. She seemed impatient today. She usually loved being at these meetings where she could tell everybody when they could and couldn't speak. Like that ever worked for long.

"I wanted to let you know about a couple of changes we'll be making," Jola began. "The healing center and the yoga studio are going to combine skills. A great deal of my studies at UW Madison centered around a more holistic and preventative approach to healthcare."

"I love this idea," Morgan breathed with a happy sigh.

"Does this mean you'll combine into one building?" Violet asked.

"No," Jola said, "neither building is large enough for that. We would like to bridge the two properties, since they're next door to each other, by constructing an outdoor pavilion of sorts."

Mr. Powell immediately perked up at this idea. "What do you intend to do in this pavilion?"

"Outdoor yoga and tai chi," Jola explained. "Classes of various sorts. We'd also like to construct a labyrinth that people can wander while meditating."

Morgan let out another happy little

squeal and clapped her fingers together. "I vote yes."

"It does sound like a wonderful idea," Violet agreed. "I vote—"

"I haven't called for a vote yet," Flavia snapped.

"Oh, for heaven sakes," Maeve slumped back in her chair. "Call for it already, then, so we can vote yes."

Flavia pushed her shoulders back and pursed her lips. "Those in favor?"

Clearly thinking his company would be constructing both the pavilion and labyrinth, Mr. Powell shot his hand into the air, the seam in the armpit of his shirt ripping out as he did.

Since it seemed no vote could ever be unanimous with the council, Donovan and Flavia voted in the negative, claiming they wanted to see blueprints and more specifics before they could vote. The rest of us, however, voted yes and passed the motion.

"This is wonderful, thank you." Jola placed her hands palms together in front of her heart and bowed her head. "The healing center and yoga studio staff will draw up those blueprints and outline the specifics. I'll have them ready for you to review at the next meeting."

"Before you go," Cybil said thoughtfully, "we need to fill Janessa's spot on the council."

"What does this have to do with Jola?" Flavia tapped her pen on the table.

I knew what it had to do with Jola, and I was one hundred percent in favor. Before Cybil could say another word, I said, "I move that Jola fill the vacated council position."

"Jola?" Donovan asked. "She barely knows anything about the village."

"On the contrary," Effie said, "she grew up here. You wouldn't know that. You didn't grow up here."

Donovan glared across the table at Effie. This wasn't the normal council member bickering; there was something more behind the statement. I had recently learned that Donovan came from an Original family; his grandmother was one of the first to move here. I knew Donovan hadn't grown up in the village, but I didn't know why.

"Jola is young and energetic." I said this like at twenty-six I was so much older than her twenty-two. "She has ideas that will spark new life into some of our older village customs. I can practically guarantee our younger tourists will love this current proposal."

"I couldn't agree more," Morgan said. "Without question, I second that vote."

When all votes were cast, the only voices of dissension were Donovan, probably because Effie had embarrassed him in front of everyone; Maeve because she didn't feel two family members on the council was a good idea; and Flavia because she was Flavia.

"Welcome, Jola." Violet, who also clearly loved this new direction for the village, bounced in her chair. "We're thrilled to have you as the thirteenth council member."

"Sheriff." Flavia raised her voice above the excited chatter going on around the table. "Are you ready to give us your report? Unless anyone else has anything important to discuss, of course."

Heads shook in unison, so I took a sip

of my coffee and stood to speak.

"It's been relatively quiet the last two weeks," I began, "until yesterday afternoon." I filled them in on what had happened with Barry. From the panicked, pale expressions on a few faces, I knew what they were thinking. "I have no reason to believe he was murdered."

"Then what happened to him?" Sugar asked.

"I honestly can't say yet. Dr. Bundy is doing an autopsy, and at this point I'm not even sure how to proceed. I know a few of the villagers had contact with this man, so I'll speak with them. Other than that, it's been standard patrol issues—breaking up a few fights, helping a kid find his family, and locking up a few drunks that needed to sit in a cell and dry out for a while."

"Any luck on a deputy?" Laurel asked.

I filled them in on the telephone interviews I'd done. "Sadly, no one from that batch is going to work out. My former captain is expanding his search for me."

"Martin is ready to come back to

work," Flavia said in a singsong voice followed by a *tsk-tsk* sound. "The poor boy is sitting at home bored to death. Are you ready to consider him yet?"

I had two issues with Martin Reed returning as deputy sheriff of Whispering Pines. First, he was Flavia's son. The thought of her trying to insert herself into my business didn't sit well with me. I could handle Flavia, though. The bigger issue was his lack of experience.

"I'll consider Martin," I began, "if he's willing to go through some training with me. We all know that Sheriff Brighton gave Martin the title of deputy but the responsibilities of an administrative assistant. I need someone in the station who I can trust to back me up when necessary."

"Sounds like a reasonable request," Effie said while dabbing at scone crumbs on her napkin.

Murmurs of agreement came from around the table.

Flavia's face twisted in some strange representation of a smile. "I'll pass that along to him."

"I need to get someone on board with me soon." I felt exhausted just thinking about being the only law enforcement person in the village. "If he agrees to my conditions, I'm willing to give him another chance."

Good lord, what had I just committed to?

Chapter 7

INSTEAD OF SCATTERING AFTER THE meeting to the four corners of Whispering Pines like usual, the council members gathered to personally welcome Jola. Mr. Powell attempted to lean in to shake Jola's hand from four feet away, went off balance, and like a bowling ball into pins, nearly took out the entire group. Fortunately, Laurel caught him before disaster ensued.

"You look fabulous," I told Jola.

She and I had a history in that I had rescued her from the woods near the UW Madison campus. She had "gone missing" according to Effie who'd had a vision about her granddaughter that led me right to her. The last time I'd seen her, Jola was dehydrated and loaded with scratches and bug bites. Now, she could be on the cover of a health magazine.

"Thanks, Jayne. Oh, sorry, I should call you Sheriff now." She bypassed my outstretched hand and gave me a firm hug instead. "I'd love to sit and catch up with you sometime."

"That would be great," I agreed. "Let's have dinner one night. We can meet here in the village or you can come out and we'll have a cookout."

Actually, a cookout with various villagers sounded like a lot of fun. Tripp and I could take them on a tour of the house to see the renovations. We'd be ready for the grand opening in a few weeks. I liked this idea and made a mental note to mention it to Tripp.

Meeka and I slid through The Inn's lobby and had just stepped onto the red brick pathway that encircled the pentacle garden when I felt an arm slip into mine. There was only one person who did that, and it meant she wanted to have a chat.

"Jayne," Morgan said with gentle concern, "are you sure that bringing Martin back as deputy is a good idea?"

"Glad I'm not the only one to see the potential problem there."

"Trust me, it's not just you and I."

I tilted my head side-to-side to release the tension in my neck. "I think it's worth a try. If nothing else, he can take care of the administrative duties for me. Honestly, I'm getting desperate. Any help I can get is welcome."

Morgan pondered this as we walked a little further around the garden toward Shoppe Mystique and then nodded decisively. Considering Morgan was a green witch, I had a good idea what she was thinking.

"I agree that you need help. I also agree that Martin could do a good job. Therefore—"

"You're going to cast a spell. Or make a charm bag. Or conduct some midnight ritual involving fire and preferably a full moon. Clothing optional."

She gave me a sly smile. "You know me so well."

She didn't comment on which option she was planning but gave me a wink and a little over-the-shoulder finger wave and hurried off to her shop.

"Since we're out here," I told my K-9 companion, "we should see if anyone can tell us anything about Barry."

Meeka wagged her tail in response. She'd choose being out on patrol to being stuck inside the station anytime. The problem was, it was still early so the commons was mostly empty. One small group was gathered around a bench near the pentacle garden. I stopped to ask if any of them knew Barry.

"The Speedo-wearing violin-playing unicyclist?" a millennial with long hair braided and hanging in front of her shoulder wanted to know. "I talked with him at the pub a few nights ago. Why do you ask?"

I explained that Barry had died under mysterious circumstances and that I was trying to get any lead I could on what might have happened. The woman immediately burst into tears.

"She didn't know him that well," said

another woman sitting cross-legged on the ground in front of the bench. "She's sort of emotional this morning. We were with a group at the Meditation Circle last night. It was a real spiritual experience, if you know what I mean. She hasn't come down from it yet."

While I had never attended one of the nighttime gatherings at the Meditation Circle, I was fairly certain the "spiritual experience" involved certain substances that were legal in some states but not yet in Wisconsin. Meeka's I-smell-something posture all but confirmed it. I should probably go and check into that sometime. As a law enforcement officer, of course.

"Did any of the rest of you know him?"

An even number of nods of agreement and heads shaking in the negative passed through the group.

"Is there anything in particular about him that stood out?" I asked.

"Other than the fact that he wore a Speedo while playing the violin and riding a unicycle?" asked a man with a flat top haircut.

"That's how he blew off steam," I explained. "Or so I've been told. What I meant was, did he fall outside the norm? Was he unusually quiet? Was he unusually friendly? Did you ever notice him arguing with anyone?"

"No. He was just an ordinary guy," the crying woman wailed and held a hand out to Meeka. Meeka sniffed from three feet away but didn't get any closer. She was in K-9 mode right now. And she didn't like crying people. They usually wanted to hug her.

That there was nothing out of the ordinary about Barry didn't surprise me. Nothing about this case was making sense. Other than a history of bitterness with his old college roommate, Angel, I had nothing that came close to a motive for murder.

"Are any of you familiar with the nun on the bicycle?" I asked.

"Sure." The flat top man gave a sideways glance at the crying woman and emphasized, "She's hot."

"She's a nun," I said stupidly. Just because they wore habits didn't mean nuns couldn't be hot. "Barry used to follow her around town while she rode her bike. I'm wondering if they had a connection at all."

"Couldn't say," the man said. "She hangs out at the beach, though. Might be there now. I think she likes the peace of the morning before the crowds come."

I scratched down a few notes, thanked them for their time, and headed southeast for the public beach. We hadn't gone thirty yards, when I noticed a crowd gathered on the opposite side of the pentacle garden near Grapes, Grains, and Grub. I changed directions, unintentionally jerking Meeka's leash, which earned me a doggie scowl.

"Sorry. We'd better go check out whatever's going on over there."

As we approached, I saw that the crowd had gathered to listen to a monster of a man who was standing on the front porch of 3G. He was in the middle of a lecture about pigeons.

Six foot four, long white hair and beard, bulbous nose, approximate age late-seventies.

"If you just think about it for a minute, you'll see that I'm right." The man held his hands out to the crowd in a pleading *listen to me* gesture. "Have any of you ever seen a baby pigeon? I'm telling you, they take them."

"Who takes them?" a man in the crowd called out.

The bearded man lowered his voice, leaned into the crowd, and said, "The government. They snatch them up as soon as the egg is laid. Then they put them in incubators and as soon as they hatch, they insert chips."

"What kind of chip?" a woman asked, matching his tone.

Smirking and laughing behind their hands, the crowd seemed amused by this guy. Their questions were encouraging, like they wanted to prolong the show.

The man on the porch pinched his fingers together into a beak shape and then jabbed them repeatedly at his own eye. "They insert tiny little cameras into their eyeballs and use them as spies."

"Why would they do that?" another man asked, as the crowd laughed softly, slightly uncomfortable now.

"To watch us, of course. They're always watching us. You all think you're safe in your fancy suburban homes. You think they don't know what you're doing?"

"They're watching us through the eyes of pigeons?" the same woman asked.

Maeve showed up then, charging over from the direction of The Inn. "Willie, get off my porch."

"Maeve!" The man threw his arms wide and wrapped himself around the pub's owner.

"Good god, Willie, you stink." She pushed him off and then flapped her hands at the crowd to disperse. "What kind of crackpot conspiracy are you spouting now?"

"It's not crackpot," Willie whispered. "And it's not a conspiracy. Well, it is. It's a conspiracy against citizens. You didn't hear everything from the start." He leaned in close, looked left and then right, and asked, "Have you ever seen a baby pigeon?"

Maeve held up a hand in a stop gesture

and then pointed north. "Go home, Willie."

Willie grumbled as he descended the porch steps. He crossed close to us as he left, and Meeka must have gotten a whiff of him. She whined, backed away, and hid behind my legs.

"I gotta get supplies," Willie objected.

"Then get your supplies," Maeve stated calmly, "and go home. You're upsetting people."

The man did as she said and walked away, mumbling to himself about the government the entire time.

"Who is he?" I asked.

"We call him Blind Willie," Maeve said with a tired sigh.

"He's a villager?" How long would it take before I had met everyone who lived here?

"Not only is he a villager"—Maeve deadheaded a pot of petunias on the deck—"he's an Original."

"You're kidding."

"Not even a little bit. Apparently, he showed up one day shortly after Lucy let people move here."

"Let me guess, Gran let him stay because he had nowhere else to go."

"It was less that he had nowhere else to go and more that they couldn't make him leave. I guess he's super rich but decided he didn't want to deal with society any longer. He built himself a little shack at the far northwest edge of Whispering Pines. He promised to not bother anyone if your grandma let him stay. It doesn't hurt that he gives the village a boatload of money every year to let him stay on that little plot of land."

"Has he always been like that?"

She paused, debating her response. "Not like this. He's become socially awkward in the extreme. He gets flustered around people and has a hard time expressing himself. I'm not exactly sure what his set up is up there, but he seems familiar with what's going on in the world. He's staying connected somehow."

"Why do you call him Blind Willie? He's not blind."

Maeve shook her head and tossed a handful of dead petunia blossoms over the side of the porch. "We nicknamed him 'Blind Willie' because he says we're all blind, that we don't see the truth of the world."

"So he's a fortune teller?"

"No, he's just a crazy old conspiracy theorist."

That made as much sense as anything else in this village.

"This is the first I've seen him," I said. "Does he come around often?"

"No. In fact, his visits are so seldom, I forget about him until he shows up again. I guess he's got a stockpile of supplies up there. Probably a fallout shelter in case of nuclear war as well. He wanders into town when he needs something, or if he has a new threat he feels we need to know about."

Unable to hold back any longer, I laughed and then felt bad. "Sorry. I shouldn't laugh at someone with mental problems."

"I don't think it's a mental thing," Maeve assured. "He's just happier alone. He never causes any harm, other than offending people's nostrils. Don't think the man ever takes a bath." She gestured toward the pub. "I've got to get to work. See you later, Jayne."

I looked down at Meeka who was looking up at me. "See? Stopping by a gathering around here is always worth the trip. Let's go find that nun."

~~~

As the guy with the flat top had said, the nun was at the beach. It was early enough in the day that there were only a few parents with kids there. She looked so peaceful sitting by herself in a secluded spot, facing the water. She appeared to be meditating with her legs crisscrossed and her habit hiked up above her knees. I almost hated to disturb her.

"Excuse me?" I kept my voice soft, didn't want to scare the poor woman.

She turned slowly, as though she'd known I was there and was waiting for me to say something. Her face split in a big smile.

Five foot six, blue eyes, straight teeth, straight nose . . . nice knees.

I couldn't tell much more about her due to the habit.

"Sheriff O'Shea. Blessed be. How lovely to finally be face-to-face with you. I'm Agnes Plunkett."

The few times we'd seen each other, she was always riding through the commons on her bike. I'd wave and smile. She'd shout out "Blessed be" or "Beautiful day, isn't it?" The juxtaposition of the Roman Catholic attire and the Wiccan greeting only further piqued my curiosity about this woman.

"Please, sit." She gestured at the sand next to her.

I hadn't planned to sit but didn't feel like I should disobey a nun. "I'm sorry to bother you, but I've got a couple of questions I need to ask you."

"Certainly." She extended her legs straight in front of her, revealing hot pink polish on her toenails. "What can I help you with?"

"There was a man who used to follow you on a unicycle—"

"Barry," she confirmed. "Quite a character, isn't he?"

This coming from a nun with hot pink toes.

"I'm sorry, but I have to ask, are you really a nun?"

"A nun?" She looked at me like I was nuts. "No."

No? "Why do you wear a habit then?"

"I used to be a nun. They kicked me out."

Was it the pink toes? "Dare I ask, why?"

"Oh, you can ask. Never any harm in asking. I don't care to talk about it though."

"Why do you still wear a habit?"

"Just because they didn't want me to be a nun doesn't mean I don't want to be one."

I considered this for a moment. "Can you be a nun without a church?"

She sat tall and pushed her shoulders back. "I set up my own. An un-church, really, since it's not affiliated with anything organized. We pray together and mostly discuss the benefits of being a good person."

"Here in Whispering Pines? I haven't

heard of it."

"I don't advertise." She leaned over to me. "You're probably aware, there's another religion that dominates here."

"Every time I see you, you shout out 'blessed be.' I figured you were Wiccan."

"I find their greetings charming." She smiled and gave a content wiggle of her shoulders. "Not everyone here is Wiccan. Are you?"

"No. I'm not affiliated either."

"Oh," she clasped her hands together, "you should come to un-church. Tell me, what are your feelings about religion?"

"Another time, maybe. What do you know about Barry?"

Her shoulders sagged and her smile drooped. "Uh-oh. Did he get himself into trouble?"

As gently as I could, I explained what had happened. Halfway through my explanation, Agnes clutched a rosary and began rocking back and forth while whispering softly. Praying, I assumed.

"Agnes? I'm sorry to interrupt, but I need to figure out what happened to Barry."

"He was a good person," Agnes offered. "Conflicted about many things in his life, which was why he came to unchurch."

"What was he conflicted about?"

She gave me a look that left little doubt that she was indeed a nun. Or used to be. "I can't tell you what he told me. I can assure you, he wasn't doing anything illegal."

"Was a man named Angel part of his conflict?"

She considered this a moment. "You know how there are sometimes people in your life that you can't seem to stay clear of even though you don't care to have them around?"

I nodded.

She nodded.

"You really can't tell me anything about Barry that might help explain his death?"

She closed her eyes, seemingly debating the request, and rocked slowly, forward and back, her hands clasped in front of her heart. After a minute, she opened her eyes.

"I can't think of anything that would indicate his death was due to nefarious circumstances." She gave a single nod, letting me know that was her answer. Then, probably sensing my frustration, she added, "If I felt there was something going on, I would direct you to someone who could share what I cannot."

Really, I was more frustrated that everything regarding Barry led to a dead end than that Agnes was bound by a self-imposed confidentiality agreement.

"Thank you for your time, Agnes."

"Not at all. Consider coming to un-church sometime. It may benefit you."

I responded with a smile and then whistled for Meeka who had been entertaining herself by chasing the little waves washing up on the beach. Every time she did that, I thought of the hot lava game we played on the monkey bars at recess. *Don't touch the ground. It's hot lava!* In Meeka's case, *Don't touch the water. She'll give you a bath!*

A thankfully un-smelly Meeka and I made our way back to the station where we found Lupe Gomez sitting on the bench by the station's front door. She was here for the summer to report on our little village for *Unique Wisconsin*, the online magazine she worked for.

"Morning, Lupe. Let me guess why you're here."

"I hear there was a death yesterday. What can you tell me about it?" Her accent, usually slight, was strong today, which told me she was agitated over something.

"Your late-breaking instincts must be on the fritz. It took you this long to find out about it?"

"No. I was on deadline last night to turn in my next article for the website." She dropped her head back and smoothed her hands over her normally tidy, now disheveled braid. "It was giving me a hard time. Took forever until I was happy with it. Anyway, I'm moving on from the circus carnies to the fortune tellers."

"They're great." I unlocked the front door, crossed to the strip of light switches on the wall to my right, and Lupe followed me inside.

"They are, but they aren't why I'm

here. What's the deal with this death? Is it another murder? Do you need help finding answers?"

A few weeks earlier, two of the village carnies were murdered. It shook the entire village. I had just taken over as sheriff, had no deputy, and desperately needed help. Lupe, being the ace reporter she was, used her investigative skills to help me get answers from the other carnies. She ended up using those interviews to write short biographies about the carnies.

"I don't know what happened this time," I told her as I took a seat at the deputy's desk straight across from the door. The station was a simple rectangular building with a large central room and two jail cells to the left of the front door. My office, a small bathroom, and an interview room to the right. People had a tendency to sneak in and startle me if I sat in my office, so for now I used the desk in the central room. "This one is confusing me. I can't get any traction on what happened to him. If you want to dig around and ask questions, I'm happy to take the help."

I explained all that I knew regarding Barry, holding back on the specifics of where and how his body was found. It aggravated Lupe that I held back, but that way only the guilty party and I knew those details. If someone supplied that information to her during an interview, it could mean we had our killer.

We were just finishing a very short list of people she could talk to when the front door opened and Martin Reed walked in.

Chapter 8

IT HADN'T EVEN BEEN AN HOUR since the council meeting ended. Flavia must have run all the way home and told Martin to get his butt over to the station. I could just see it. Her shin-length, tent-like dress hiked up to her knees, her blonde hair coming loose from the bun normally pulled so tight her eyes were squinty, as she raced through the commons, over the bridge that crossed the highway, and all the way to the last road on the left just before the creek. Now that was a show I'd stop everything to watch.

"I hear you're looking for a deputy."

Reed gave his standard cocky grin, and all I could think was *please, don't let this be a mistake.*

"You're looking good, Reed." I matched the grin the best I could, but no one could pull off cocky like Martin Reed. When I first met him, he was pale, scrawny, and sickly-looking. Much like his mother. I figured he had a disease of some kind or he was wasted from drug use. Turned out, he simply didn't take care of himself. Now, a healthy tan replaced the pastiness. His medium-blue eyes sparkled. While he was still thin, he also had developed some muscle. "Looks like you've had an awakening of some kind."

"Almost dying was good for me, I guess," he said. "The doctors told me that if I wanted to recover fully from the poisoning, I had to treat my body well. I work out every day now and turned vegetarian."

Lupe stood in front of me, her nut-brown eyes wide and blazing, her mouth hanging open. "Who's he? He's hot."

My stomach turned a little bit.

"Lupe Gomez, village reporter at large, meet Martin Reed. Martin used to be the deputy here."

I stood back and distracted myself with happy thoughts—*Meeka playing in a field chasing butterflies on a warm spring day*—while Lupe and Martin checked each other out.

"So, Reed," I interrupted the budding ... whatever it was. "You really feel ready to come back to work?"

"I'm begging you," he clasped his hands together. "I need to start working again. Being at home with my mother all day is making me crazy." He paled, glanced at Lupe, and turned red. "I've, you know, been staying with her while I recover. Getting back to work, earning a paycheck again, will let me get out of there again."

Again? He was so full of it. Reed was twenty-three years old and had never left his mother's house. Nothing like the desire to be alone with a girl to kick the motivation for one's own place into overdrive.

"Lupe"—I stepped between the two of

them—"I need to chat with Martin alone for a bit. If you don't mind."

She glanced around me at Reed and gave him a smile I had never seen on her face before. Sweet and sappy didn't begin to describe it.

"No problem." She giggled. Something else she'd never done in my presence. "I'll come back later."

Oh geez. I knew there would be a problem of some kind bringing Reed back here; I had no idea it would be of a romantic nature.

I gestured for him to follow me into my office. I sat at my desk, and he took the chair across from it.

"I assume your mother discussed my conditions for you coming back?"

"She did. Look, Jayne—"

I held up a finger, stopping him before he could say another word. "First rule, you need to call me Sheriff now."

He gave a humble nod. "Sheriff, I've thought a lot about all of the complaints you had about me. Mother has told me everything you said at the council meetings. I think I know more than you give me credit for, but I understand why me not having formal training is a problem for you."

He was saying the right things. Did he mean them? Or was he simply *really* tired of living with Flavia? I fully understood the desire to get away from that woman.

"I'm not expecting you to apply to the academy or anything like that. I do want you to have a better understanding of the law and the expectations of a deputy. If you're willing to review some online material I found, I will deputize you. You'll do everything you used to do for Sheriff Brighton and probably a little more." I paused so he could consider the proposal. "That's it. That's my offer. Do you agree?"

"Yeah, sure. I'll agree to whatever you want if it means I can come back to work."

I printed out a list of all the online things I wanted him to review and handed it to him.

"All of this?" he asked of the two-page document.

"Fortunately, the tourists are behaving

themselves, other than our standard drunk and disorderly folks. It shouldn't take you that long. If you agree to review everything on that list, I will put you back on the payroll right now."

Reed jumped to his feet and stood at attention. It was cute, really.

"Yes, ma'am," he said with a salute. "I promise, you won't regret this."

"I will hold you to that. I can get a list of candidates from Madison in a heartbeat."

I was about to expand on that but bit it back. He just said Flavia told him everything that went on at the council meetings. If that was true, he knew the difficulties I'd been having finding someone.

"Your computer login hasn't changed," I told him. "Start studying. I have paperwork to do."

A couple hours later, I realized I'd forgotten to pack a lunch. I went out into the main room and whistled for Meeka who appeared from beneath her preferred cot.

Reed jumped, startled by my whistle.

"Sorry," I said. "That's her favorite place to sleep, especially when it's hot outside."

"Is she gonna be here all the time?" Reed and Meeka never really got along.

"The Whispering Pines Sheriff's Station officially has a K-9 unit." I gave him a big grin and a pointed look. "Do you have a problem with that?"

He mumbled that he didn't, and something else I couldn't make out, and returned to whatever he was reading on his computer.

"I'm going to grab some lunch. Can I get anything for you?"

"No, thanks. Mother said if I wasn't back in an hour she'd assume I got the job and would bring me something." He held up a hand before I could say what I was thinking. "Don't worry, she won't be coming by often."

Meeka and I walked to Grapes, Grains, and Grub where I sat on the pine tree-shaded deck with a few dozen tourists and enjoyed a bacon, lettuce, avocado, and tomato wrap, fries, and a vanilla shake. Meeka got to play with a group of other dogs in the fenced-in area Maeve had set up for her patrons' furry companions.

We headed straight back and had barely entered the station when Reed announced, "Dr. Bundy called, about half an hour ago. He's got news on your dead guy from yesterday."

"Already? He said it might be a few days."

Reed held his hands up in a *don't know* gesture. "He said he has to leave early today so wouldn't be there for much longer."

I went to my office and immediately dialed Dr. Bundy's number.

"I was going to give you another five minutes," Dr. Bundy said in lieu of a standard greeting.

"You found room in your lineup for my dead guy?"

"Deaths in Whispering Pines are rarely what they seem. I admit, curiosity got the better of me and I bumped him ahead of a few others. But you didn't hear that from me."

"Thanks, Doc. So? Does this one fit

with the other recently deceased from here?"

"Honestly, it was a bit of a letdown for me. I'm betting you'll find it interesting, though."

"Was he murdered?"

"No, he wasn't murdered. Care to guess again?"

"You said you were about to leave the office. Unless that means you've got a couple of hours for me to take stabs, you should probably tell me."

"True. We're having a little gathering at our place tonight. My wife is making pot roast for dinner. I love her pot roast. Nice and rare."

The fact that a man who cut up dead bodies all day enjoyed near-bloody meat for dinner didn't surprise me nearly as much as it probably should.

"Hang on." He shuffled through some papers. "Want to make sure I've got the right info for you. Like I said, I've had a lot of bodies on my tables lately." More shuffling. "Okay, got it. He drowned."

"What? No, you must have the wrong file. I rescued him from drowning.

Remember?"

"It's called secondary drowning," Dr. Bundy explained. "Some call it dry drowning, but that's a different set of circumstances. During his struggle, your guy got just enough water into his lungs to impede proper oxygenation."

"All those hours later, nowhere near water, he drowned?"

"That's what I'm telling you. His symptoms probably included chest pain, tiredness, coughing, and irritability. Basically, his breathing became impaired and he asphyxiated. It's common for victims to live for many hours before expiring. Your guy fits the profile, so to speak."

"You found nothing else suspicious on his body? No injuries of any kind?"

"Nothing that could have caused him to asphyxiate. That's what I'll be listing as cause of death."

"What about that white stuff around his mouth and nose? It looked like pillowcase fibers to me."

"It was foam residue. Another common thing in drownings. Foam bubbles up from inside and exits through the mouth and/or nose. I found trace amounts of foam on his face, too, which tells me there was more initially, and someone wiped it away."

"One of his friends performed CPR. She probably removed it before beginning."

"That would be my assumption as well." He paused, flipping through papers, probably checking to see if there was anything else he needed to tell me. "That's all I've got."

"Okay, if you're sure." This explained why no one I interviewed could provide any helpful information.

"You sound disappointed, Jayne."

"Do I?" I laughed. "I guess after the other ultra-involved deaths here, this one is rather tame. Not that I wanted there to be another murder here."

"I understand what you mean."

I paused a second before asking, "Doc? Did I miss something? Did I do anything wrong?"

"You told me that when you came across this man he was tangled up in some weeds, correct?"

"Right, he was in a little cove. The water is warm and still there, which is why the weeds grow so thick in that spot."

"I found tiny bits of plant material in his lungs. The damage was done before you got to him."

"I understand that." I still felt sad about the situation. Nice guy, my age, headed for a bright future. "After such a traumatic event, I feel like I should've taken him in to get checked out."

"Did you ask if he wanted to go?"

"Yes, but—"

"We're talking about a full-grown adult man. You couldn't have forced him."

"I know. But if he would have gone?"

"Then he would probably be alive right now. Don't beat yourself up over this, Jayne. You didn't do anything wrong." He waited to see if I had anything else to say and then changed topics. "I have something that might cheer you up."

I took a deep breath and shook my head, forcing thoughts of Barry out of my mind for now.

"Cheering up would be nice. What have you got for me?"

"Maybe 'cheering up' isn't the right term, but I got a hold of someone in records. Your grandmother's autopsy report should be in your inbox now."

I spun to my computer and wiggled the mouse to wake it up. Sure enough, the subject line of the last item to hit my inbox read FULL AUTOPSY: LUCY O'SHEA. I slumped with relief as my adrenaline level soared at the same time.

"This is great. Thank you so much, Dr. Bundy."

"I'll send over the preliminary autopsy on your guy before I leave for the night. Let me know if I can help with anything regarding your grandmother. I didn't have time to look over the report, so I have no idea what you're about to see."

"Will do. Go enjoy your pot roast."

Try as I might, I couldn't get myself to read Gran's report slowly. I flipped through the pages at lightning pace and then went back to the start. Among the many details and photographs, two things stood out to me like a neon sign in the middle of the village commons.

First, my grandmother didn't drown like we'd been told. Unlike poor Barry, there had been no water in her lungs. This meant she was already dead when she ended up in her bathtub. Which meant someone put her there. As the reality that someone had killed my grandmother took hold, my vision tunneled and I felt like I was going to pass out. I leaned forward in my chair, putting my head between my knees, and waited for things to clear.

Meeka, who'd been wandering around exploring the station, was in front of me in a flash. She pawed at my hands dangling off my knees, her little claws gently scratching me. When I didn't respond, she licked my hand.

"I'm okay, girl. This is a nightmare, though. Someone killed Gran."

As though she understood, Meeka let out a mournful whine.

Once I was sure I wasn't going to pass out, I sat up and turned back to my computer. The second thing that stood out to me in this report was the image currently on the screen. I'd seen it before, someone had drawn it all over the walls of my house. A lower case "y" with an extra-long straight tail, a horizontal line crossing the tail near the bottom. Below the line and to the right of the tail was what looked like a lower case "m." Beneath it all, a lower case "w."

Morgan had identified it for me as a symbol from the Theban or Witch's Alphabet. She said witches used to use the alphabet, a few still did, as a sort of encryption in their spell books to keep others from being able to read it. This particular symbol meant full stop or period. As in, at the end of a sentence.

The fact that this symbol had been drawn over the heart of the dead woman I found in my backyard had delivered a chilling message: full stop, end of life. The fact that it had been drawn in the same place on my grandmother, according to the picture on my computer screen, led me to believe it had to be the same person.

Chapter 9

REED LOOKED UP FROM HIS computer with an expression I recognized. It was the same one my sister used to get when she had information to share. Usually, being the older sister, it was something I already knew, but I let her share anyway. It was easier than dealing with her demanding, at the top of her lungs, that I never let her talk. Like I could ever stop her from talking. Right now, whatever Reed had learned, I wasn't up for a discussion about law enforcement rules and regulations.

He opened his mouth at the same moment he must have registered the look on my face and course corrected. "I take it you got in touch with Dr. Bundy. Bad news?"

I gave him the quick rundown on the autopsy results for Barry.

"Really? Never heard of secondary drowning before." He studied me for a moment. "That's not what the look on your face is for. Care to share?"

Good question. "Tell me something first. I need to know that hiring you was the right decision."

"You won't regret it. I know we started out kind of rough when you first got here, but you saved my life. And that's not being dramatic. If you wouldn't have figured out—"

"I know." I halted what could turn into a mushy moment. I wasn't up for that either. "I'm glad I was here for you."

"I feel like I owe you." The tops of his cheeks pinked a little and he tried to shrug it off. "Not like, you know, I am indebted to you forever." Another shrug. "I just appreciate what you did."

Who knew Martin Reed was such a softy?

"Okay, here's the deal. I'm sure you're aware that your mother and I aren't exactly crazy about each other."

He laughed. "Yeah, I noticed."

"Then I'm sure you can understand why I was wary of bringing you back on as my deputy." He nodded but didn't reply. "If this is going to work, we need to trust each other. Like I did with my old partner in Madison, I need to know you've got my back. That means you can't tell your mother things that go on here. Just like I can't tell Tripp everything."

I waited while Reed analyzed my comments.

"I can agree to that, but in return can I ask that you don't hold my mother against me? She's my mother and I love her, but I understand how people feel. She's not my fault."

Another side of Reed I didn't anticipate. "How about we proceed with the theory that we will trust each other until there's a reason not to."

"Deal." Reed stood and held his hand out to me. "Now do you want to tell me what's got you so upset?"

We had an agreement going forward, but full confidence had not yet been achieved. Like I did when explaining a crime to Lupe, I held back the crucial information that only the killer would know.

"I received new information regarding my grandmother's death. Turns out it wasn't accidental."

"You're saying she was murdered?"

"That's what I'm saying. I have no idea where to start investigating this. My gut is telling me that the reason is tied to something that happened long ago."

My gut and the fact that two people, Sugar and Reeva Long, had told me the same thing. Reeva was Reed's aunt; no way was I ready to connect those two dots yet.

"If that's the case," Reed said, "you should start with those who were here years ago. The Originals."

I smiled, pleased with his logical reaction. Maybe bringing him back was the right choice.

"As Tripp and I have been renovating the house, I've been going through my grandparents' possessions. I think my grandmother kept journals but I don't know how far back they go. If I can find them, they might help. So, if you don't mind—"

"I've got probably another hour and I'll be through with this first website you gave me. Who knew learning about the law would be interesting. I'll close up tonight if you trust me to do that."

All I wanted at that point was to get home and talk to Tripp. "That would be great. We'll review what you've been reading tomorrow."

Before leaving, I printed Gran's autopsy report and tucked it into Gran's file, which I took home with me, then Meeka and I left through the station's back door.

"Crap." I groaned and let my head fall back. Once again, I had forgotten that we brought the van into work this morning. It was either take the van home again or walk all the way to the marina to get the kayak. "Might as well go for a walk or we'll have to deal with this again tomorrow."

~~~

The marina was packed with tourists when we got there. Some were checking in their rentals for the night, but since closing was still a couple hours away, there were plenty of people just heading out onto the lake. Either way, this meant Oren and his dad Gil were dealing with boat rentals. My kayak was on the rack inside the building where Oren had put it yesterday. I grabbed my dry bag from the cargo well and went out to the changing hut to get out of my uniform. Even more than not wanting to get it full of lake water if I tipped, I was ready to be off duty.

Once changed, I stepped out of the little hut to find Lily Grace scratching Meeka's ears. My first reaction was to hide. I was almost in the clear, all I had to do was grab my kayak and go. But then I remembered Lily Grace's vision of the lady in the water.

"Hey." I pointed at her hair. The not quite blonde, not quite brown, not quite curly, not quite straight mane had expanded to nearly the size of her boyfriend Oren's Afro. "Problems with the humidity?"

She rolled her eyes. "Don't get me started."

I smiled. "Can I chat with you for a second?"

She gave Meeka's ears a final fluffing and stood. "Sure. What's up?"

I led her off to the side where no one could overhear us. "I got some news about my grandma today."

Confiding these things to Lily Grace presented a quandary for me. First, she was a teenager. Second, I didn't believe in the woo-woo of fortune telling. Except, her visions had been spot-on, and regardless of my personal beliefs, the cop in me couldn't dismiss tools that helped solve cases. In this situation, the personal collided with the professional. If Lily Grace could help me figure out what happened to Gran, I didn't care where the information came from.

"She was murdered?" Lily Grace looked as shocked as I felt. "That sucks.

Why are you telling me?"

"I'm not sure, to be honest. Do you remember the second reading you did for me?"

"Told you before, I don't hold on to all that. My head would explode if I tried to remember the details of every reading."

"That's what I figured. What you told me was that you saw a lady in the water and that she had 'black stuff' on her."

She looked at me and blinked, waiting for more details.

"At the time," I said while flipping through papers in Gran's folder, "we thought maybe you had seen a tourist who had drowned. Would drown. Whatever."

"And I was right? Didn't some guy drown yesterday?"

"Yes, but it was a guy not a lady."

"You know my visions aren't that exact." Her tone said she needed patience when dealing with me. "I saw someone drown and someone did."

"Maybe," I pushed, "but you said you saw a lady *in* the water. You didn't see someone who was dead in the water."

I walked her through how the position of Gran's body, face up in her bathtub, combined with the placement of the lump on her forehead didn't add up. It wasn't possible for her to have hit her head on the bathtub in that spot and ended up face up.

"You're saying," Lily Grace concluded, "that you don't think she drowned in the bathtub?"

"That's what I'm saying, and that's what the autopsy proves. There's also this 'black stuff' you saw on the lady in the water." I showed her the picture included in the report of the symbol drawn over Gran's heart.

"Huh." Lily Grace sounded both surprised at this revelation and pleased that she had foreseen it. "That kinda qualifies as black stuff, doesn't it? So what is it that you want from me? Another reading?"

She held out her hands, as though prepared to read me right here on the beach, and I shook my head.

"Not yet." I couldn't believe I was even considering using a fortune teller to help solve a case. "I mostly wanted to tell you about the connection between your vision and Gran's death. If my trail runs cold, I'll stop by The Triangle and see what you can see."

The Fortune Tellers' Triangle was an area of Whispering Pines not far from my house where Lily Grace and all the other fortune tellers lived.

She held my gaze, her big turquoise eyes full of emotion. "Jayne, I knew your grandma. Not, like, intimately, but she was my grandma's friend. She was around a lot, and I went to her house . . . your house pretty often. I really liked her." She blinked and cleared her throat before continuing. "If I can help you figure out what happened, I'm all over that."

With emotion clogging my own throat, I nodded my thanks and motioned toward the marina office. "I need to grab my kayak and head home. I know there's something somewhere in that house that can help me with this."

She walked with me. "I'm waiting for Oren. We barely see each other during the summer season. His dad agreed to let him take off a little early tonight. We're going to have a picnic by the lake."

The two teens were so cute together. I had no idea how many high school sweethearts stayed together forever anymore, but I hoped these two would. They were good for each other.

A few minutes later, Meeka and I were securely in the kayak and Lily Grace gave us a gentle push onto the lake. Meeka, always in tune with my moods, sat in the well between my legs. Normally, she stood with her front paws on the edge of the boat, looking over the side for fish. Tonight, she sat there and looked mournfully at me instead.

"I wish you could have met Gran. The two of you would have loved each other."

She gave a sharp exhale and leaned against my leg in reply.

The next thing I knew, I was standing on the dock at home, pulling the kayak out of the water. Normally, getting out of the thing was a huge exercise in caution. I was always afraid of tipping and ending up soaked. Tonight, I hadn't even thought

about it and hopped right out. Success
tended to come much more easily when I
didn't overthink things.

Chapter 10

I WAS SO ANXIOUS TO GET INSIDE and talk to Tripp, I thought, for about two seconds, of leaving the kayak on the deck. With all the tourists in the area, that was a really good way to lose a nice kayak. After taking two minutes to put it back in its proper spot in the rack inside the boathouse, I rushed upstairs to drop off my dry bag and give Meeka some food. I found Tripp in the house putting the finishing touches on dinner.

"Oh good," he said as he glanced up at me, "you're just in time. Since it's been so hot, I thought pasta salad with plenty of veggies and little cheese cubes sounded like a good idea. What's the matter?"

While he dished up the pasta salad and set a plate in front of me on the kitchen bar, I told him about the autopsy report.

"I'm sorry," he said, "but you're not really surprised, are you? I mean, we already figured something was suspicious."

A few weeks earlier, while cleaning out Gran's bathroom, I came across a harlequin doll that was meant to represent Gran. Donovan, village council member and owner of Quin's clothing shop, supposedly had the ability to foretell death. He claimed he would go into a trance whenever this knowledge came to him and he'd create a porcelain harlequin doll that resembled the to-be victim in death. I'd had no doubt that Donovan's precision with the Gran doll was accurate, right down to the tiny blue fingernails and large lump over the doll's left eye. While I didn't for one moment believe his knowledge of impending death was supernatural, I had no way to prove how he knew these things. Regardless, that doll was what made me realize the police report my family received didn't make sense.

In his report, the late Sheriff Brighton explained that his conclusion was that Gran had slipped on water on her bathroom floor or tripped on the bath mat, hit her head on the edge of the tub, and fell into her already full bathtub where she drowned. As I'd just told Lily Grace, Tripp and I walked through that scenario step-by-step, numerous different ways, and decided that the report couldn't possibly be accurate.

"I haven't studied the autopsy report in detail yet," I told Tripp as we settled in to eat, "but it supports the conclusion you and I came to. And, there was no water in her lungs. She didn't drown."

"You're saying that someone staged it to make it look like an accidental drowning?" Tripp's smile turned into a wince. "Sorry. Didn't mean to get so excited about that."

"Don't worry about it. That's probably the same reaction I have when clues in a case come clear to me." I chewed and swallowed a mouthful of pasta salad. "This is good, by the way."

He smiled his thanks at me.

"I have to figure this out," I insisted. "I have to find out the truth of what happened to Gran, and I have to catch whoever did this to her."

"I know you do and wouldn't even think of trying to stop you." He waited a beat before adding, "Because I know you, I have to say I'm a little concerned that it will consume you."

I shrugged off his worry while sipping iced tea. "There's something in this house that will help, I know it. I'm going to find it."

"Just don't let yourself become so involved with this hunt that you get sidetracked from getting the bed-and-breakfast ready. As you've told me a dozen times, we're on the clock."

He meant the deadline my parents had given us. We had one year to at least break even, or they were putting the house up for sale. That meant the two thousand acres Whispering Pines occupied would also be sold. The villagers would have first chance at buying the property, but if they couldn't and whoever did buy it didn't want to host a village, everyone would have to leave. No pressure on us whatsoever.

"I'm all set with my Pine Time stuff," I promised. "Everything is ready to go. All I have to do is hit the go button on the website and the ads. Once I figure out what happened to Gran, I'll be able to focus on the house and running the B&B."

Tripp gave me a skeptical smile but didn't argue.

I finished dinner, helped him with the dishes, and told him I was going up to the attic.

"I'm going to finish looking through those boxes tonight. If there's something up there that will help me, I will find it."

"Tonight? You do realize how many boxes you have left?"

"I do. Which means I need to get busy. It's not like I'll sleep otherwise."

Anticipating a long night, I made coffee and filled a travel mug.

The attic occupied the third level of the house and had never been finished. Once everything else on the first and second levels was complete, our plan was to create a caretaker's apartment for Tripp to live in up there. We hadn't decided if we would include a kitchenette or if Tripp would simply use the first-floor kitchen, but there was plumbing for a bathroom. It was almost as though my grandparents had anticipated this very thing. Putting in an apartment or another room, not Tripp living there.

There was a ton of furniture in the attic; Gran's obsession. I had already moved the lighter weight pieces to one side of the space. I hadn't been as organized with the storage boxes, however. I took a few minutes to set aside the boxes I'd already looked through and then called Tripp to help me with some bigger pieces of furniture.

"What exactly are you looking for?" he asked as we set down a sofa and went back for a heavy steamer trunk.

"Anything that will tell me about the history of the village. Gran mentioned journaling in the emails she used to send me, but I don't know if she ever did that.

If she did, I'm hoping the journals are up here."

"You really think that would uncover her killer? Lift with your legs."

I grunted as we hoisted the trunk. "Sugar, Reeva, and Briar all told me that's where I needed to start. At the beginning."

"So, we're looking for a bunch of books."

I smiled at the way he was suddenly a partner in this excavation, and gratitude spread over me like a thick blanket on a cold winter night. With the attic better organized, I realized there weren't as many boxes left as it had seemed when they were spread out all over the place. We started at opposite ends of the pile and methodically worked our way through every box. Many of them, like those I'd already gone through, were filled with holiday decorations. Those, we set in a corner; I'd decide what we wanted to keep and what to get rid of later. Other boxes held photo albums, filled with pictures of my grandparents when they were young, my dad as a little boy, and the many trips Gran and Gramps had gone on once Dad had left home.

"These might be helpful for you." Tripp held up two photo albums, both with the Triple Moon Goddess symbol on their covers. The symbol—a full moon with a pentacle inside flanked by crescent moons on the left and right—was the one the Originals had adopted for their logo, of sorts.

"What's in them?" I asked.

"I'm just guessing," he said as he flipped pages, "but they look like they were taken here in Whispering Pines. There's a lake and trees everywhere." He looked closer at one picture. "This looks like the pentacle garden mid-construction." He turned another page. "It's so weird to see this place without all the buildings."

My heart skipped a beat and I asked him to set the albums near the stairs. "I'll look through them later. Let's finish the boxes."

Two hours later, we finished the last box but hadn't come up with anything else even remotely helpful.

"You're sure she kept journals?" Tripp asked.

"I'm not sure of anything," I snapped then blew out a slow breath. "Sorry. It would be nice if answers could come easily, just once."

"Don't give up yet. You know there's more in the basement and in the loft over the garage."

"True. I forgot about the garage. Maybe I'll go start there."

"Jayne, it's almost midnight. Whatever is there will still be there tomorrow. Go get some sleep. We have to work in a few hours."

"Fine," I reluctantly agreed. "I'll look at the pictures in those albums before I go to sleep. It'll be like a bedtime story."

~~~

Tripp was right, some of the pictures showed the progress of the pentacle garden during construction. I recognized Gran and two fortune tellers that I was sure were Effie and Cybil, their preferred clothing styles of monochromatic gypsy skirts and button-up blouses hadn't changed much in the last fifty years.

One young woman, with wavy, raven-black hair that fell almost to her waist looked a lot like Morgan, so I guessed she was Morgan's mom, Briar. No, that couldn't be right. I did a quick calculation. This had to be Dulcie, Morgan's grandmother. The woman responsible for this plot of land turning from a single-family homestead into a village. I had to show these to Morgan and Briar.

A second album was filled with pictures of the kids who lived here. A few pictures had just one or two kids in them, but most were of a group. Along with my dad, I spotted two blondes that had to be Flavia and Reeva but couldn't decide which was which. Two younger girls with red hair were probably Sugar and Honey. The others who showed up in many shots with Dad—three boys and three girls—I couldn't identify.

Mixed in with the regular photographs were a few Polaroids, the instant-developing kind. Most of those were of the adult villagers, all in Wiccan robes. They probably took Polaroids to capture memories of their rituals, rather than bringing film in to be developed, to keep them private. People still thought Wicca and devil worship were synonymous. So not true.

I'm not sure how long I sat there looking back through the photographic history of Whispering Pines because I fell asleep on the loveseat in my apartment sitting room. I woke with a jolt at three in the morning with a thought screaming at the front of my brain.

"Steamer trunk," I exclaimed loud enough to wake Meeka. She scowled at me, stood, spun in two circles, and then lay down again.

We had searched through every box and every drawer of every piece of furniture. I had tried to open that steamer trunk, but it was locked. I'd made a mental note to get the keys and find out what was inside, but my mental note-taking app must have been on the fritz because I never thought of it again.

As I was preparing to drive up to the

village from Madison, just before Memorial Day weekend about two months ago, my mother had given me a keyring, the diameter of a grapefruit, loaded with dozens of keys.

"Your grandmother has an addiction to collecting antique furniture. And it seems every piece has a lock." Mom had said this with a stiff shake of her head, indicating how impractical she found Gran's collection. Mom was much more of a minimalist; less clutter and less to clean. She handed me the keyring pinched between two fingers, as though the entire set was infected with a communicable disease of some kind.

"What does the color coding mean?" I'd asked of the three keys with silicone disks around their heads.

"My understanding is that the blue key is for the front door. Purple for the backdoor. The green one is for the garage. Good luck figuring out which goes to what otherwise. Once you do, I suggest identifying them somehow or you'll have to go through the entire ring every time you need a key for something."

Right now, my problem was that I couldn't remember where I put the keyring. I searched through each of the eight drawers in the dresser Tripp and one of the crew guys had brought over from the attic for me. I checked in the three kitchenette drawers with no luck. Then I remembered, "Side table."

This time, Meeka woke with an angry bark.

"Sorry. I need to find those keys." I opened the only drawer on the table in the sitting area, reached to the very back, and, "Success!"

I nearly tripped running down the stairs on the outside of the boathouse. Then, I nearly tripped over Meeka as we ran through the yard. She seemed to think this was a new middle-of-the-night game of some kind.

"We aren't playing," I scolded as we ran. This didn't stop her, she just ran in bigger circles around me, barking the whole while. By the time I made it through the house and up two flights of stairs to the attic, I was completely winded. I bent at the waist, hands resting on my knees, and waited for my heart rate and breathing to slow.

Then came the painstaking process of going through all those keys one-by-one. By the time I was on key number twenty-something, I heard a voice shouting from the bottom of the stairs.

"Jayne?" It was Tripp. "Are you up there?"

"Yeah, it's me."

I listened to his footsteps pounding up the stairs as I continued trying keys. He appeared wearing nothing but a pair of light cotton lounge pants. The sight of him shirtless almost made me drop the keyring.

"Seventeen minutes after three in the morning," Tripp announced, his own breathing a little elevated. "That's the time, in case you were wondering. What are you doing up here?"

"We forgot about the steamer trunk. This thing is so heavy, something is obviously in there."

"This couldn't wait until morning? No, never mind. Stupid question. Of course it can't."

"Why are you up at seventeen minutes after three?"

"I was sound asleep until I heard Meeka barking." He scowled at her, and she turned her back in shame.

Finally, four keys later, I found the one that opened the trunk. With wide eyes, I turned to Tripp who was kneeling next to me now. I released the latch on the right as he undid the one on the left and then we lifted the lid.

I gasped. "Jackpot."

Inside, were dozens of books of various sizes and colors. Some leather, some linen, and all of them tossed inside in no sort of order.

"Any chance you'll wait until later to organize these?" Tripp asked with a look that said he already knew the answer. "I'll go make coffee."

Chapter 11

BY THE TIME THE CREW ARRIVED AT seven o'clock, we were organizing the last of the journals. We had forty-five chronological stacks of journals, each stack representing a year, set neatly against the far wall of the attic. Some years contained a single book, others as many as five.

"One year is missing." I stood by the first stack on the left. "The journals start at 1966, the year Gran and Gramps moved here. I'm not sure when other Originals started coming." I walked along the row, past twelve years' worth of journals, and came to a gap. "This is

1978." I took a step, spanning the gap, to the next stack of books. "This is 1980. Where are the books for 1979?"

"They're not up here. We've checked everywhere. It's not like you can't start reading. We don't have to keep looking now, do we?"

I gave him what must have been a withering look, because he backed a couple steps away. I was so tired of there always being holes to fill.

"No, not now," I agreed, "but I need to find them."

Rebounding from the glare, he moved closer and wrapped me in a hug. I hadn't realized how tense I'd been until the strength of his arms and the warmth of his body relaxed me. I felt like I had so much to prove to so many people. Mom and Dad were expecting me to make the B&B a success. So was Tripp. The entire village expected me to be a good sheriff. They didn't know the terms of the B&B— be a success in a year or sell—but I think a few had a feeling something big was riding on this. It was getting to be too much.

"I think," Tripp said, "we've looked through everything we can possibly look through up here. You'll need to start with what you've got because we both need to go to work soon. We'll look in the basement and garage tonight. How does that sound?"

Logically, that made sense. I was exhausted, though, so I only felt the frustration of needing to find the year of missing books.

"Come with me." He grabbed the first three stacks of journals, six in all of varying thicknesses, then took my elbow and led me downstairs. "Just in case you have some time today, and you want to start reading, I'll put these in your car. You go get ready for work."

I stood in the middle of the yard and watched as he carried the books to the Cherokee. I'd never had anyone in my life before who took care of me the way he did. My mother probably did when I was little, but by the year I started middle school, she decided to open the salon. My dad spent more and more time at his dig sites with each year that passed. I was the

182 | SHAWN MCGUIRE

bigger sister, so it was always expected that I would take care of Rosalyn.

As for Jonah, my ex-fiancé, it became clear that he wanted a traditional, old-fashioned marriage. He loved coming home to dinner on the table, even though that usually meant pizza, carry out, or something from a box that I warmed up in the microwave. He was so determined to live out his dream, he gave me cooking lessons for Christmas one year, presumably in the hopes that I'd be a topnotch hostess when it came time to throw dinner parties for all his political cronies.

It was obvious that I'd struck gold with Tripp. What was I waiting for?

Twenty minutes later, I was showered and dressed in my uniform. I needed coffee, about a gallon of it. Tripp, of course, knew this and had it ready for me when I re-entered the house.

"I made it extra strong." He handed me a mug and grinned. "Do me a favor and don't make any important decisions today, okay?"

"Or operate heavy machinery?" I felt

instant gratitude as I took the first soothing sip. "Why is it that you always know just what I need?"

He didn't respond, just locked eyes with me over his own steaming mug.

He quickly scrambled some eggs while I warmed up some blueberry muffins in the microwave—my preferred kitchen appliance—and we settled onto our bar stools.

"I never asked how your day went yesterday," I said, embarrassed. "How are things coming?"

"Destruction goes a lot faster than reconstruction," he explained. "We had a good day yesterday, but you wouldn't notice much if you looked. We fixed lots of plumbing issues and should be able to start on the tiling soon. I'm going to interview tilers today."

"You're going to stay away from heavy machinery, too?"

"I got more sleep than you, but that's probably a good idea." He popped a piece of muffin in his mouth.

"When will we be able to start with the tiling, then? You know my mother likes to be updated on our progress."

Tripp ran a hand through his curly hair and stretched, his T-shirt tugging tight against his chest as he did. "Mr. Powell assured me that the people he's sending over are all very talented. I'll make the decision based on design ideas. Did you want to see those before I choose someone?"

We'd gone back-and-forth with ideas for weeks and had looked at hundreds of pictures on the internet. Pinterest was my new favorite thing. "You know what I like. I trust you to make the right decision."

He smiled, clearly pleased with my confidence in him. "Mr. Powell also assured me that we can get inventory quickly. He uses a place in Wausau, drives down there once or twice a week for small things. They deliver the big orders. I'm guessing we'll be able to start with the tile next week."

"That's great. Looks like we're staying right on schedule."

"No. Don't say that." He held his hands out to me with two fingers crossed in an X.

"What's that supposed to mean?" I poked his crossed fingers. "Are you placing a hex on me?"

"You'll jinx it. Never say anything about a schedule when it comes to construction work."

I finished my eggs and glass of orange juice, dumped my remaining coffee into a travel mug and topped it off with more of Tripp's extra strong brew. Still, I sensed at least one trip to Ye Olde Bean Grinder coming today.

"Sorry to keep you awake last night," I said as I screwed on the lid, "but I'm glad to have had your company. Good luck today. I hope the schedule falls apart completely."

He put his hands over his ears. "Stop talking about the schedule. Go, get out of here."

He pointed in the direction of the garage, and I left before he physically removed me from the house.

I opened the back of the Cherokee and Meeka jumped in and crawled into her crate. I glanced up at the garage in front of me. In particular, at one of the windows in the loft area up top. While cleaning out the house to start on renovations, Tripp put some things up there for safekeeping during construction. That's when he found Gran's altar table, sitting in a little alcove beneath a window that overlooked the lake.

Meeka whined when I still hadn't closed the crate's door after nearly a minute. I looked down at her and scratched her neck beneath her collar.

The adults told Rosalyn and I that Gramps' workshop was in the loft. They said it was full of dangerous tools that could hurt us, so we needed to stay out. Naturally, this meant we had to sneak up there and explore. Late one night sixteen years ago, that's what we did and found Gran up there performing a Wiccan ritual. She let us watch, as long as we promised not to tell anyone what we saw. We agreed, but the next morning, Rosalyn told Mom everything. The little snitch. Minutes later, we left Whispering Pines, and I'd never been back until two months ago.

After we learned the truth, as much truth as a twelve- and eight-year-old could understand, Rosalyn started calling the loft Gran's secret clubhouse. A club of one, unless Gramps had also been Wiccan.

"Clubhouse."

Meeka gave another tiny whine and pawed at my arm, confused as to why we weren't leaving.

People kept special things, secret things, in clubhouses. My instincts were telling me Gran had done the same thing.

"Come, Meeka. We need to go check this out."

Gran's car, a sporty baby-blue hardtop convertible Lexus, was still parked in the garage next to a more practical Subaru SUV for the winter months. Dad would need to decide what to do with them. Rosalyn would want the convertible, but I'd argue that it belonged to the estate and claim it as the B&B owner.

I flicked the switch at the bottom of the stairs and lights in the loft above turned on. Meeka raced ahead of me as we climbed up. Kitty corner from the top of the staircase, in the left-hand corner of the loft, was Gran's altar table. It was still full, like it was the day Tripp found it, with Gran's Wicca tools, or whatever they were called. A blue cloth with a silver pentagram covered the table. One purple and one silver taper candle along with a white pillar candle stood at the back of the table. A goblet, a small black cauldron, something that looked like a magic wand, a dagger, and an incense burner also lay where Gran last set them.

My gaze continued past the altar to the large antique armoire in the corner positioned. If Gran had kept anything personal up here, in there would be a safe bet. While I crossed to look through the armoire, Meeka trotted over to explore the corner with all the pictures and statues and other items Tripp brought up here for storage.

"Don't break anything."

She sneezed, but I was pretty sure it was because she'd gotten dust in her nose instead of being a response to my warning.

I stopped just outside a circle that had

been either drawn on or burnt into the floor. I didn't know what it meant, but I knew it was a Wiccan thing. Was crossing into it like entering a church? Should I genuflect? Cross myself? I seriously had no idea what the protocol was. Or if it even mattered for a non-Wiccan.

Morgan had a small altar room hidden behind the bookcases in the reading room at Shoppe Mystique. I'd been in that little room twice, to provide Morgan with positive energy as she made spell bags. Morgan never made a big deal about entering the little room, and she never stopped me from just walking in. So, hopeful that lightning wouldn't strike me, I breached the circle.

Inside the armoire, two beautiful velvet ritual robes were hanging in a skinny compartment that ran the length of the left side. On the right side were a set of shelves. The top shelf was loaded with candles of various colors and sizes. The next held boxes of incense and oils and other tools of the Wiccan trade. A third shelf held folded altar cloths, also in a variety of colors and designs.

Beneath the last shelf was what appeared to be a box. It looked like the woodworker had intended to put a fourth shelf there; the space was the exact height and width of the others, but for whatever reason it had been boxed off instead.

I backed up a few steps, to the middle of the circle, and took in the open armoire in its entirety. From this distance, I could tell that all the interior wood was different from the wood that had made up the rest of the cabinet. Or at least it was a different color. The main cabinet was a beautiful, gleaming—if not for the layer of dust—mahogany-brown. The shelves were a flat chocolate-brown. Gran had customized the interior. But why would she make a box at the bottom instead of a fourth shelf? Was something inside it? Maybe I could break through the wood and find out.

Meeka trotted past me to investigate the armoire. She stood on her back legs and sniffed the altar cloths. She sneezed again, this time her nose surely overwhelmed by the incense and oils that had permeated the fabric over the years.

Then she dropped back down to the floor. As she did, I tracked her movement and noticed very faint scuff marks in the wood floor near the base of the armoire, only visible because the morning sun was shining in the windows. Any other time of day, between the layer of dust and the simple dim lightbulbs, I wouldn't be able to see the scratches.

I took hold of the back corner of the cabinet and pulled; much like Morgan when she pulled on a section of the built-in bookcases to reveal her hidden altar room.

Gran must have installed glides of some kind on the bottom of the cabinet because it pulled easily away from the wall. On the backside, in the same location of the box, was one of those finger-pull latches that folded flat into the wood. I stuck in my finger, pulled the latch, and found four journals inside the drawer. A peek inside one confirmed they were the missing year: 1979.

Chapter 12

DESPITE MY FIERCE CURIOSITY over why Gran had hidden those four books, I started with the first journal from 1966. Best to know everything from the start, or I'd likely miss something important and end up confused.

My grandparents had lived in Oconomowoc, Wisconsin, a small town between Milwaukee and Madison, before moving to the Northwoods. It seemed that the move to the property on the water was a good thing for her.

Of all the two thousand acres we acquired, no other spot speaks more to us than this little ten-acre piece that juts out into the lake. If we position the house just right, I'll be able to see water from every window. Naturally, all Keven can talk about is getting a fishing boat.

As much as I'll miss my friends, I just can't handle all the people anymore. Milwaukee has been expanding further and further westward. Oconomowoc is still small, but it's only a matter of time. I don't want Dillon to grow up with all that chaos and congestion. I want him to have the freedom to run and not worry about cars and neighbors and noise. Keven agreed to move as long as there was some place for him to fish. When he heard about this plot, we didn't hesitate and bought it sight unseen. He's so determined to get that boat, we're building the boathouse first. Also, that will give us a place to live until the main house is ready. It's going to be a big house, one we can fill with children and someday grandchildren.

I hadn't realized the boathouse was built first. Gramps and his fishing. Every chance he got, he was out on the lake. I'm sure there were days when he didn't even drop a line in the water, he just wanted to be out there. I also hadn't realized my dad was born before the move. If I'd taken the time to do the math, I would have realized that in 1966, he would have been four or five years old.

The rest of the first journal was filled with the trials and tribulations of building a home in the middle of nowhere. The closest grocery store was a good thirty miles away. Clearing the trees off the "piece of land" took months. The driveway, from the country highway down to where the garage now stood, had to be laid. Electrical, sewer, and telephone lines had to be run; I couldn't even imagine how expensive that must have been. When summer turned to fall, and the warm days turned to frigid nights, Gran took Dad back to Oconomowoc until the spring.

Construction hadn't stopped over the

winter, but it slowed drastically. By springtime, when they were ready to return, the house was still nowhere near finished.

Spending time with friends over the winter was nice, but we've been so anxious to return to our new home. Keven had warned me that only the first floor was usable. We have a kitchen and bathroom and rooms to sleep in so really that's all we need. I could spend all day every day in that kitchen, it's the one of my dreams. The bedroom and bathroom near the kitchen will suit Keven and I fine for now. A room at the other end of the house will eventually be Keven's den, but it's big enough for Dillon to use as a bedroom. And the living room! I've never seen a room so large. Dillon will be able to run around in it on days when he can't be outside. It's truly like a little piece of heaven here.

That explained the mystery of the one bedroom on the main level.

A few weeks after they had sold the house in Oconomowoc and were permanently in their new home, Gran made a less than shiny entry:

I hate to say it, I hate to even think it, so I will only mention it on this page. Now that we're here, I worry about Dillon not having any other children to play with.

"Careful what you wish for, Gran," I whispered.

"Jayne? What are you doing out here?"

I looked up from the journal in my lap to find Tripp standing next to the Cherokee. Why . . . What . . . Oh, yeah. After getting in the car, I picked up the first journal from the seat next to me. I'd only planned to read the first page or two. That was two journals ago.

"I came out to throw a load into the dumpster and saw your car still here."

"I found the books from 1979. They were in the armoire upstairs." I pointed to the upper level of the garage. "That bedroom on the first floor? That's where

Grams and Gramps stayed while the rest of the house was being built. My dad used the den for a bedroom."

Tripp leaned into the open driver's side window, the trace of a smile on his mouth. "Couldn't help yourself, hey? Had to start reading."

"Yeah. Guess I lost track of time."

"Don't you think you should go to work now?" He said this gently, as though speaking to a kid who had put off starting her homework for way too long.

I blinked. "What time is it?"

"Almost eleven."

"Are you serious?" I tucked the ribbon secured to the back of the journal between the pages to mark my spot. "I had no idea. Yes, I need to get to work." My mind transitioned to law enforcement as I set the journal on the passenger's seat with the others. "Did I tell you that I hired Martin Reed yesterday?"

"As your deputy? Is that a good idea?"

"So far but ask me again in a day or two."

~~~

I found my deputy sitting at his desk reading the online material I had assigned him. He looked up from his computer and gave me a nod. "Sheriff. Something going on you need my help with?"

"No, why do you ask?"

"Because it's nearly lunchtime and this is the first I've seen you today."

My first thought was to snap at him. I was the boss. What business was it of his when I got into the station? He was my deputy, though, and yesterday I had made a big deal about us needing to be able to trust each other.

"I got distracted with something at home," I explained. "Normally, I'll be here by eight. How's the reading coming? Learn anything interesting?"

This led to a half hour discussion on crowd control followed by another on how to properly pull over and then approach a vehicle to ensure the safety of not only the officer, but also the driver and passengers in the vehicle.

"Have you heard of touch DNA?" he

asked.

"I have." His enthusiasm amused me. "What did you learn about it?"

Reed leaned back in his chair with his hands clasped behind his head. "When you pull someone over and are approaching the vehicle from behind, you touch the back of the vehicle, preferably the trunk."

"And why do you do this?" I hoped I'd come across as an instructor and not, as Rosalyn would have accused, like a condescending big sister.

"Couple reasons. First, if anyone is waiting in the trunk to ambush you, by pressing down on the trunk lid, or the tailgate of a larger vehicle I suppose, you'll lock the person in."

"And," I added, "if you announce your presence to the driver while tapping on the lid, in the rare event that someone is being held captive in the trunk, they'll hear you and make a noise of some kind, letting you know they're in there."

"Huh. Hadn't thought of that." He nodded his approval. "The other reason is to leave your prints or DNA on the car.

That way if the vehicle leaves the scene, you can prove you had contact with the vehicle."

"Fortunately," I added, "we've got dashboard cams to back us up now as well. The touching thing is old-school, but some of the best techniques are the old ones."

"I like knowing these things, even though I'll probably never use ninety percent of these tactics around the village."

"Probably not, but if you ever decide to move away—"

"I'll never leave the village," he insisted while shaking his head.

That's what he said now. I never thought I'd leave Madison. If things went well, maybe he could take classes in the off-season and then enroll at the academy. Maybe I'd be content running a B&B with Tripp, and Reed could step up here at the station. But I was getting ahead of things.

"Glad you're finding the reading valuable." I pointed at my office. "I'll be doing some reading of my own. Feel free to take off for lunch if you'd like to. You can do a patrol of the area while you're out there."

"Yes, ma'am. I'm just going to finish this chapter."

I smiled as I settled into my office. From the start, I had the feeling that Reed was never encouraged to do much. He certainly hadn't been well respected. I'll never forget Sheriff Brighton's description of him: *The boy isn't capable of investigating his way out of this building without a map. I'm basically a department of one.* Shame he didn't recognize "the boy's" potential. No wonder Reed was so crabby when we first met.

There were only about fifty pages left in the journal I'd been reading when Tripp stopped me. I probably should have left it at home, but since Reed was going to patrol and it seemed like an otherwise quiet day, I didn't see any harm in quickly finishing up those pages.

There's not much I can do inside the house at this point. I've subscribed to a few decorating magazines and am collecting ideas from them, but until the second floor is done, there's no sense even starting. What I can do is work on the landscaping around the house and boathouse.

That entry was written in early spring, shortly after they had moved into the house. A week or so later Gran wrote:

Landscaping is more involved than I realized. I'm capable of pots on the deck, but if I'm going to do justice to this house, I'll need help.

Morgan had told me that our grandmothers met at a gardening show. That had to be what was coming next. I could hardly wait to meet Morgan's grandmother.

"Good afternoon, Sheriff Jayne."

I looked up to see Lupe standing in my doorway and my heart sunk a little. I liked Lupe and enjoyed the spirited conversations we sometimes had, but right now all I wanted to do was read.

She looked casually around the station, poked her head in my office, and then frowned.

"He's not here," I said.

"Who's not here?"

"Reed. He went to get lunch and patrol the village."

She slumped into the chair across from my desk. "I stopped by earlier today. Martin told me you weren't in yet. Were you out investigating that death?"

"You mean Barry? No, I spoke with the medical examiner late yesterday afternoon. Turns out it was accidental. There's nothing suspicious about his death."

I filled Lupe in on the preliminary results and how there was nothing further to investigate. She looked heartbroken. As much fun as she was having putting together her pieces about the village for the online magazine, village life wasn't for everyone. I got the feeling that Lupe Gomez was really a big city, hard news reporter at heart.

"Is the enchantment of Whispering Pines wearing off for you?"

"It's not." She shrugged. "I don't know. I like it here. I like the people."

"But?"

"But I'm starting to feel like I am regurgitating the same story over and over. 'Tell me about your childhood . . . Have you lived in Whispering Pines your whole life . . .? No? What brought you here, then?"

"I thought you were moving on to the fortune tellers. They've got to have some interesting stories for you."

"Maybe. I don't know." She slumped further into her chair. "I didn't make it over there yet."

"Don't you have a deadline?"

"Four o'clock tomorrow afternoon."

She really was in a funk. "Have you met Lily Grace yet?"

"Doesn't sound familiar. Who is she?"

"Teenage fortune teller. She'll give you a great story. Her 'gift' turned on a few months ago, so unless her elders have instructed her otherwise, she'll give you the real scoop on what it means to do a reading for someone. Go talk to her. I'll be shocked if she doesn't give you something good."

"Okay, I'll give her a try." She sighed like she doubted it would work, but I saw a little gleam in her eye. "Otherwise, I might have to hide a body somewhere just to have something juicy to write about."

I stared at her. "You do remember that I'm the sheriff? I arrest people for things like that. Then you'll have to write about life from inside the pokey."

She made a face, like she was considering the option, and then smiled at me. "And you know I'm joking."

The front door opened then and Newt James, the village delivery guy, poked his head in the doorway.

Late-twenties, six foot two, beachy blonde hair, blue eyes, athletic build.

"Hey, Sheriff." He jerked his thumb over his shoulder. "I've got boxes for you."

"Excellent." I stood and went to hold the front door open for him. His battery-operated delivery cart was fully loaded today.

"I thought vehicles weren't allowed in the village," Lupe said from behind me.

"We make an exception for Newt," I explained. "He's the only delivery guy for the entire village, except for the restaurants. They've got a separate food service. Some days Newt has so many items to deliver, it would take him all day if we forced him to use a handcart. Mr. Powell rigged a golf cart with a flatbed, bumper hitch, and small trailer. It's battery-operated so there's minimal noise and no emissions. Nature lover approved." I turned to find Lupe's eyes lingering on Newt's wide shoulders and muscular arms. "I thought you were hot for Martin."

She blinked. "What?"

"You never order this much," Newt said. "Planning something special?"

"It makes you a little crazy sometimes, doesn't it?" I asked. "You're sort of like Santa, but you have no idea what's in the packages."

He laughed. "At Christmas time I wear a red coat and elf hat."

I swear, Lupe drooled a little bit.

"I don't think he meant that's all he wears," I whispered to her.

"How do you know I don't know what's in the boxes?" He flashed Lupe a grin and a wink. "These, for example, have walkie-talkies."

He set four matching boxes on the simple wooden bench next to the front door.

"That's because," I pointed out, "there's a picture of walkie-talkies on the outside of the box."

"That does help." He went out and came back in with a large, flat box. "I have no idea what's in this one."

"Portable whiteboard," I explained. "Helps me think better when I can scribble ideas on something bigger than a piece of paper. I ordered one for the house as well. Did it—?"

"Yep, delivered it about an hour ago."

"Great. They said one was on backorder. Must've found an extra."

Newt gave me a little salute as he dropped two final boxes with office supplies on the bench and left the station. "See you next time, Sheriff."

"Walkie-talkies?" Lupe asked.

"Since cell phones don't work around

here," I explained, "and I'm not always in my office, I figured I would distribute these to various businesses. This way they can call me if they need me."

"Smart." She stood, hands shoved in her pockets, looking bored. "Where did you say Martin went?"

"To patrol the village. If you head over there, you might run into him."

"What makes you think I—"

"Hate to tell you this," I interrupted, "but you are as easy to read as a front-page headline."

"He worked for the station before? Was he a deputy then, too? Has he always lived here? What else can you tell me about him? Have you ever noticed how super-hot he is? Wait, do you have a thing for him?"

"Stop." I held both hands up in front of her face. It was like a floodgate opened, and the last thing I wanted was to be caught in a flood. "First of all, I'm his boss. Second, not my type. Third, I have—" I almost said Tripp.

"So Martin is available? Do you know if he has a girlfriend?"

Fine. I'd deal with this now or the topic would keep coming back at me. "As far as I know, Reed is single. Why don't you go find him and ask him for yourself? If you hang out at the pentacle garden, you'll probably see him."

The normally bold and daring Lupe Gomez was rendered speechless. Literally. She opened her mouth, and nothing came out. Really? She was shy around guys?

"Guess I need to go that direction anyway if I'm going to meet up with this teenage fortune teller of yours. What did you say her name was?"

At that moment, Reed entered the station. He froze as soon as he saw Lupe standing there, then cleared his throat, and continued to his desk. No way was I going to hang around and watch the two of them making googly eyes at each other again. Besides, I hadn't done any actual police work yet today.

"Right on time," I said. "The walkie-talkies I ordered just arrived. I'm going to deliver them. Would you plug in two of the units to start charging? One is for me, the other for you."

"Walkie-talkies?" Reed asked.

I explained my plan to him.

"Good idea. Tracking down Sheriff Brighton could be a nightmare sometimes."

He looked impressed with me for the second time that afternoon. First my knowledge of touch DNA and alerting potential victims locked in the trunk and now this. I was on a roll. That meant I should leave before I did something stupid and he took points away from me. Besides, the googly eyes had started.

Chapter 13

SINCE THE HEALING CENTER/YOGA studio was literally one hundred yards from the sheriff's station, I delivered the first walkie-talkie unit to Jola. Next, my trusty K-9 and I jumped into the Cherokee and headed for the east side of the village. First stop there was Sundry, the general store, and then to the area the villagers referred to as Hotel Row. The four hotels, right along the lake, had been there for almost ten years now. I didn't know anything more about their history than that, but Gran used to complain that the modern buildings didn't fit in with the village's Old World atmosphere. At least the hotels were short, none of them taller than three stories, and they all honored the "dim outdoor lights only" rule the village established long ago. The villagers liked having as little interference with the night sky as possible. It took me a little while to get used to minimal lighting, but I had to agree with them; seeing that many stars every night was amazing.

Since I only purchased twelve units, ten of them already spoken for, I flipped a coin to see which of the hotels would get one. Technically, they were outside of the village limits and needed to contact the County Sheriff if they had problems. If there was an emergency, however, I would come over and do what I could to help.

My last stop on the east side was the rental cottage office, a tiny one-room building that looked like it had been plucked from the rolling emerald fields of Ireland. It even had a thatched roof, although I was pretty sure the thatch was cast cement; had to be mindful of fires around this many pine trees. After leaving a unit with them, I drove past the rental cottages and patrolled the area.

When I came through the area the first time, to investigate Barry's death, I was focused on the investigation and didn't pay attention to the area. Now I saw that almost all the cottages scattered around the twenty heavily-treed acres that made up the rental grounds were an eclectic mishmash of styles and sizes—cottage, log cabin, Cape Cod, Tudor . . . All, as was standard for the village, were charming.

I stopped at the two A-frames where Barry and his friends had been staying. There were no cars, but someone was sitting at the picnic table by the fire pit.

"Angel? Are you here alone?"

He looked over his shoulder at me, slowly, as though it took a great deal of effort to do so, then turned away again.

"Everyone else left, but I wasn't ready to go yet." His voice dragged as much as the rest of him. "We still have both rentals for another week."

It had only been a couple days since I'd seen him, but he looked like he'd been through hell and back in that time.

"Are you okay?"

214 | SHAWN MCGUIRE

"I guess . . . Maybe . . . I don't know."
He said nothing for a minute. "Barry and
I knew each other longer than anyone else
in the group. When I think about the
stupid reasons we'd been going at each
other for the last five years . . . I don't
know if I'm more pissed off, embarrassed,
or sad." He put his head in his hands,
elbows on knees. "That first year we were
roommates, we were good friends. The
annoying stuff was just that, annoying.
More like brother stuff. You know? I
figured I had a lifelong buddy."

Technically, their friendship had
lasted a lifetime. Sadly, one of those lives
hadn't been very long.

"I've been sitting here trying to figure
out what happened." He looked up at me,
his eyes red rimmed. "I wish I could take
it all back and have another chance."

"I understand. We all wish there were
things we could take back or do again."
He barely registered that I'd spoken, so I
moved to stand in front of him. "You look
like you're in rough shape, Angel. Are you
eating? Sleeping?"

He shrugged and answered with a

simple, "Some."

"Would you do something for me?" He just stared without answering. "I'm worried about you. I'd like you to go to the healing center."

A small fire ignited in him. "That the place you wanted Barry to go? The place that would've saved him if you insisted he go?"

I felt a little nudge of guilt at his words. Dr. Bundy had assured me I'd done nothing wrong, that getting him to the healing center wasn't my responsibility. Dr. B had never been anything but honest with me, so I chose to believe him on this one and stopped the guilt from creeping any further. Angel was in the anger stage of grief now and taking that anger out on me. That meant I was not the person he should talk to.

"That's the place. Go there and ask for my friend Jola. I'm guessing you have a lot of questions, and you've clearly got a lot of emotion going on right now. I think Jola can help you."

I gave him directions and repeated that I was worried about him. He grunted at me.

"You'll go find Jola? I'll take you there right now if you want." I waited, but he didn't respond. "You're not thinking about doing something stupid, are you?"

"I'll go," he snapped.

I stood there, deciding if he was a danger to himself or just really angry. He said he'd go, and there wasn't much more I could do other than check on him again later. I could give Jola a call. Maybe she'd come over here.

"Don't do anything that can't be undone," I begged. "Okay?"

He grunted again, and after standing with him for another minute or so, I went on my way.

~~~

The next walkie-talkie unit was for Creed and Janessa up at the circus. By the time I got there, everyone was preparing for the afternoon performance in the big top, which meant I shouldn't bother them.

"Is it okay if I leave this with you?" I asked Colette at the ticket booth.

Colette was big, as in, she stood nearly seven feet, with red hair that was probably as long as I was tall.

"No problem," she said in her deep voice. "I'll drop it off with Janessa later."

Meeka tugged hard on her leash. She loved the circus grounds. Big cats to watch, food scraps to eat, and about a million smells to decipher. I let her retractable leash extend as far as it would go.

"How's everything going up here?"

"Little better every day." Colette looked down at her hands, which were twice the size of mine, and sniffled. "I miss them. All four of them. Especially Joss."

Full of empathy, I answered, "I know you do."

Creed had told me that the wounds from the deaths were healing, but that most of the carnies were still mourning the loss of their "family" members. I was proud of them for remaining professional and continuing to give the tourists what they came for.

"Do you have a new closing act yet?"

"Not yet," she confirmed, "but rumor has it that there's a woman who's stepping down from a Cirque du Soleil show that's been touring in Vancouver. I think she's coming to do a tryout for Creed next week."

"That's good. Bringing in new talent will help everyone move forward."

We chatted for another couple of minutes, Meeka tugging on her leash the whole time. I gave her a gentle tug back, and then we were on our way.

"No lions and tigers today, girl. We need to deliver more walkie-talkies."

She snorted, a sound that said she couldn't care less about walkie-talkies.

"Even if it means we get to see Violet and Morgan?"

She looked up at me, ears perked and tail suddenly wagging double time. Violet and Morgan were two of her favorite people in the village. And not just because one always gave her dog biscuits and the other always scratched her ears with her long, black fingernails.

~~~

We dropped the Cherokee at the station and made our way around the pentacle garden, dropping off units at The Inn, the marina, and Grapes, Grains, and Grub.

At Treat Me Sweetly, not only did Meeka get a dog biscuit, I got a scoop of ice cream. While Honey prepared my lemon-lavender cone, I stepped across the store to where Sugar was placing raspberry-filled pastries into the display case.

"Do you remember when you told me to dig into the village's history?" I asked.

She looked over her shoulder at me. "I remember. Are you trying to find out what happened to Lucy?"

I made sure no one was close enough to hear us and leaned in even closer to her. "I got her autopsy report. It wasn't an accident."

"That's what I thought, too. Accidents happen, but no way would Lucy have an accident related to water." She glanced past me and held up a finger, signaling her customer she'd be right with her. "Your Gran was a water witch, you know."

I didn't know. Nor did I have any idea what that meant. I played dumb, pretending that I did, and made a note to ask Morgan about it later.

"I found Gran's journals last night."

Sugar took me by an arm and pulled me into a corner behind the counter.

"Be careful, Jayne." She was serious, almost angry. Then she relaxed and seemed almost sad. "And keep an open mind. You are going to learn things that will surprise you, and possibly rock your beliefs."

"My beliefs? About the village?" Or worse. "About Gran?"

"Look, Honey and I were just little kids at the time. I don't remember the details anymore."

"Details about what? What are you talking about?"

"Never mind." Sugar turned to help her customer. "I shouldn't—"

"Sugar, stop trying to protect me. My grandmother was murdered, this is a legal matter." I stopped myself before saying *Don't make me bring you in for questioning.* "I can tell you're battling with whatever this is. If it's this hard for you, that seems like an even bigger reason to tell me."

She closed her eyes and after a few seconds admitted, "Let's just say that Yasmine Long was not the first murder in this village." She put a big smile on her face and spun to her waiting customer. "Welcome to Treat Me Sweetly. What can I treat you with today?"

"Here you go, Jayne." Honey handed me a cone stacked high with two generous scoops of lemon-lavender. "You okay, hon?"

My gaze drifted from the cone to Honey's concerned face. I considered asking her what she knew about the years in question. Sugar was the older sister, though, and if she couldn't remember details, Honey probably had no recollection whatsoever.

"I'm fine." I narrowed my eyes at her and held up the cone. "I thought I asked for one scoop."

"Did you?" Honey tapped her ears. "I don't always hear so well."

"Right," I smiled and headed for the

door. "Remember to plug-in that walkie-talkie. I hope you never need to use it."

I sat on a bench between the sweet shop and Shoppe Mystique to eat my ice cream and give Meeka some water. She was okay with lavender but didn't care for lemon so wasn't interested in the ice cream. As I ate, my mind fired off one question after another: A murder near Whispering Pines' inception? Who was the victim? Why were they killed? Who was the killer? Was it somehow related to Gran's death?

"Jayne?"

I looked over my right shoulder to see Morgan standing on her front porch looking quizzically at me.

"You're so deep in thought. Did you even notice the people greeting you?"

I looked at the crowd that had just walked past me, gave a little wave, and turned back to Morgan. "Do you have a minute?"

"Of course. Come on in."

I shoved the last bite of cone into my mouth and followed her inside. I handed the walkie-talkie unit to Willow, Morgan's long and lanky assistant, and gave her instructions to plug it in and set it to channel six. Then I asked Morgan, "You're sure this is a good time?"

She gestured around the shop. My gaze skittered over the cases loaded with bottles of dried herbs and flowers; a table full of Morgan's handmade lotions and beauty potions; the racks of candles, crystals, and stones; more racks of oils, incense, amulets, and talismans. Among all that were a handful of shoppers.

"We usually get a lull in traffic at this time of day," Morgan explained. "We'll get another little rush just before dinner, but for the most part, our business is done for the day. Come into the reading room with me."

I followed her to the small, cozy room at the back of the shop, off the main sales area. The room was big enough for only the stone fireplace on one wall, two wingback chairs flanking it, a small coffee table set on a braided rug in the middle of the floor, and the worn velvet loveseat that was my preferred place to sit. On the wall opposite the fireplace were bookshelves, behind which was Morgan's hidden altar room where she created personalized charm bags or witch balls for her customers.

In an attempt to try something different, I sat on one of the wingback chairs. That lasted for approximately five seconds before I moved across to my usual spot on the loveseat. Funny, this put me in a position to have people sneak up behind me. That was never okay anywhere else. Why was it okay here?

"How come no one is ever in this room?" Maybe that was it.

"This room is almost always full." Morgan winked. "Maybe it just knows when you need it."

She waited patiently, hands resting in her lap, as I sat for a minute with my eyes closed. I breathed deeply, taking in the aroma that came from the dozens and dozens of dried plant bundles hanging from the rafters all around the shop. I never understood why all the different scents didn't overwhelm. Instead, they combined into the aromatic version of a hug.

"Did something new come up regarding the man you rescued from the lake the other day?" Morgan asked. "Is that what you were thinking about outside?"

I shook my head and debated about making a cup of tea from the shop's complimentary tea stand. The "Chill Out" blend always helped settle my mind. "I was a little in shock over something Sugar just told me."

Morgan sighed and shook her head. "Goddess bless her, she means well, but Sugar's words are often double sided. What did she tell you this time?"

The first time Sugar's words had upset me was when the village council voted me in as sheriff. Sugar was one who had voted against me, but not, she claimed, because she didn't have confidence in my law enforcement.

"Remember during the vote," I began, "she told me that she didn't want me getting messed up in the muck?"

"I remember well."

"Did you know that part of 'the muck' is that there was a murder in the village decades ago? I'm not sure when exactly, but Sugar said that she was a little girl at the time."

"I didn't know." Morgan sat forward and looked as shocked as I felt. "If that is the case, my mother must know about it. She was here from the start."

Literally from the start. Morgan's grandmother, Dulcie Barlow, and Morgan's mother, Briar, were the first two people my grandmother let come here.

"I think I'm going to meet your grandma today." I laughed at the confused look on her face and told her about finding the journals. "So far, she's talked mostly about the joys and struggles of moving to undeveloped land. I'm at the point where Gran needs landscaping help."

"It's a safe bet that means she contacted my grandmother. At the risk of sounding arrogant, my skills as a green witch are good, but they're nothing compared to what Grandma Dulcie knew."

"Don't they say that the teacher always

holds back a little from the student?"

"Possibly. I prefer to think it's a matter of getting a good foundation and then learning as you go." A distant, fond smile brightened Morgan's face. Surely, remembering times with Grandma Dulcie. Then she blinked her heavily black-lined eyes and returned to me. "Is that why you look so tired today? You were up reading all night?"

"Last night, I was up all night searching the attic for the journals. On the plus side, the attic is better organized now. Tonight, I'll be up reading."

"Would you like a cup of tea? It might perk you up."

"Your tea doesn't have caffeine. I need the strong stuff today." I patted the walkie-talkie unit next to me on the loveseat. "There's a reason I saved Violet for last."

"I'll understand if you say no," Morgan began, "but I'd love to look at those journals sometime."

"I almost forgot, I found photo albums, too. There is one raven-haired beauty in those pictures that has to be

228 | SHAWN MCGUIRE

Grandma Dulcie. She looks just like you. I'll bring those over for sure."

Morgan placed her hands palms together and inclined her head in a little bow of thanks.

"Speaking of the journals," I said, "I'm itching to get back to them. You'll ask Briar if she remembers a murder forty-some years ago?"

"I'll ask her tonight. I'm surprised she never told me before. You know she prefers that we do our research first before she fills in with her knowledge. She'll probably tell me she remembers the death and leave it at that. She's such a tease."

I left Shoppe Mystique, popped in to Ye Olde Bean Grinder to drop off the walkie-talkie, and left with an extra-large mocha with an extra-espresso shot and a bag of dog biscuits. Meeka and I returned to the station to find Reed at his desk reading on his computer and both jail cells occupied.

"What's going on here?"

"They were fighting over a canoe at the Marina." Reed said of the two men as he rubbed his red eyes. "Couldn't tell you why that was something worth throwing punches over. There were plenty of boats on the racks. I brought them in to chill out for a while."

The first thought that entered my head was *great, more paperwork.* Then I realized I now had a deputy who seemed very interested in learning all the rules and regulations of law enforcement.

"Did you ever do the paperwork for Sheriff Brighton?" I asked him.

Reed lit up like a kid being offered an early Christmas present. "Never. The only thing I got to do with paperwork was file it."

I waved a hand over my shoulder as I walked into my office. "Follow me. This sounds like the perfect time for a lesson."

Chapter 14

REED WAS AT HIS DESK, HAPPILY filling out the paperwork that I passed off to him. Since both jail cells were in use, Meeka couldn't crawl beneath her favorite cot and had to find another napping spot. She chose beneath my desk at my feet. As she softly snored, I returned to the journals.

Dulcie and I met approximately eighteen months before Keven and I bought the property up here. I'll never forget that day; it was one of the most inspiring of my life. We had both attended a seminar at a new garden center in Oconomowoc. At that point, the only thing I knew about gardening was how to buy plants. This was still five or so years before hippies had taken over the country, so bra-less Dulcie with her bare feet and wild hair stood out like a rose in a weed patch in the crowd of women wearing shirtdresses and sweater sets.

I was drawn to Dulcie the moment I got there. All I wanted was to be in the aura she projected, so I chose the closest seat to her I could get. We learned about plant zones and how to properly prepare the soil and why it was important to put shade-loving plants in shady areas instead of bright sunshine. I didn't even know that there were shade plants and sunny plants at that time.

Dulcie and I had chatted throughout the morning's seminar, and once it was done, I asked if she wanted to go get coffee with me. She accepted immediately, and we spent the rest of the afternoon talking about plants and politics. I never considered myself uneducated or uninformed, but I felt like such an ingénue in her presence. In a good way, she sparked something to life in me. When Dulcie hinted at this religion she recently started following, I knew we were going to have to get together again very soon.

"How about tomorrow?" she asked in this gorgeous throaty voice.

I swear, it was like I was having an affair, not that I would ever do that to my Keven, but I lay awake all night that night in anticipation of getting together with her again the next morning. Keven knew something was going on and was happily surprised when I told him I'd made a new friend.

Gran went on to describe their meeting at the same café again the next day. I swear, if I closed my eyes it was like I was sitting right there with them. And the way Dulcie explained Wicca to Gran sounded like an echo in my ears.

"People don't understand us," Morgan had told me the day I re-met her two months ago. "Most think that we worship the devil, perform human sacrifices, and dance naked in the moonlight. That's not at all true. Well, some dance naked, but that's entirely personal preference. If a comparison helps, Wicca is similar to Native American spirituality in that both revere nature and its gifts. That's a very simplistic explanation, but this was the discussion our grandmothers had."

If she only knew how right she was. The comparison to Native American spirituality was exactly what Gran wrote in her journal. Like Morgan and I had, Gran and Dulcie became close very quickly.

It didn't take long for me to realize that Wicca just made sense to me. Dulcie called herself a green witch. This means she has a connection to plants and nature, not that she can perform hocus pocus like a magician. The more time I spent with her and the more she explained her religion, the more it felt like the right path for me. I always wondered why I felt so much calmer, so ready to take on my day, so much more like myself after a day outside. Seems I have a connection to nature I never fully appreciated.

"Sheriff?"

I looked up from the book on my desk to see Reed standing in my doorway. "Yes?"

He pointed behind him, in the direction of the cells. "These guys have calmed down. I don't think they're going to cause any more trouble. I'm going to let them go, okay?"

"Yeah, that's fine. Give them the standard warning about how we'll ticket them if they do it again."

He paused, then stood a little taller, a little prouder. "Okay."

He'd probably expected me to handle the release process. For an offense more severe than fighting in public, I would have. If Reed really wanted to be of help to me, he could handle these little things.

"It's almost time to close up shop," he added. "After I have a little chat with them, I'm going to head on home."

"Be sure to take your walkie-talkie. Unfortunately, as a department of two, especially during tourist season, we're never really off duty. Keep it with you at all times."

"Will do. Good night, Sheriff."

I gave him a little salute and returned to the journal.

My desire to be outside and connect with the natural world turned quickly from an interest into an obsession. Keven saw it. He could tell the days when I was able to spend time in the park with Dillon versus the days when we were trapped inside the house. When I told him that I wanted to move somewhere we could be surrounded by nature all the time instead of the constant buzz of the city, he didn't argue. The only thing he cautioned me about was that there would be many times when I would be alone with our little boy. Keven had to travel for work, I knew that. I told him that wouldn't be a problem because we would soon have plenty of children for Dillon to play with and keep me company. I couldn't imagine anything more joyful than a big house full of family.

That dream never happened. My dad was an only child. Why?

Today, nearly a year to the day since we broke ground here, I called Dulcie and told her I needed help with landscaping. She didn't hesitate. She'll be here in two days and is bringing her little girl, Briar. I'm not sure who's more excited, me or Dillon.

I looked away from the journal to find Meeka sitting at my side. She whined pitifully at me.

"Is it dinner time? How long have I been sitting here?"

A quick glance out the windows showed me that it was getting dark. I'd completely lost track of time and had probably missed dinner again. Didn't Tripp say this morning that he'd make something tonight? Because I said I'd be home in time. I gathered together the journals, turned off my desk light, and the overhead light in the main room.

"Okay, let's get out of here and hurry home. I think I'm in trouble with Tripp, too."

She didn't hesitate. She raced to the back door and as soon as I had opened it, she ran to the Cherokee. I'd barely gotten the back open when she leapt inside and went directly to her crate. Poor dog. She really was hungry.

A few minutes later, we pulled to a stop in front of the garage next to Tripp's rusty old F-350. I let Meeka out of the back, looked toward Tripp's popup, and spotted a Porta-Potty in my yard.

Chapter 15

AS I STOOD THERE, STARING AT THE portable toilet set up near Tripp's popup, I noted that the house was dark, but the lights were on in the trailer. Tripp was probably watching movies. One of the crew members sold him a laptop for a ridiculously low price—something about warning his son that he'd get rid of it if his grades kept falling. Not only was Tripp learning about some new technology that had hit the world while he'd been off the grid for the last few years, he also discovered Netflix. And Hulu. And a few other streaming apps.

Meeka appeared at my feet and gave

me a short, crisp bark. A sound that clearly meant, *the dog is hungry.* She trotted toward the boathouse, stopping every ten feet to look back and give another warning *yip.*

"I'm coming."

After giving her a generous helping of food, she'd waited so patiently while I read today, I took the time to change out of my uniform and into a pair of lightweight pajama pants and a tank top.

"Tripp?" I called from outside his popup. "Are you in there?"

The trailer shook a little, presumably as he crawled out of his bed in the pop-out section tucked into the tree line. A beam of light stabbed the darkness from between the curtains as he peeked out at me.

"Jayne?"

"Who else?"

"Don't know, can't see you. It's dark out there." A moment later the door opened, and he came out. "Another long day."

"Yeah. Totally my fault this time. I got distracted by journals." I hung my head in mock-shame while Tripp chuckled, but not a lot. "Why is there a portable toilet in the yard?"

"Remember I told you not to say anything about the schedule?"

"Uh-oh."

"Exactly, uh-oh." He led me over to the folding chairs next to the trailer, and we sat. "The guys took out the old sinks, tubs, and toilets this morning. As the day went along, this nasty sewer smell started filling the house. We plugged up all the drain openings in every bathroom the best we could, but we'll need to leave the windows open until this is fixed."

"Until what's fixed? What happened?"

"Turns out there's a break in the septic line."

"How did you figure that out?"

"They have a camera that we snaked through the line." Tripp got up, reached inside his trailer, and pulled out a two-foot-long flashlight. He directed the beam of light at a trio of safety cones set up between the side of the house and the trees. Then he traced the light from the house through the yard. "The line runs out toward the trees and then angles downward underground to the septic tank about halfway into the front yard."

"What does this mean? And before you start the full Septic Systems 101 workshop, I understand what a septic system does."

"It means that the guys are going to show up tomorrow with heavy equipment, dig out the earth around the septic line from the house to the tank, and we'll go from there. Won't know the full damage until we open it all up."

"Don't hold back, tell me everything. I'm going to have to call Mom in the morning and let her know."

"Well, since we'll have it all dug up, it only makes sense to replace the entire line. It's more than fifty years old, after all. Hopefully the tank is still okay."

"That makes sense. Do we have an estimate on cost?"

"Ten."

Sometimes Tripp gave more information than any human being could ever need. And then there were times, like this, when minimalism ruled. "I'm pretty sure you don't mean ten dollars."

"No. It'll be around ten grand. More if the tank needs replacing, too."

I cringed, already imagining Mom's reaction. She hated everything about this place—the house, the village, and the people living here. If I called to let her know the house had burned to the ground, she'd probably throw a party to celebrate.

"Okay," I said. "It is what it is. We can't rent rooms in a house that smells like a sewer."

He turned off his flashlight and leaned back in his chair. "What did you learn from the journals today?"

I gave him the edited version of how Lucy met Dulcie. "Dulcie is just about to arrive here. Gran is so excited."

"And I assume, by the fact that you're bouncing in your seat, that you want to go read more."

"Do you mind?"

He paused before answering. "Why would I mind? Besides, I just started a new series about this chemistry teacher who finds out he's dying and decides to sell meth to make money for his family. Have you heard of it?"

"Heard of it. Watched it. You're going to love it. Go, watch your show."

Halfway back to the boathouse, I thought again about how it had been a while since Tripp and I had sat out on the deck at the end of the day. He said that he didn't mind if I went to read, but he paused before answering and his voice was flat when he did. I stood next to the garage, watched the light go out in his popup, and silently vowed to make dinner on the sundeck a priority for tomorrow night.

A few minutes later, I settled onto the loveseat in my apartment with the next two years' worth of journals. The coffee table in front of me was loaded with chips and guacamole, cheese sticks, chocolate covered peanuts, and a Sprecher Irish Stout, my favorite of their beers. Not only was the flavor great, it made me think of Milwaukee's Irish Fest, a celebration my family used to attend every summer when Rosalyn and I were little. We stopped attending the fest around the same time we stopped coming to visit Gran and Gramps.

I thought of other happy times with my family, ironically becoming sadder by the second, so I opened a journal and slipped even further into the past.

Dulcie and Briar arrived yesterday afternoon. I can't begin to express how wonderful it is to see her again. Dillon and Briar fit like two snug little bugs into his temporary bedroom. Fortunately, Dulcie is a trooper and is happy to camp out on the sofa. I wish I had somewhere nicer for her to stay.

For the rest of that journal, Gran explained in painstaking detail the process she and Dulcie went through to create the gardens around the house. There were dozens of sketches among the entries that detailed their plans. While they were doing the actual work, the entries became shorter, just a few sentences about their progress for the day and the mischief Dad and Briar got into. By the time the landscaping was wrapping up, Dulcie was regretting the fact that they had to go back home.

I should have put this past Keven first, but I asked Dulcie to move here. Once finished, the house will be more than big enough for her and Briar to stay. They can each have their own bedroom and bathroom. She immediately said yes but then backtracked, saying she needed to think it through first. What would she do up here, she wanted to know. How would she make money? Before I could say anything, she insisted that they would not sponge off Keven and me. She also insisted I put this past Keven first.

A few days later, she wrote:

Keven got home from the job site today. The first thing he saw was the new landscaping; it couldn't be missed. Once all those perennials fill in, the gardens will be amazing.

They had been showstoppers. Now, they needed attention. I'd have to hire someone to come over and revive the beds. My green thumb was wilted.

The second thing he saw was how happy I was. I'd barely gotten halfway through my planned pitch regarding Dulcie and Briar when he said yes. "I'm gone a lot in the summer. I don't want you to be alone all that time. It will ease my mind to have her here with you."

It's late, but I couldn't wait until the morning. I just called Dulcie to tell her the good news. She says they'll be here in two weeks!

The rest of the journals for that second year were filled with entries about life for the two women and their kids. They taught Dad and Briar not only the standard reading, writing, and arithmetic, but they also delved deeply into gardening.

Dillon loves to dig the holes. He

pulls the dirt out and Briar puts the pretty flowers in.

That must have been the start of Dad's archaeology obsession. Give a kid a shovel when he's five and he'll keep digging stuff up for the rest of his life.

As much fun as it was to read about the beginnings of Whispering Pines, there was nothing in these first years that gave any indication of an impending murder. Would this really get me to the truth about Gran's death, or was I wasting my time with these journals? The only way to answer that question was to keep reading.

Chapter 16

I WOKE UP ON MY LOVESEAT—ONE journal next to me, others on the floor, still more cluttering the coffee table—to the beeping sound of trucks backing up. Considering the crew showed up every morning at seven o'clock, it was a safe bet that was the time.

I got up, let Meeka out to do her business, and jumped in the shower. Crossing the yard, with still-wet hair, I found the crew laying heavy tarps in a line across the yard while a backhoe dug a narrow trench, depositing scoops of dirt on the tarps.

"Not going in to work today?" Tripp

tugged on strands of my wet hair and indicated my shorts and T-shirt ensemble.

"I know the station is only ten minutes away, but I figured I should be here just in case."

"And it gives you an excuse to keep reading?"

"Can't hide anything from you, can I?"

He winked. A gesture that sent a shiver up my spine. "I made pancakes, they're in the fridge."

I ran inside, warmed up a stack of blueberry-almond pancakes, slathered them with honey butter and maple syrup, then brought my plate to the front porch to observe the process. I was halfway done when Mr. Powell pulled into the driveway.

First, he went over to inspect the digging and promptly fell into the trench. Two of the crew helped pull him out and pointed him in my direction. I couldn't hear them but imagined they said something like, *Why don't you go talk with the customer? That way you can't hurt yourself.* That would be optimistic.

There was almost no situation that couldn't result in Mr. Powell hurting himself or needing rescue. Violet had told me that one morning he knocked his alarm clock off the nightstand. It skittered beneath his bed, and somehow he ended up getting stuck beneath the bed when he tried to retrieve it.

"Good morning, Mr. Powell."

"Good morning, Jayne." He gave me a little salute and put a scratch across his forehead with his thumbnail. "Quite a job they have to do for you."

"I'm just glad this happened before we opened the B&B and were full of guests."

"Nice way to put a silver lining on that dark cloud." He dabbed a tissue over the little droplets of blood seeping from the scratch.

"Here, let me help." I took the tissue and wiped away the droplets as well as the tiny pieces of tissue now stuck to his eyebrow. "Tripp tells me this should run about ten grand?"

"That's about right. Little more, little less, depending on what they find."

I chatted with him for a few more

minutes then went inside to call my mother with the report. First, I picked up the walkie-talkie.

"Deputy Reed, pick up, please." I waited a few seconds and tried again. "Deputy Reed?"

"This is Flavia Reed, who is this?"

Great. Just the way I wanted to start my day, talking to Flavia. "It's Jayne. I need to speak with Martin, please."

"We do have a telephone, you know. This is rather invasive, don't you think?"

"You're right, Flavia." Sometimes it was easier to take the blame and move along. "I'll use the telephone next time. Would you hand me over to Martin, please?"

A grumble and a short wait later and Martin's voice came over the device. "This is Deputy Reed. Is there an emergency, Sheriff? Over."

"Not as far as Whispering Pines is concerned. I'm having a bit of an issue at my house, however."

"Anything requiring my assistance? Over."

He sounded so eager to help. And so

formal. Must be trying to impress his mother.

"No, thanks, though. I'm going to stay here for the day. If there are any problems, give me a buzz and I'll be right there."

"Will do. Over and—"

"One thing, what's your phone number? No need for me to contact you this way when you're at home."

The biggest reason not to use the walkie-talkies at home? Flavia could hear everything I was saying. She now knew there was something going on over here. Who knew what rumor she would have circulating around the village by lunchtime.

Reed gave me his number and took mine for the boathouse. "Got it. Over and out."

When I'd finished giggling over Reed's military-style walkie-talkie protocol, I called the day spa.

"Melt Your Cares, this is Tiffany, how can I help make your day beautiful?"

"Good morning Tiffany. This is Jayne. Is my mother available?"

"She's in her office," the receptionist replied. Then, in a whisper, "She's in a mood today."

Great. "This is important. I need to speak with her regardless of mood."

"Alrighty." Which was a nicer way of saying, *you asked for it.* "I'll put you through."

A few seconds later: "This is Georgia."

Oh boy. Tiffany was right. I could hear the mood in those three words.

"Hi, Mom."

"Jayne, I'm at work. "

"I know. That's the number I dialed."

"Call me back at home tonight."

"This is kind of important. There's a problem with the house."

A clattering, like she had dropped the phone onto her desk, sounded in my ear. I could picture her, elbows perched on the desk, hands to her head with her index and middle fingers pressing on her temples. Next came a humming sound that meant she was attempting to vibrate away a sudden, oncoming headache. Best for me to give her a minute.

Finally, "What happened?"

I told her what I knew. "Fortunately, it will only take a day or two to fix so it won't interrupt our construction schedule. However—"

"How much will it cost?" The question came out as an impatient hiss.

"Approximately ten thousand." A squeak sounded over the line this time. In preventative defense of the Pine Time bed-and-breakfast, I quickly added, "This would've been caught in the inspection if we'd put the house up for sale. At least this way we stand a chance of making that money back through rentals."

She blew out a slow breath that sounded like it came from her toes. "Fine. Contact the insurance company and see if it's covered. In the meantime, I'll transfer *more* money into the fund to pay for this."

"Thanks, Mom. Trust me, this is the last thing we wanted to deal with. We're so close to being able to take reservations."

"After you have an answer from the insurance people," she said as though I hadn't spoken, "send your father an email. Like Jonah from the whale, he has emerged from the desert for two weeks."

A bible reference from my agnostic mother? My familiarity with the story consisted only of hearing it referred to in passing, but I was pretty sure it didn't apply to Dad the way she wanted it to.

"Not your Jonah, of course," she added.

"He's not my Jonah anymore."

"At any rate," her voice rose with irritation, "if there's anything you need to speak with him about, now is the time. He's likely to disappear into the sand again without notice."

Good idea. Maybe Dad could tell me about the village's history. Sending that kind of information in an email could be a hassle, and there was always a significant chance of misinterpretation. A phone call to Egypt, or wherever, would be far too expensive. Could we video chat?

"Jayne!"

I snapped to attention. "Present." How long had she been trying to get my attention?

"I've got work to do. Is there anything

else you need?"

For half a second, I thought about asking her how she was. How Rosalyn was doing with her summer internship. Just . . . chatting with my mom. But she was at work. "Nope. That's about it."

"Very good."

"Wait." Could she tell me anything about the village's history?

"What is it, Jayne?"

She sounded as though continuing this conversation was the last thing she wanted to do. Well, since I'd already annoyed her . . .

"I found a bunch of Gran's journals when I was going through the attic. She started keeping them when they moved here. They're really interesting. Do you know anything about Whispering Pines' history?"

"Far more than I care to."

"There's a reason I'm asking, not just because I'm curious. Gran was murdered."

"Not every death is a murder, Jayne."

"No, Mom, I've got her file here and—"

"I understand you calling to tell me

about the house, but the last thing I wish to discuss while at work is anything relating to your grandmother's death. In fact, I don't ever care to discuss your grandmother. Or anything relating to that village. You know how I feel about it."

I thought I did. I called it a feud, but I thought it was just hurt feelings or a nasty disagreement. Maybe it was more. Right now, it seemed her feelings toward Gran bordered on hatred.

"It's really that hard for you?"

Quietly and with great sorrow, she said, "It's that hard."

"I'm sorry, Mom. I wouldn't have asked if I'd understood that." I waited for a response of some kind but got nothing. "Okay, well, if you can transfer the money into the account, I'll take care of everything else."

"Very well. Have a pleasant day."

I found myself standing in my little kitchenette, shaking with emotion that I couldn't label. I was somewhere between extreme sadness and extreme anger. I mean, I knew my mother could be stubborn, but hatred of a sweet old woman?

Staring at my two kitchenette cabinets, I tried to remember if there was anything in there to eat. Specifically, something chocolate. Then I remembered a package of cookies I'd shoved up on the top shelf. Standing on a chair, I found the cookies at the very back. I'd inhaled three of the chocolate discs and was devouring a fourth before realizing they were stale, as in, no longer even a little bit crisp. How long had they been up there? I spit out the cookie in my mouth and looked down to see Meeka looking up at me with sad eyes.

"I haven't done that in months." I brushed crumbs off my hands into the sink and swallowed the sour lump that had formed in my throat. "Seems the less contact I have with my family, my mother in particular, the better off I am."

Meeka took a few steps toward me and pressed her little head against my leg.

"This much anger toward Gran can't possibly be because of the Wicca thing. What could Gran possibly have done?"

I shoved the package of cookies into

the garbage can and found the contact information for the insurance company. The very polite woman on the other end of the call informed me that no, the septic system was not covered under our homeowner's insurance. Basically, these things wear out, and it's up to the owner to replace them.

"Like any other appliance," she said.

Not sure a septic system should be placed in the same category as a refrigerator, in any possible situation, but there it was.

Sitting at the little dinette table, I passed that information, along with an update on the status of the renovations, to my dad via an email. Then I told him about Tripp and how I'd been named sheriff of Whispering Pines. I told him about my friendship with Morgan and gave him a quick update on the other villagers he likely knew. I had no idea if he cared any more than Mom did, but I felt like he should know. Then I told him about the journals and how I was learning about his life as a child here. By the time I was done, I'd composed what would be five pages if he printed it. I read it over one more time, deleting comments and then putting them back, and finally hitting send before I changed my mind on everything but the house stuff.

Since I was staying home from work for a reason, I decided I should probably keep an eye on what was happening out front. So I gathered together the next two journals and headed to the house's front porch.

"Come on, Meeka. We get to watch a show today."

She was excited until she saw what "a show" meant. Quickly bored with just watching, the little Westie decided to entertain herself by taking running leaps back and forth over the trench. After I had scolded her for the third time, one of the men told me not to worry about her. I got the feeling they were waiting for her to miss and fall in and give them a show. Not going to happen; Meeka never made a misstep.

Satisfied that my dog wouldn't be in the way, I slipped back into the journals. As I had expected, nothing of any importance pertaining to a murder, either Gran's or the mysterious first one, happened during those initial years. By the end of that second summer, Dulcie had asked Gran if her friend Fern and Fern's daughter could come up.

I met Fern at a gardening workshop I attended with Dulcie one time. She's a lovely lady and her little Laurel is adorable. I told Dulcie it was fine for them to come. We have plenty of room in the house now that the second floor is finished. I need to stay in control of this, though. If I open to a few, how many more will come?

"Oh, Gran. If you had any idea . . ."
I knew that Laurel was an Original, but I didn't realize she was one of the first to come here. As I read further, I became so involved in these stories I didn't even notice the equipment in the yard next to me.

A few weeks after Fern and Laurel, Rupert and Gregor came with their son Horace. Then Oksana and Juergen and their daughters Flavia and Reeva. With every new family that came, Gran became happier.

I always dreamt of laughter and happiness filling my house, I just never anticipated it coming from other families. We've gotten requests from two more women who'd like to come. Effie and her daughter Rae, and Cybil with her son Gabe. With them, all the rooms will be full. I told Keven that if any more people want to come, we'll have to start building more houses! He didn't find that funny. Then again, he didn't object.

Not long after Effie and Cybil and their kids get here, the autumnal equinox will be upon us. The Mabon harvest celebration is by far my favorite with all the focus on gratitude for the past year. I plan to put everyone to work ensuring we have enough supplies to last because winter will strike the Northwoods soon after that.

Good Goddess, I make it sound like

we're pioneers stranded in the middle of the prairie with no way to obtain food. The nearest grocery store isn't on the corner—it's thirty miles away— but there are six vehicles in my driveway with which to get to it. I'm sure we'll be fine.

"Ms. O'Shea?"

I blinked, the words on the page blurring as my vision shifted from the book to the man in muddy jeans standing before me.

"We've done all we can for today," he explained. "Mr. Powell is in Wausau right now waiting for me to call with the exact order for supplies. He'll make sure they deliver everything bright and early tomorrow morning."

"That's great," I said as Tripp walked up and stood at the man's side. "Thanks for working so hard today. Anything else I need to be aware of?"

"Only that the water to the house has been shut off. I understand you stay in the boathouse?"

"Right. There's a small apartment

above it."

"Everything's fine over there. There's a separate water line running to the boathouse and sewer line from the boathouse to the septic tank. You should be fine for the night."

A strange look came over his face, then. One I'd seen plenty of the male students at UW Madison give each other.

"What?" I asked with narrowed eyes.

"Mr. Bennett here is going to have to use your shower until we're back up and running."

Chapter 17

I SAT ON THE LOVESEAT IN MY apartment with the next journal resting on a pillow on my lap and tried to concentrate on reading. This was nearly impossible because Tripp was currently in my shower. My eyes kept drifting from the page to the wall between the sitting room and the bathroom. All I could think was that on the other side of that wall, Tripp was naked.

Meeka let out a little bark that sounded like a laugh.

"Really? You're laughing at me? Tell me you wouldn't have a hard time concentrating if a really hot male Westie was sitting a few inches away."

She tilted her head as though considering this and then trotted over to her water dish.

The other problem with concentration was the journals were getting a little boring. It was a lot of daily life with ten families living in what was now the village.

Houses are slowly being constructed. Dulcie and Briar are happily tucked away on a little plot of land near the stream that runs through our two thousand acres. Having a constant supply of water for their garden just a few feet away will be perfect for them. Fern and Laurel have a suite of rooms on the main level of The Inn. Laurel keeps telling everyone she has the biggest house in the village.

We decided it was only fair to build homes in the order in which people arrive here. This means that a place for Rupert, Gregor, and Horace is currently under construction. In the meantime, everyone else is living either here with me or at The Inn.

The bathroom door creaked open.

"Fair warning, I'm coming out and all I've got on is a towel." Tripp peeked around the corner. "I forgot to grab clean clothes."

Such a dilemma. I could look respectfully away. Of course, I'd seen him wandering the house in the same outfit a few weeks earlier. He'd just come up from using the basement bathroom, I'd just entered from the back patio.

"I could put my work clothes back on," he said as he emerged, "but then I'd need another shower. Be right back."

Since he seemed to be enjoying showing off for me, I did him the favor of watching him do so. His lean torso was even more developed than it had been a few weeks ago. Good thing I was at a point with these journals that I was skimming. Even then, I had to reread the next few lines three times before I could concentrate fully again.

Oksana, Juergen, Flavia, and Reeva finally moved out. I like Oksana a lot and Keven and Juergen seem to get along well, but I get a strange feeling around Flavia, like a premonition or something. I wouldn't say this out loud, because I wouldn't want to hurt Oksana's feelings, but that girl of theirs is trouble. She demands constant attention and becomes irrationally jealous if Reeva receives so much as a smile from anyone.

In another entry:

Oksana told me that both of their girls are practicing Wicca. Dulcie observes them when they go over to visit Briar. She says that Reeva seems to be developing the skills of a fine kitchen witch, while Flavia is following her parents' more traditional leanings. Problem is, she thinks that Flavia's intents are turning darker.

Morgan had told me that about the sisters' witchy talents. It was common knowledge that Flavia liked to influence events to benefit herself, but I didn't realize she had always been that way. I thought it started with her obsession over becoming the high priestess of the coven.

A man who looks like a cross between a mountain man and a hippie who dropped out years ago wandered into the village while we were working on the pentacle garden today. He seems nice enough, told us he decided living in society wasn't working for him anymore. He wanted to know why we were all gathered here in the middle of nowhere. We explained that we were a group of friends who had decided the same thing about society he had.

"So, you're a bunch of people living together because you don't belong anywhere else."

It seemed like he'd fit in, so I asked if he wanted to stay.

He admitted that there could be a

benefit to having people around, like in case of accidents. He didn't say it, but I think he was worried about loneliness, too.

"Don't know that I want to live right here next to you all," he said. "That's a little too much like a society for me, but I sure would like to live among these whispering pines of yours."

An audible gasp rose from the group. All eyes turned to me and a shiver rushed through my body.

I asked the man his name.

"Name's Will Haggerty. You can call me Willie."

I asked all ten families and our newest member, Willie, to gather around the beautiful white marble well Rupert and Gregor had constructed at the center of our garden. We joined hands, and I declared our motto: A place for those who don't belong.

I told them that we were a society and while Keven and I owned the land, they, the original settlers, would always have a voice. Then I said, "This will be the first of many votes we will make together. I move that we call our village Whispering Pines."

The vote was unanimous.

"I put chicken in the fridge to marinate last night," Tripp announced as he walked back into my apartment. "Are you crying?"

I nodded and flung a hand at the journal. "Just learned how Whispering Pines got its name. It was kind of cool."

Not only was Tripp fully clothed now, he was holding a tray loaded with chicken and the fixings for a salad.

"That looks great." I sniffed, marked my place in the journal, and stood. "Do you want to grill or prepare the salad?"

"You're going to leave me hanging? You have to tell me how the village got its name."

I smiled. "I'll do that while we eat."

Tripp took care of the salad, and I was happy to take chicken duty. The grill was my second favorite appliance.

The only issue with being outside as

the sun went down was the mosquitoes. They thrived in the muggy weather and traveled in swarms. We needed both bug zappers, one at each end of the deck, and a little spray to keep them under control.

As Tripp and I settled in for dinner on the sundeck, a thrill of excitement rushed through me. It had been far too long since we'd spent a night taking in the lake and the surrounding nature. How had we let that happen?

While enjoying the savory chicken and crispy salad, Tripp listened while I told him about the naming and what I'd learned in the journals today. He'd become as interested in the unfolding drama as I was. Once up-to-date, he laughed and shook his head.

"Ten families? How do you keep all of them straight?"

"It's not that hard, I already know half of them. I guess keeping all the parents straight with their children is a little challenging." I glanced at the unopened box sitting just inside my apartment. "The whiteboard I ordered arrived. Would you like to help me with a village family tree?"

After we had the board set up, I dictated while Tripp wrote the names on my board. When he finished writing, I stepped back and looked at the list.

Lucy and Keven with Dillon
Dulcie with Briar
Fern with Laurel
Rupert and Gregor with Horace
Oksana and Juergen with Flavia and Reeva
Effie with Rae
Cybil with Gabe
Velma with Priscilla
Yolanda and Kent with Karl
Ruth and Jonathan with Sugar and Honey
Blind Willie

There they were, the Originals. Village royalty. I grabbed a different color pen and lightly crossed out those who I knew had died. Then with another color, I circled Dillon, Briar, Laurel, Flavia, Reeva, Sugar, Honey, and Blind Willie.

"What do the circles mean?" Tripp

asked.

"They're the ones who are still around. The ones I can talk to about what happened when I find out who was murdered. These folks"—I underlined Rae, Gabe, and Priscilla—"I'm not sure where they are."

"You said your mom wasn't willing to talk about the village. Do you think your father would?"

I gazed up at my dad's circled name at the top of the board. "I have no idea. I sent him an email this morning and asked if we could do a video call before he leaves civilization again. I'll try then."

Tired from all the reading I'd done today, I rubbed my eyes.

Tripp took the marker from my hand. "Enough working for today. We haven't hung out on the deck in a long time."

"I was thinking the same thing."

When Meeka saw us taking our usual seats outside, she barked, spun in a few excited circles, then ran down the stairs to do laps around the backyard. Looked like she missed her routine, too.

"Will they be finished with the septic

system tomorrow?" I asked.

"Shh."

He reached over and placed a finger to my lips. My entire body froze, except for my heart which stuttered at his touch and then raced double time. Time seemed to pause as his skin, rough and calloused from hard work yet still tender, pressed against mine. He pulled away a second later, looking peaceful as he leaned his head against the back of his chair and stared at the sky. I, however, needed a few minutes to calm my still-racing heart.

Chapter 18

AFTER AN HOUR OR SO OF TIME together on the deck, Tripp said he was heading to bed. "The crew will be back before I know it."

I settled in with a couple journals. After the naming of the village, the population of Whispering Pines seemed to change weekly.

I don't know how they're finding out about us, but people keep coming. There seems to be someone new showing up at my door every week asking if they can stay. Lately, we've had an influx of fortune tellers, complete with crystal balls and tarot cards in hand! I'm going to gather the Originals to discuss this. We're going to have to implement regulations. If we let in everyone who wants to live here, soon our two thousand acres will be full and we'll be elbow-to-elbow. That's why we left!

Some of the daily life entries gave me a further glimpse into my dad's childhood. I smiled at comments like:

Dillon is so happy here. He's always hanging out with the other kids. I've nicknamed them The Pack. The twelve of them—Dillon, Briar, Laurel, Rae, Gabe, Flavia, Reeva, Horace, Karl, Priscilla, and the tagalongs Honey and Sugar—are inseparable. They start their days together in their one-room schoolhouse, separate for as long as it takes to eat dinner, and then wander through the village as a single unit until bedtime. They even do homework together, the older kids

278 | SHAWN MCGUIRE

helping the younger ones with assignments.

And:

The Pack has created their own version of a clubhouse. Befitting the Whispering Pines way, they call it the Meditation Circle. They've made seats out of tree stumps and circled them around a fire pit, so they not only stay warm when it's chilly outside, they also have light by which to do their homework. Dillon told me they're going to build a table or two next because a flat surface would be easier than balancing notebooks on their laps.

Also:

As happens with teenagers everywhere, hormones have flared. Not only do the older kids tend to fight with each other now and then, romance is also in the air. Dillon tells me that Rae and Gabe are an item, *that Flavia can't decide if she likes Horace or Karl better—Goddess help them both—and it seems that Dillon is enamored with one of the girls. He won't tell me her name, so I'll have to watch closely and see if I can figure out who she is.*

Before I knew it, I had read twelve years' worth of journals. I had one more book to go and I'd be ready to start on the ones I had found hidden in the armoire. I glanced at the clock; it was already one-thirty in the morning. As tired as my eyes were, the rest of me was wide-awake. I had to keep reading.

Growth led to change around Whispering Pines. It seemed that the fortune tellers were the ones who got everything started. People came for readings and wanted to stay for the night or the weekend and sometimes the week. Soon, The Inn was full all the time, so rental cottages were built. Dulcie had, with Briar's help, opened Shoppe Mystique which quickly became popular with the tourists. Sugar and Honey's parents, both talented kitchen witches, opened Treat Me Sweetly. The carnies decided to get in on the money flow and started their circus.

Throughout all the change, Gran's opinion of Flavia remained the same.

I can't believe how different siblings can be. Reeva is the most even-tempered girl I've ever met. Everyone in the village adores her. This, of course, infuriates Flavia who seems to want to be queen of the village. I told her that the other day.

"I would be an excellent queen." She strutted around doing a royal wave and then with an evil gleam ordered, "Off with their heads."

She's just a self-centered teenager, I know that, but I couldn't let that pass without comment. I informed her that Whispering Pines is my kingdom and I am the queen here.

I imagine the awful child ran back home to work some sort of hex against me. Guess I'll need to keep one eye open at all times with her around.

"She did it." I slapped the book closed, startling Meeka awake.

The little dog jumped up on the bed, stood with her front paws on my crisscrossed legs, and licked beneath my chin. I grabbed her gently by the scruff of the neck and looked her in the eye.

"Flavia has been evil since birth. She killed my grandmother. I know it. Now, how to prove it?"

Meeka studied me for a minute, then jumped off the bed and returned to her cushion with dog bones embroidered all over it. She stood there looking pointedly at me and then at what I assumed to be the lamp on my nightstand and then back at me. It was now nearly three in the morning.

"Message received." I yawned and turned out the light. As I drifted toward sleep, images of Flavia in her own altar room practicing spells of *negative intent*, as Morgan would call them, filled my head.

~~~

"Sheriff O'Shea?"

In the distant, fuzzy regions of my brain, someone was calling my name. I rolled onto my side. Was I dreaming about work now? Not a good thing.

"Sheriff O'Shea? This is Jola Crain over at the healing center. Are you there?"

As Jola's voice called out to me again, I felt something wet press against the back of my hand. I opened an eye to find Meeka sitting at the side of my bed, nudging my hand with her nose.

With a groan, I tucked into a ball and pulled the covers over my head.

"Sheriff?"

Realizing that the voice was coming from my walkie-talkie and not from somewhere in my sleepy brain, I flipped back the sheet and grabbed the unit next to the clock on my nightstand.

"I'm here. This is Sheriff O'Shea. What's going on, Jola?" I rubbed the sleep out of my eyes while waiting for her response.

"I've got a man in here, Angel Delgado."

I sat straight up. "Angel? Is he okay?" Damn! I forgot to call Jola about him. The last time I'd seen him, when I stopped by the cottage, he'd been so down about Barry's death.

Please, let him be all right.

"He's not in immediate danger, but we're keeping an eye on him," Jola explained. "Honestly, I'm concerned. Could you come over to the center? It'll be easier to explain things face-to-face."

"I had a late night so I'm not ready to go yet. I can be there within the hour. Unless you need me there now."

"Within the hour is fine. Like I said, we're watching him. Thanks, Sheriff."

Why were they watching him? What happened?

I let Meeka out and jumped in the shower ... and thought of Tripp being in here last night. A simultaneously pleasant and frustrating image. Once dressed, I dropped some kibble in Meeka's dish, left the door open for her, and crossed the yard to the house to get some breakfast. I found Tripp in the kitchen and immediately pictured him naked in my shower.

Stop it. You need to be professional now.

"You made breakfast sandwiches?" My voice caught as I reached for a travel mug in the cupboard.

Tripp placed a neat disk of scrambled eggs on top of a biscuit along with a thick slice of ham and a square of cheese. "We're getting closer to Pine Time's opening. I figured I should start coming up with more breakfast options. I want to create a signature dish for us, but at the same time, we don't want to have the same thing every day."

"This is the right morning for a portable breakfast. I just got a call from Jola over at the health center. I need to run over there."

"Problem?"

"I'm not sure. She says it isn't an emergency, but she needs my help. Speaking of my help, do I need to be here at all today for the septic system work?"

"Nope, I've got it. If anything, other than what they already told us about, comes up I'll call the station."

He handed me a ham, egg, and cheese biscuit along with a cluster of green grapes tucked into a parchment paper sleeve.

I inspected his package. *The* package. *Seriously, Jayne. Get a grip.* I inspected the breakfast bag and wondered if the day was already getting hot or if it was just me.

"This is kind of swanky. Are you planning to have these available for the guests?"

"That was my thought. People like to get up early and go hiking or fishing or just get on the road. Send them off with a nice to-go breakfast, a cup of coffee or tea, and a smile . . ."

"They'll remember you forever. I knew you'd be good at this." I held up my breakfast-in-a-bag in thanks. "Hope everything goes well today. For both of us. See you later."

I stepped outside and whistled for Meeka. While I was ready to hit the road, she wasn't. She'd finished her breakfast but hadn't finished her morning routine of inspecting the yard for whatever might have invaded the perimeter last night. I took that time to sit on the patio below the sundeck by the boathouse and watch the early morning sun sparkling off the small ripples on the lake. At that moment, I was grateful that Meeka was so particular about her schedule. Tripp had been right the other morning, it was nice to take in a few minutes of quiet and a little nature before starting the day. A line of heavy dark clouds was just starting to roll in on the horizon. Looked like we'd finally get some rain today.

It was also good to have a few minutes of quiet to think about my life. To take inventory, so to speak. Something I hadn't done in a while. My professional life seemed to be back on track, which was great, but my personal life was still a mess. I liked Tripp, a lot, and he gave every indication of wanting to be with me. My inability to take a chance with him was making me crazy. He couldn't be happy about it either. It was time I got out of my own way. Tonight. We'd talk tonight.

~~~

I parked the Cherokee in my spot behind the station, and we headed straight over to the healing center. The slightly crooked cottage echoed the others around the pentacle garden. Where each of the commons area buildings were surrounded with a riot of colors from overflowing flower beds, here the landscaping was natural, with weeds scattered among a few purposely placed plants, but still tidy and aesthetically pleasing.

Beneath nearly every pine tree was a small wooden meditation platform, most sized to fit one person but a few could fit two. Bamboo wind chimes hung from low hanging branches while small trickling water fountains created a peaceful atmosphere. Or so they claimed. Listening to trickling water just made me need to go to the bathroom.

Inside, wood accents, a big stone fireplace, and overstuffed leather furniture created a welcoming, rustic, log cabin feel.

288 | SHAWN MCGUIRE

"Jayne." Jola appeared from down a hallway across from the door. "You're here. Good."

"What's going on? Is Angel all right?"

She held her hands up in a not-sure shrug. "First, I should state that he asked me to call you and has given me permission to talk with you."

"Why me?"

"You took the time to talk with him. He trusts you."

"And all his friends left, making me the only one in the village he knows even a little bit?"

"Could be. Look, I'm worried about his mental state. You know he's suffering from some pretty severe guilt. He feels like it's his fault that his friend died."

"That's exactly why I suggested he come here."

"He thinks that the man pushed himself when they were swimming that morning because he, Angel, was giving him a hard time."

"Right. What is it that you want me to do?"

"A friend is coming to pick him up, but

she's coming from Kenosha which is a good six hours from here. We don't really have a secure room for him to wait in."

She let me connect the dots.

"You want me to put him in a cell? Do you think he's going to hurt himself?"

"I don't know, but I don't want to take the chance. Guilt is a powerful emotion, Sheriff. When it's severe like this, you can't predict what the sufferer will do to either themself or someone else."

"Going off the legal definition now, do you think he did something? As in, do you think he was in any way responsible for Barry's death?"

If Dr. Bundy's findings were accurate, and I had no reason to doubt them, there was nothing Angel could have done to cause this. The cop in me, however, couldn't stop wondering about other possibilities.

"No, but he feels like it was his fault."

Well, he made it this far because of my suggestion. I sure wasn't going to abandon him now.

"All right. Hand him over, and I'll keep an eye on him."

When Angel appeared from one of the rooms down the hall, he looked sleep deprived. His hair was greasy, his beard thick, his eyes dark and heavy. Had he looked like that yesterday? Fortunately, he made it here in time.

"You'll come quietly, right? I don't need to slap the cuffs on you, do I?" I kept my voice light, trying to ease some of the heavy tension hovering around him like a storm cloud.

He gave a weak smile. "No cuffs."

During my drive to the station, a gentle misty rain had started. While I was inside the healing center, it had turned into a downpour. Jola lent me an oversized umbrella that I promised to return.

As Angel and I walked along the Fairy Path toward the station, he said, "You were right about Jola. You probably can't tell by looking at me, but I'm doing a little better. Thanks for suggesting her."

I echoed Dr. Bundy's words to me. "Don't beat yourself up over this, Angel. You didn't do anything wrong."

"I know that here"—he tapped his

head with a thick finger and then his chest over his heart—"but not here, yet. I'm so damn competitive. I couldn't beat him in his finance world, so I figured I'd bring him into mine."

"You're the stronger athlete?"

"For sure. I mean, that's what I do. It wasn't a fair race, I knew that. Barry kept in shape, but he rode a desk chair all day." He looked off into the woods and shook his head. "In college, he was as competitive as I am. That worked for us. At first, it was just fun stuff, but it turned ridiculous. It got to where our mutual friends chose sides." He shook his head again. "So stupid. You know what I mean?"

Schoolyard squabbles that turn friends into enemies. For me, that was Melanie Coulter, my elementary school best friend. At least she was until I got picked to be pitcher for the kickball competition between the two fifth grade rooms, and she was sent to the outfield. Afterward, not only did she refuse to speak to me, she spread the lie that I kissed Bobby Jenkins, our class captain, and let him touch my butt to get the pitcher position. Fortunately, there was only a week left of the school year to suffer the humiliation, but during that week Melanie stole half my friends and they treated me like a tramp. Then on the last day of school, Bobby Jenkins cracked from the teasing and redeemed my reputation by telling everyone loud and proud that he'd rather touch a steaming pile of poo than my butt. To this day, there are former classmates living in Madison who call me Janie-poo."

"I understand exactly."

A quick sob escaped Angel. "What if this *was* my fault? I kept pushing and pushing . . . What if he died because he was determined to beat me?"

"Look, I understand why you're feeling the way you are, but you've got to let it go. You can ask yourself 'what if' for the rest of your life and never know the truth. Barry died due to an unfortunate set of circumstances, not because you pushed him to race."

Angel stared, devoid of expression, down the path. "I pushed him. Now he's dead."

He really was in this deep. "I agree with Jola, you need to talk with someone or this guilt will destroy you."

A few yards later, we were on the covered front porch of the station. Meeka shook, spraying water droplets everywhere as I opened the door. Inside, we found a sopping wet deputy Reed and a familiar-looking man sitting in one of the jail cells.

"Why do I know him?" I asked. "And why are you all wet?"

"Downpour started when I was on the way back with this guy. Didn't have my rain jacket. He was in earlier for the fight over the canoe."

"Oh, yes." I led Angel to the other empty cell and asked him, "Do you need anything? Water?"

"I'm good." Angel sunk down and seemed to melt into the cot. "I just want to sleep."

Two seconds later, he was out.

"What did he do?" Reed asked.

"Basically, we're doing a psych hold." I filled him in on the details. "What's going on with our repeater?"

"He ran into the same guy he got into the fight with before. Apparently, the other guy was looking at this one's girlfriend. Laurel called my walkie because no one was here yet and you weren't answering yours."

Reed gave me a pointed look.

Oops. "Sorry. Forgot mine at home. And yes, I see the irony."

"Anyway," Reed continued, "she said the two were getting into it in the middle of The Inn's restaurant. Food went flying, Sylvie went flying."

"Sylvie? Is she okay?"

"She's fine. Ended up with oatmeal all over her uniform so had to go home and change. Other than a small bruise, that was the worst of it for her."

I stood in front of the repeater's cell. "I think it's time for you to go back to your home."

"Already goin'," he growled.

"He and the girlfriend were staying at The Inn," Reed explained. "Laurel gave her half an hour to pack up the room and get out."

"Is she mad? The girlfriend."

"Furious," the guy in the cell called. "We were here for her birthday."

"And you get to ride home with her?" I asked.

He nodded like he'd just received a ten-years-to-life sentence. "All the way to Chicago."

I put a hand over my mouth to disguise a smile. "That's a good eight hours. Trapped in a car with a ticked-off girlfriend. You better sit there and treat these next few minutes like a vacation, my friend."

"Should we charge him with anything?" Reed asked.

"Nah. Laurel will bill him for damages. The girlfriend will take care of the rest."

Reed's eyebrows scrunched together. "You have an interesting way of executing justice."

"Anytime we don't have to be the bad guy, I'll take it."

Reed considered that and nodded. "Good plan."

"I'll be in my office if you need me for anything."

Meeka, not happy that The Repeater was in her cell, preventing her from crawling beneath her preferred cot, sat outside the cell just out of arms reach and growled at him every time he moved.

"Is your dog gonna bite me?"

"Probably not," I called from my desk. "I recommend not sticking your hands outside the cell, though. And don't make her mad, she can squeeze between those bars."

I replied to a few important emails and then dug out the journals from 1979.

Chapter 19

I SAW NOTHING IN THE FIRST WEEKS of the 1979 journal that would justify, to me, hiding the books. Then I came to mid-February and the entry Gran wrote after the monthly village council meeting.

It seems that this will be a year full of ... excitement? Drama? Yes, drama is guaranteed, we do have a horde of teenagers living here, after all. Regarding one of those teenagers in particular, Velma dropped a bombshell on the council today. Turns out her daughter Priscilla is seven months pregnant. None of us suspected. The weather turned cold earlier than normal this year, so the girl has been able to disguise her condition by wearing baggy sweatshirts and heavy sweaters. They decided now was the time to let us know. They haven't, however, told us who the father is. I'm not sure if they're hiding this fact or if they don't know. I sincerely hope it's the former.

A scandal in the village. Oh my! I'm sure after twelve years there were plenty of other events of the scandalous variety that had happened around Whispering Pines, but nothing worthy of mention in Gran's journal. And nothing between the children. For something to happen to one of the Original families made it all the more gossip-worthy, I'm sure.

A commotion in the main room caught my attention, so I went out to investigate and found that the repeater's girlfriend had arrived. He'd been spot on; she was furious. She ranted and raged about how long they'd been planning the weekend and how much money they spent on it.

Wisely, he said nothing. Then she'd say, "Come on, let's go," but would take two steps then turn and chew him out for a few more minutes. After this happened the third time, Reed stepped in.

"Go, both of you. No one pressed charges, so you're free to leave. Don't do anything stupid and turn this into a legal matter." He guided them to the door. "Or if you do, wait until you're way out of Whispering Pines' jurisdiction."

As the couple left, we could hear her yelling all the way around the building and to the parking lot. We stared at each other, burst out laughing, and then Reed said, "That wore me out. I'm going to go get lunch and patrol the commons."

Before I could say a word, he was out the door.

Angel Delgado had his back turned to the chaos and continued to sleep. Meeka crawled under her cot the moment the repeater was out of the cell and was now also sleeping. I returned to 1979.

Turned out I was wrong about the "scandal" of pregnancy being an issue in this village. The villagers, the Wiccans in particular, didn't have the same taboos around sex that the rest of society did. While everyone agreed it would have been better that Priscilla wait until she was at least out of high school to have a baby, no one chastised her. They did harass her about revealing who the father was, but the bigger problem that arose in the village had nothing to do with her.

Dillon tells me that Flavia has started experimenting with dark magic again. Or rather, negative magic. Dulcie doesn't like me to call it dark. Whatever the term, Flavia has been trying to manipulate events again. Her latest obsession are her school grades. Reeva is not only the top of her grade, she's the top of the school and always has been. That's what Flavia is after, top ranking. The problem is, Flavia isn't trying to help herself do better, she's trying to make Reeva fail.

Sisterly rivalry. I could identify with that only too well. It wasn't that I wanted to be like or be better than Rosalyn, it was that my mother wanted me to be more like her. Guess that wouldn't be sisterly rivalry, then. It would be a child not living up to her parent's expectations. I didn't realize that was my responsibility.

Dillon reports that a rift has formed among the members of The Pack. Dillon, Briar, Sugar, Laurel, Rae, and Gabe are on one side. Flavia, Priscilla, Horace, Karl, and ten-year-old Honey whom, Dillon reports, has a crush on Horace are on the other. Reeva has not chosen a side. In fact, Dillon says it's been weeks since she hung out with the group.

What could have caused this fracture? I wonder if it's Flavia's continuing fascination with darker spells. Dillon says her determination to outdo her sister is growing, although nothing she has tried is having an effect. Instead, it seems to be coming back on Flavia herself. Her grades have fallen instead of rising. It seems that Flavia will need to learn

the lesson of negative intent the hard
way before she'll stop.

This had to be the do no harm rule of Wicca Morgan had told me about. She said that "The magic a witch performs comes back to her or him. If I were to perform negative magic, I would attract negativity and become negative myself."

In other words, it was a karma thing. Forty years later, Flavia still hadn't learned. She was still driven to control circumstances and be queen of the village. She'd be working through a backlog of bad karma until the end of her days.

A few entries later, Gran revealed that Flavia might be trying to manipulate more than just Reeva's schoolwork.

Dillon feels that Priscilla is staying
close to Flavia because Flavia protects
her. From what, I don't know. The
fact that she won't reveal the father's
name isn't that big an issue. As for
why Karl and Horace have taken
Flavia's side in this rift? Dillon thinks

she offered them sex. I wish I could say this comment surprised me, but it doesn't. Oksana and Juergen have been trying to get her on a straighter path, but so far nothing has worked.

"Hey. What are you doing in there?"

Voices from the main room pulled me from The Pack's problems. I left my office and found Lori standing near Angel's cell, talking with him.

"You're here," I said. "That was fast. The woman at the healing center told me you were coming from Kenosha."

"No," Lori said. "I live in Kenosha, but I was in Green Bay at my parents' house. That's only like three hours."

I motioned for her to follow me into my office. "Come talk with me."

Once seated, she said, "Jola . . . is that her name?" I nodded. "Jola told me what was going on. I'm glad Angel didn't have a car here."

Now she was worried? I bit back my irritation the best I could. "You all left him here. Didn't you notice something was wrong with him?"

Lori matched my irritation and countered with defensiveness. "You know, we were all pretty messed up right then. We were all devastated by Barry's death and couldn't handle being here anymore. Angel refused, I mean he flat out refused to get in a car. He said he wanted to stay and work through things. Said he'd figure out his own way home."

The look on her face as she talked about Angel struck me. "You didn't want to leave him, did you?"

"Of course not." She shifted positions in the chair. "I've been really worried. That's why I went to my parents' house, so I'd be a little closer. Stupid cell phones don't work here, so I kept calling the cottage to check on him. Yesterday, he didn't answer, so I called the rental office. They told me they thought he went to the healing center. I called there, and Jola said he needed a ride."

I watched her expressions and body language. She felt more than friendship for this man.

"You went through a lot to find out if he was okay," I said.

"Yeah, well . . ."

"You're in love with him."

She started to deny it and glanced out toward his jail cell.

"He can't hear you from here," I promised. "Just keep your voice low."

She nodded, blushed, and wouldn't look at me. "You guessed my secret."

"Things are kind of a mess with your group, aren't they?"

Lori snorted a laugh and lifted her head. "You aren't kidding. Angel liked Marissa but that upset Barry. Then Marissa hooks up with Rochelle which only makes the other two more determined to get her. I honestly feel like the only reason either Barry or Angel wanted Marissa was to keep the other from getting her."

"So now what?" I asked.

Lori smiled. "I know this will probably sound inappropriate considering the circumstances, and I don't mean it to be. I'm hoping now that Barry isn't a factor anymore, maybe Angel will move on from Marissa and notice me." She shrugged. "That's awful, isn't it?"

"No, I understand what you mean."

Total mess. Hormones have flared, Gran had written about The Pack. Romance was in the air.

Or was it rivalry? Like that guy in high school who only wanted to go out with me when I was dating someone else, maybe Angel and Barry simply couldn't stand for one to have what the other couldn't.

Was that what had been going on with Flavia, too? She simply couldn't stand for Reeva to have what she didn't?

"Sheriff?"

I blinked to find Lori looking at me like she wondered where I'd gone. "Sorry, lost in a thought. You'll make sure that Angel gets help, right?"

"Jola made arrangements." She pointed in the general direction of the healing center. "I stopped there first. There's a clinic outside of Milwaukee waiting for him. I'll bring him straight there."

Before letting him go, I spoke with Angel as well.

"I get that it wasn't my fault," he said from inside his cell, "but I can't help thinking that Barry died because I couldn't let stuff go and walk away. I'm too wrapped up in myself. I gotta start thinking more about other people."

"You're saying the right things. That's a good start." I couldn't help but think it sounded rehearsed, though. "For now, I want you to get home safely. Lori's going to take you to a clinic."

Angel nodded. "Jola told me. If I don't show up at that clinic, she's gonna call the police."

"Then I won't ask you to call and check in with me."

I let him out of the cell, wished them safe travels, and sent them on their way.

It was past noon by the time they left. I was torn between wanting to go get lunch and wanting to continue with the journal. As it had at nearly every turn, the journal won, and I settled for a lunch of two who-knew-how-old granola bars Sheriff Brighton had left in a desk drawer and water from the cooler in the interview room.

From late April:

Priscilla's baby was born last night. A little boy. We'll have a blessing ceremony for him at the next full moon.

From mid-June:

Dillon reports that there are new tensions within The Pack. Now that Priscilla's baby is here, she wants a family. Velma keeps assuring her that the three of them are a family, but Priscilla wants a father for this baby. She still hasn't revealed the birth father, but Dillon says that her sights are now set on Gabe. Problem is, Gabe is devoted to Rae.

The rest of the summer passed along with this tension hanging over the group members. Everyone wanted Priscilla and her baby to have a good home, but everyone also wanted Gabe and Rae to stay together. Everyone except for Flavia. Just when I was sure I would never find out the real reason that Gran hid these books, I came to the final weekend of summer 1979.

I don't know exactly what happened last night, but Priscilla is dead, and Dillon claims Rae is responsible. Around moments of sobbing so hard he couldn't speak, he told me what happened.

Flavia summoned Rae, Gabe, and Priscilla to the Meditation Circle last night proclaiming that the love triangle drama between them needed to get straightened out. Rae told Briar, who gathered the rest of The Pack, but by the time they got there, things were already very heated. Flavia had positioned Priscilla and Rae face-to-face and told them that if they both really wanted Gabe they needed to plead their cases to him.

Teenagers never cease to boggle the mind. The entire village knows that Gabe and Rae have been together for a long time. A person can't 'plead their case' and take someone's partner. But it seems that Priscilla wanted Gabe, and Flavia was determined to make it happen.

As the rest of the group circled around, Rae and Priscilla shouted horrible things at each other while Flavia egged them on. If anyone from the group tried to put a stop to the face-off, Flavia would silence them, saying they needed to resolve this. By the time the rest realized things were going to get violent, it was too late. There was a lot of pushing and shoving and Priscilla ended up falling and hitting her head on one of the large rocks that make up the fire ring. The kids immediately tried to help her, but it was already too late.

I stood from my desk, my mind spinning as much as Gran's must have been at this revelation, and paced my office, Meeka following me like my shadow.

"So, Flavia—" I started to say out loud and then realized Reed was back at his desk again. And Reed, I'd learned, had the hearing of a bat.

"What about my mother?" he called.

There was no way I could involve him in this. What was I supposed to say? *I'm pretty sure your mother was complicit in a girl's death nearly forty years ago.* Yeah, that would go over like a spotlight at a new moon ritual. I tried ignoring him and hoped that he'd let it go.

He appeared in my doorway. "What did you say about my mother?"

The thing was, as Briar had so perfectly pointed out to me not too long ago, any information gathered from a witness to a crime were the events filtered through the witness' point of view. This was why, as a police officer, I spoke with everyone who'd been in the area where a crime had been committed. Then I'd compare all the statements I'd gathered with those the other officers had taken, keep the things that matched, and get rid of the outliers. The only thing I could keep from Gran's written statement, a recounting from an emotionally distraught mother which had been filtered through her emotionally distraught son, was that Priscilla had died and a crowd had been there to witness it.

If I wanted to figure out the truth of what had happened to Priscilla, I needed to talk with everyone who had been there that night.

"I've been reading my grandmother's journals," I told Reed. "Did you know that an Original named Priscilla was murdered in 1979? Well, that's the accusation. I don't have proof that it was murder. Could have been accidental."

If the report in Gran's journal was accurate, Rae might be guilty of involuntary manslaughter, and Flavia could be charged with aiding and abetting. Unless, of course, Flavia had wanted Priscilla dead. Or, maybe Rae had been the intended target and Priscilla got caught in the crossfire.

I shook my head. "I'm getting ahead of myself."

Reed's forehead wrinkled with confusion. "Ahead of yourself about what?"

I had to stop expressing my thoughts out loud. I tapped my head. "I'm trying to figure out what happened the night this Priscilla girl died." I glanced at him. "Did your mom ever mention that incident to you? According to the journal entry, she was there."

Reed leaned back, arms crossed over his chest, seemingly scanning his memory. "No, can't say as I remember hearing about that."

"I need to figure this out. There are people in the village who were there at the time. I'm going to talk with them." I grabbed my car keys, Meeka's leash, and the raincoat on the back of my office door. "I'll be at The Fortune Tellers' Triangle."

Chapter 20

FROM THE PARKING LOT ON THE west side of town, Meeka and I followed a well-trodden path that ran beneath the highway and through the forest until we came to a clearing. There, a dozen brightly colored wagons and a few canvas tents were scattered about, and twenty or thirty people waited patiently to have their fortunes told. Despite the steady falling drizzle, the area was relatively dry due to a heavy canopy of pine branches overhead.

Large signs on each wagon, hand painted with fanciful fonts, revealed the teller within. Effie and Cybil, being the *grand dames* of the fortune tellers, had prime front and center spots for their wagons. Because The Triangle was so busy at that moment, I figured I'd be waiting a while before I could talk with either of them, but it turned out wearing a sheriff's uniform afforded privilege.

"Well, Jayne, what a surprise," Effie crooned as she stepped out of her wagon. The woman following her was crying what appeared to be happy tears. The man behind her looked shell-shocked. Effie leaned in close to me, "I just told them that by this time next year, they'll have triplets."

"That explains the look on his face," I empathized.

"What brings you here, dear?" Effie asked.

"I need to talk with you and Cybil." I quickly added, "I don't need a reading."

She gasped and placed her hands palms together, seemingly excited by this. "Official business. That bumps you to the head of the line."

"Oh, no, these people have been waiting."

She leaned in to me again. "And if they truly want their futures foretold, they'll wait as long as necessary." She held a hand out toward her wagon. "Go on inside and make yourself comfortable. I'll catch Cybil as soon as she's done. And before you ask, of course, Meeka is welcome."

Effie smiled down at my little dog. If we were anyplace else in the world, I'd wonder how she'd known what I was about to ask.

I was relieved to find that the inside of her wagon did not match the outside, which was top-to-bottom shades of purple from the palest lavender to the boldest violet. I understood having a signature shade, but if I had to sit inside an all-purple room day-in and day-out, I'd get nauseous. Instead, the twelve-foot by twenty-foot space was a bohemian dream. Multicolored scarves covered the windows as well as the round table at the back half of the wagon. Two simple wooden chairs sat on one side of the table while a beautiful tapestry-covered armchair—Effie's throne, I assumed—sat on the other. A clear crystal ball, about the size of a bowling ball, sat on a silver filigree stand at the center of the table. A deck of tarot cards and candles in various shapes and sizes surrounded the ball.

The front half of the wagon resembled a living room. An old overstuffed loveseat, also covered in tapestry fabric, sat to my right. Two overstuffed chairs across from the loveseat were covered in shades of all lavender.

"Wouldn't be complete without an all-lavender something."

It seemed that because nothing matched, it all went together perfectly. Like the herb bundles in Morgan's shop. Or the people who lived in this village. I chose the loveseat while Meeka decided that beneath the covered crystal ball table was the best place for her.

A minute later, Effie entered the wagon with Cybil in tow.

"The sheriff is here," Cybil stated as she dropped with a groan into one of the lavender chairs across from me. "We must be in trouble."

"No trouble," I assured her. "Thanks

for bumping me to the front of the line. This shouldn't take long; I just have a few questions. First one being, did either of you know that Gran kept journals?"

The first sign that I was on to something helpful was the fact that they instantly looked at each other instead of me.

"Effie knew," Cybil said.

Effie swatted her arm. "You did, too. Yes, Lucy proudly took on the role of village historian. That's really what her journals were, after all. Her version of the history of Whispering Pines."

"Interesting that you call it 'her version,'" I noted. "I'm here to get your versions of some events I read about. What can you two tell me about The Pack?"

Again, they looked at each other.

Cybil spoke up first. "That was Lucy's nickname for our kids. They were constantly together. A single cohesive unit."

"They were the best of friends," Effie recalled with a fond smile. "It started out with Dillon . . . your father, and Briar

Barlow. They were the first two kids here and really only had each other, but as more and more came, their circle grew."

"Your dad and my son Gabe got to be good buddies," Cybil said.

"Don't forget Horace," Effie reminded. "He was in with them as well. Thick as thieves those boys."

"I could tell from Gran's journals that the group was very close. Then something happened to divide them. Do you know what caused that?"

Effie inspected her long, multicolored fingernails. Cybil shook her head.

"What caused the divide?" Something between sadness and anger flashed in Cybil's eyes. "Two things. I assume you read about the pregnancy."

"You mean Priscilla's," I said.

"Yes, Priscilla's. Everyone in The Pack, and in the village, wanted to know who the father was. The girls, I believe, were afraid that she had been attacked and wanted to know who to be wary of." Then Cybil chuckled, a mischievous sound. "The boys probably wanted to know who to get instructions from."

320 | SHAWN MCGUIRE

"Cybil." Effie swatted her again, shocked by the crass statement.

"Stop hitting me. I'll be black-and-blue."

"The kids," Effie amended, "wanted to know because they cared about their friend. They were worried that she'd been assaulted and wanted to help. I'm sure you know how it can be when all you want to do is help and that's the last thing the person will let you do."

Barry and Angel. Not exactly the same thing, but I fully understood the desire to help only to be shut out.

"Had Priscilla been dating anyone? Gran never mentioned a boy in the journals."

The two turban-wrapped heads shook in unison.

"What happened to the baby?" I asked.

"Velma sent it away," Effie said with a dramatic sweep of her hand. "Couldn't handle caring for a baby at her age."

It, not *he* or another more endearing term. This was a baby we were talking about. There was more behind her statement. Much more behind this entire situation.

"The other thing that caused the divide," Cybil continued, "well, I'm sure you can guess."

I made a mental note to come back to the baby and said, "Flavia."

"Flavia," Cybil confirmed. "She was obsessed then, as she is now, with being at the top of the leaderboard."

"Gran wrote that Flavia and Priscilla were close." They nodded but didn't reply verbally, so I prodded for more. "Something other than the pregnancy happened to Priscilla."

"The poor girl." Effie blinked her eyes again and again.

"Do you know what happened?" I asked. "I mean, I know that she fell and hit her head. I know that's how she died. Do you know how the fall happened?"

Cybil cleared her throat. "Do you mean, do we know who pushed her?"

Pushed her? I didn't say anything about her being pushed. I gave a small nod but remained quiet, jotting the word *pushed* in my notebook and circling it a few times while waiting for them to

322 | SHAWN MCGUIRE

supply more information.

"What we know," Effie said, "was that there was a misunderstanding—"

"Misunderstanding?" Cybil blurted. "Effie, come on. If you're going to tell the story, tell it."

Effie closed her eyes and released a weary sigh. She tapped her long multi-colored fingernails together, almost like a meditation, and then looked me square in the eye.

"Priscilla and my daughter Rae disliked each other." She held a hand up to Cybil who was about to interrupt again. "Some might say they hated each other. What I know, as does anyone who was here then, is that my daughter and Cybil's son were an item."

Softly, Cybil interjected, "They were crazy about each other."

Effie patted her friend's knee. "Priscilla set her sights on Gabe. Rae said that Flavia put the thought in Priscilla's head that out of all the boys in the group, he could give Priscilla and her baby the best life."

"He did have a bright future," Cybil

said, smiling like a very proud mama. Then she picked up the story. "Gabe told me that Priscilla would corner him. She'd ask him to walk her home and then try to seduce him right there in the woods. The little tramp."

"Mm-hmm," Effie agreed.

"And you felt that Flavia was somehow involved with this?" I asked.

"We know she was," Cybil said.

"Priscilla and Flavia were in cahoots," Effie stated.

"And how were they going to separate Rae and Gabe?" I asked. "Were they holding something over Gabe's head?" I look to Cybil. "Was he the father?"

Cybil glared, not happy with my accusation of her son. "He most certainly was not."

The conviction in her voice made me believe her.

"Like we told you," Cybil continued, "Gabe and Rae were crazy about each other. They intended to get married after college. Gabe planned to become a chemical engineer. Rae wanted to be a nurse."

"Where are they now?" I asked. "I've never met either of them."

"After Priscilla died," Effie began then paused, drifting away for a second. "Her death was too much for them to deal with. They left the village. Rae got a job at a diner to support them while Gabe attended classes and worked on that degree. Those two kids worked so hard to support themselves and the—"

"The stress of everything was too much for them," Cybil quickly added. "They split up."

They were hiding something. What made Priscilla's death so hard on the two of them that they had to leave the village? None of the other Pack members, except my dad, left. I'd probably be getting different stories if I spoke with these two separately, but seeing one play off the other was equally telling.

"Back to Priscilla's death," I said. "Do you know what happened that night?"

Cybil shook her head. "All we know, is that there was a gathering at the Meditation Circle where Flavia insisted that Gabe needed to be with Priscilla."

That was more or less what Gran wrote.

"What happened at the Meditation Circle that night?" I asked.

"Rae told me," Effie began, "that there was an argument which led to a scuffle and the next thing they knew, Priscilla was on the ground."

"Okay," I murmured, mostly to myself, "she was either tripped or pushed."

Or someone hit her in the head. Like someone had hit Gran. Had Flavia killed Priscilla nearly forty years ago in the same manner that she killed my grandmother five months ago? No, that didn't add up. Why would Flavia act as Priscilla's defender and then kill her?

"Tripped or pushed," Cybil agreed. "We don't know for sure, we weren't there. We know that Flavia was the ringleader. The kids weren't sure if orchestrating the fight was her goal all along or if that happened as things progressed."

"Because everyone else got there late," I mumbled and wrote in my notebook. "Was there an investigation?"

They shook their heads.

"There was no law enforcement in the village at that time," Effie explained. "Immediately after that incident, the council voted in Kent Brighton, Karl's father, as sheriff."

"Kent agreed to hold the office for a short time," Cybil said, "but he didn't want it permanently. Karl was twenty years old and looking for a career. The next week, he started taking criminal justice classes and then entered the police academy. Immediately upon graduating, we voted him in as sheriff."

Just like Reed, Karl hadn't had any on-the-job experience either. No wonder the rules around here were so flexible.

"Let me get this straight." I scooted to the edge of the loveseat. "You're telling me that an investigation into Priscilla's death was never done. You just buried her body and moved on?"

"We had a ceremony for her," Cybil offered like that made it better.

"Poor Velma." Effie wiped her eyes and looked at Cybil. "Remember how her hands shook as she marked her?"

"Marked her?" I asked.

Cybil answered with a solemn nod and started reminiscing about Priscilla's ceremony and others held over the years.

"So," I said, trying to get them back on track, "there was no investigation. You knew nothing more than what Dillon, Rae, and Gabe told you?"

"Lucy spoke with the other kids," Effie said. "Since this is her property, she made all the rules. She looked at the council more as her advisors than a governing body."

"What did she decide?" I asked.

"She called all the villagers together at the pentacle garden," Cybil recalled. "She told us that after speaking with all the kids involved, she determined that Flavia was responsible for Priscilla's death."

"That's what she said?" I almost fell off the loveseat. This could explain so much. "Were those her exact words?"

"Her exact words." Effie confirmed. "She said that she couldn't state conclusively how Priscilla fell, meaning she couldn't prove who shoved the girl, but everyone agreed that—"

"Everyone agreed," Cybil interrupted, again, "that Priscilla would not have died if it weren't for Flavia."

My brain was now vibrating with questions. Did Flavia shove Priscilla and cause her to fall? If she had been responsible, why wouldn't any of the other kids say so? Did she have control of some kind over them? Did she give them a concoction of some kind that made them compliant? Now I was reaching, but she could have persuaded someone else to push Priscilla.

Images of The Pack circling that poor girl, taunting and humiliating her, flashed in front of my eyes. Had it been a single blow or strike to the head that had killed her? Or had mob mentality taken over and they all took part in a beating once she fell, making it impossible to determine who had delivered the kill shot? That wasn't likely, but it sickened me to think of what human beings could do to each other when given the right motivation. There was no investigation, so there was no autopsy. That meant there was no way to determine conclusively how Priscilla died. All I could do was go off forty-year-old memories and journal entries.

The equally big bombshell was that Gran had decided Flavia was responsible for the death and told the entire village. She basically sentenced Flavia to a life of public humiliation. I can't imagine a worse punishment for Flavia. That sure sounded to me like a possible motive for wanting my grandmother dead.

"Thank you both," I said as I stood from the loveseat. "This was helpful."

"And what," Cybil inquired, "do you intend to do with this information?"

"Gran was murdered," I stated. "I'm sure you both know that. I don't know that I'll be able to prove exactly what happened to Priscilla, but I'll put together the best investigation I can. As for what happened to Gran, I have a strong feeling the two deaths are intertwined."

Effie stood and took my hand. "Jayne—"

I pulled away. "Don't tell me to ignore this. And you don't have to tell me to be careful. There might be a murderer in the village; I'll be careful."

As Meeka and I left Effie's wagon and headed out of The Triangle, we crossed paths with Lily Grace.

"Hey there, Sheriff. Are you here for that reading?"

I looked around at the crowd, uneasy with the public thinking that law enforcement relied on extrasensory perception to solve crimes. I was about to say no, then remembered the black stuff on the lady in the water. Just because I couldn't explain it or believe in it, I couldn't deny the accuracy of Lily Grace's visions.

She led me to a secluded grove tucked behind the wagons and tents. There, she had a temporary setup of colorful scarves tied together and tossed over ropes suspended between trees. Right now, because of the rain, a heavy-duty tarp was suspended over the whole thing. If she decided she was staying in the village, instead of going away to veterinary school, they'd reward her with a wagon of her own.

She sat on a cushion on one side of a

short round table, and I sat across from her. After a minute of breathing deeply with her eyes closed, Lily Grace placed her hands on the table with her palms up. I placed mine on top of them, palms to palms.

After a few seconds, she started humming softly and the upper half of her body began to sway side-to-side. Regardless of what she was seeing, her expression remained neutral. I did my best to help with this vision by thinking of nothing but Gran and trying to send those thoughts straight to Lily Grace. After a few seconds, I swear I felt energy pulsing between our hands. After a few more seconds, Lily Grace's swaying started to slow. Finally, she opened her eyes and, as though in a trance, stared blankly at me.

"What do you see?" I asked softly.

"I see a doll."

"A doll? What kind of a doll?"

"A porcelain baby doll. The old-fashioned kind with those dead-looking eyes that open and close." Then she blinked a few times, like she was waking up. "What did I say?"

Chapter 21

HONESTLY, I HAD HOPED FOR A LOT more from Lily Grace's reading. The face of the killer, for example, would have been awesome. The gender would narrow the options. Hair color could even be helpful. But a baby doll? What was that supposed to tell me?

Meeka whined at me from the back of the Cherokee.

"I know, the visions don't always make sense at first." Hopefully she had given me something valuable, and I simply needed to be patient and wait for the answer to come.

As for Cybil and Effie's statements, I

couldn't believe no one reported Priscilla's death. Even though they lived in the middle of nowhere, it had been 1979, not 1779. There were laws. They couldn't just bury a body and walk away. An autopsy, obviously, would've been best, but even a partial report from an amateur investigation would give me something to go on. Gran reiterated statements in her journals, but nothing else. She must have seen the body. If she would have mentioned any sort of identifying marks on it, I might be able to—

"Marks on the body!"

In the rearview mirror I saw Meeka stand and look at me, her head tilted to the side.

"Effie said Velma's hands shook as she 'marked' Priscilla."

The same mark left over Yasmine's and Gran's hearts? The mark that Flavia could instantly identify because she was familiar with the Theban alphabet?

Events were filtered through the person who experienced them, so I needed to talk to everyone who was present that night and gather all the pieces for my puzzle that I could. So far, I'd gotten statements from three people— six if I factored in that Dad, Rae, and Gabe had all told their mothers about what happened. The main thing they all seemed to agree on was that Flavia was at least partially responsible for the death.

Meeka let out a sharp bark from the back of the Cherokee. We were still in the parking lot near the Fortune Tellers' Triangle. I'd gotten lost in thought and hadn't even started the car.

"Let's go have a chat with Flavia."

This time, Meeka whined pitifully and laid down in her crate.

"I understand how you feel. Being around her isn't at the top of my favorites list either. Everyone seems to think that Flavia was responsible for Priscilla's death, though. And now I've got a motive for why she would want to kill Gran, too."

~~~

Violet had once described Flavia's house as "creepy as hell." A perfect descriptor in my opinion. The narrow three-story tall Gothic-looking cottage was stained entirely black-brown. Surely, it was the house kids in the village would label "The Witch House." Then again, in Whispering Pines that didn't mean much.

Flavia stiffened when she opened her front door and found me standing there. "What do you want?"

I tapped the shiny gold star on my shirt. "This is official business."

"Is Martin all right?" She looked panicked. "Did something happen to him?"

Her maternal concern made me pause for a beat. I softened my tone to respond. "Deputy Reed is fine."

Her whole body slumped slightly with relief, and I turned my cop-self back on.

"Something did happen to a girl named Priscilla about forty years ago." I had to bite back the smile playing at my mouth when the color drained from her face. An impressive occurrence in someone so naturally pasty. "May I come in, or should we talk about this on your front porch?"

Her hands fluttered at her throat and she frowned down at Meeka. Flavia wasn't a fan of dogs. Still, she took a step back and to the side and held the door open for us. I'd been inside Flavia's home once before, to question her about the death of Yasmine Long. I remembered thinking then that the minimally furnished house looked like it had been cleaned with steel wool and a power washer. It still did.

Flavia led me to the Quaker-style dining room table, big enough for only four people, if they didn't mind being crowded, and indicated a chair for me to sit in. The one she chose would have left me with my back to the door, something I avoided whenever possible. I chose the chair that put me with my back to the wall instead, and Meeka lay at my feet. Flavia stood there for a moment, perplexed, as she now had to decide if she wanted to sit across from me or in the chair she clearly favored which would put her next to me.

She chose the chair across from me, sat, and cleared her throat. "What is it you think you know about Priscilla?"

"I know that the two of you were good friends." Start out slow, build a rapport, hit her with the big stuff.

A smile turned her mouth; a sight I wasn't used to. "We were best friends. My family and I had been here for maybe six months when Prissy and her mother moved here. I was so grateful."

I'd never heard her speak so fondly of anything or anyone else. Except maybe her son.

"Why grateful?" I asked.

Just that fast, her features hardened. "Because Reeva stole the other girls. We hadn't even been here twenty-four hours, and she had snatched Briar away from Dillon. Then Rae and Laurel joined her little group as well. I was left alone; the only other kids being Horace and Gabe."

Or was she welcome but didn't want to put forth the effort to fit in? Kids didn't always accept new kids right away, and Reeva was the more approachable of the two.

"I have a hard time believing that none of the other girls already here would be friends with you, Flavia." Had she been

338 | SHAWN MCGUIRE

shy as a kid? She managed to split The Pack in two, so she clearly found her voice along the way. Why? What led to the shift in self-confidence? "What did you do all by yourself? Read? Wander the woods? Did you have television up here at that point?"

Flavia cringed at my mention of television. "Mostly I read and practiced my witchcraft. Like trying on dresses, I experimented with the different types, searching for the best fit."

Considering Flavia only wore shapeless, tent-like frocks that fell to mid-shin, that wasn't the best analogy for her to use.

"Morgan tells me you're an eclectic witch."

She pushed her shoulders back and sat taller. "I am. The medicinal element of plants intrigued me, so I considered becoming a green witch. The preparation of food was enjoyable, so I also delved into kitchen witchcraft." Her lips pinched together in a pucker. "Reeva has unbeatable skills as a kitchen witch, though, so that wasn't a wise choice."

"Because it was important for you to be able to beat her?"

She ignored the question, shifted in her chair, and placed her folded hands on the table. "I eventually decided that picking and choosing what I excelled at from the different practices was the wisest choice."

"Morgan says that being an eclectic witch can sometimes mean utilizing dark magic."

Flavia made a sour face.

"Sorry," I said. "Perhaps I should say, sometimes means casting spells of negative intent."

"Because one person sees things differently from another, that doesn't mean those things are negative." She swiped non-existent dust from the table. "I admit to casting a spell or two to take some focus off my attention-addicted sister, but I lived in this house, too. Wasn't I deserving of a little praise for my accomplishments?"

As Flavia clamped her mouth shut, I flashed to an afternoon during my sophomore year in high school. I'd just come home from a good day at school to find Mom gushing over her younger daughter.

"Rosalyn was awarded first chair in the violin section today," Mom had explained. "I can't remember the last time I heard you practice the cello, Jayne. Do you even try?"

"No, because I hate the cello." Quickly, before the lecture about money spent on lessons started, I blurted, "I got a 99 on my math test. Highest score in the class."

I could see the smile she gave me as clearly as if she was standing in front of me right now. The visual equivalent of a pat on the head. I cleared my throat, clearing away the memory. Beneath the table, Meeka sensed my upset and shifted to lay on my feet.

With empathy, I told Flavia, "It must've been hard to not be allowed to be yourself."

"It was all right for me to have different interests," she corrected. "Not only was that encouraged, multiple activities were required. That way I could stop one if Reeva took an interest in it and move on with another." Her mouth pursed in a tight pucker for a moment. "Goddess forbid I be better at something than Reeva."

That seemed extreme. Was that really the way her childhood had been, or was that the way Flavia chose to remember it?

"Speaking of casting spells," I said, backing the conversation up a little, "I understand you cast a love spell to make Gabe break up with Rae and get together with Priscilla."

I had no idea if she'd done that. The accusation would likely lead to the truth, though.

A dark shadow crossed her face. "Priscilla and her son needed a man to take care of them."

"Needed a man to take care of them?" I cringed internally, probably externally, too, as every feminist cell in my body protested. I was totally in favor of relationships but couldn't stomach comments like that. "*Prissy* wasn't capable of taking care of herself?"

Flavia shot me a momentary glare, then shook her head, a crisp little movement that said I had no idea what I was talking about. "Being a single mother is the hardest thing in the world. I'm the first to admit that I was fortunate to have inherited money from my parents. There was also the generous life insurance payout from Horace's death. Still, money can't relieve the burden of being a child's only parent. Raising Martin on my own, without a father figure to assist, is the hardest thing I've ever done."

"But you didn't have that understanding then. What made you decide to help Priscilla and Gabe get together?"

She didn't respond, just held my gaze, her lips tightly clamped.

"Rae must've been furious about that. There were other unattached boys in the village. Why Gabe?"

Again, no response.

"I understand that you arranged a gathering of The Pack the night Priscilla died because you wanted to settle the rift between your friends."

She flinched, the tiniest bit, at the word *friends*. "You're well-informed,

Sheriff O'Shea. Where did you get your information?"

"My grandmother's journals. I also spoke with Effie and Cybil."

"You're basing your accusations on a work of fiction and second-hand memories from forty years ago? I'm sure Effie and Cybil agreed with everything Lucy said, didn't they?" Her nostrils flared. "Those three shared a brain. Did they tell you that the only investigation done was by your grandmother?" She laughed. "You're wasting your time and mine, Sheriff. You have nothing to go on."

"My grandmother told the entire village that you were responsible for Priscilla's death."

Flavia froze, then narrowed her eyes at me. Hatred oozed from her like pus from an infected wound.

"You hated my grandmother for that, didn't you?"

"Of course I did," she insisted with a hiss that made Meeka sit up. "It wasn't true. I told you, Priscilla was my best friend. All I wanted was for her to have a happy life."

That statement sounded rehearsed, pre-prepared for moments like this. "You've been carrying that hatred around for nearly forty years."

She considered this. "I suppose I have."

"Sounds like motive for murder to me."

"Murder?"

"Yes, Flavia. As I'm sure you're well aware, my grandmother was murdered."

"No, she—"

"Drowned in her bathtub?" I shook my head. "Funny, the autopsy report was missing from her file."

Flavia stiffened, and I felt like I'd just scored the winning touchdown in the playoffs.

"Did you think Sheriff Brighton had disposed of her file?" Because she had instructed him to do so? "Reeva found it while going through his den. The autopsy report was missing, but I got another copy. There was no water in Gran's lungs. This means she was dead before she ended up in that tub." I opened a picture of the mark drawn on Gran's chest.

"Remember this?"

She squinted at my phone. "The full stop mark found on Yasmine's body."

"Velma drew this same mark on Priscilla's body before it was buried, didn't she?"

Flavia's eyes took on a far-off stare and her features softened again. "They'd been practicing the Theban alphabet together. They thought it would be fun to use in their spell book."

"This particular mark," I indicated the picture on the phone, "is on my grandmother. Over her heart. I see a pattern here. Do you?" I paused, but Flavia just blinked. "Nothing to say? You're not surprised by any of this?" Blink. "Why? Because you already knew the mark had been drawn on her?" Still nothing. "Flavia, did you kill my grandmother?"

"You'd just love it if I had, wouldn't you?" A slow smile turned her mouth. "I'm sorry to disappoint you, Sheriff, but I did not kill your grandmother. I was sick the night she died. Wracked with an awful stomach flu. Check with the healing center. They prepared a concoction for me."

"A witch of your caliber goes to the healing center? Why not prepare your own concoction?"

Perhaps she already had. One that *made* her sick.

"I told you, I was ill." She said each word slowly, as though I was dense. "Preparing medication requires precision, and I could barely stand. I had no choice but to rely on others that night."

"How convenient."

"As I said, check with the healing center."

Meeka jumped to attention as I pushed back from the table. "That's exactly what I'm going to do."

Chapter 22

JOLA PLACED A FINGER ON HER computer screen. "I can confirm that Flavia Reed was here in early February. I can't reveal more than that without a warrant or her permission."

"Can you confirm that she was here for a stomach ailment?"

Jola pondered the question while staring at the screen. "I can't not confirm it."

Good enough, Flavia told the truth about the stomach bug. "She says she was treated with a concoction of some kind."

"On occasion, the center will ask someone in the village to help with holistic treatments."

I studied her. Jola was all but begging me to understand.

"One of the villagers prepared a holistic concoction," I thought out loud. "That would require someone with skills in mixing plants, flowers, and herbs." Jola sneezed, a sound that sounded suspiciously like, *Yes.* "Someone I know in the village who has skills with mixing plants, flowers, and herbs would be a green witch."

She held a tissue to her nose, her thumbs up in an awkward sign of affirmation.

"Thanks for your time, Jola. Wish I had a warrant, so you could confirm everything you didn't tell me." I gave her a wink and a grin as I left the center.

~~~

It was getting late, so I decided to suspend my investigation until tomorrow. Meeka and I were on the way home when we came to the highway where a figure dressed in head-to-toe flowing black was crossing the bridge. It had to be Morgan. I pulled over to the side of the road and waited for her to finish her journey.

"Hop in and I'll give you a ride," I said after lowering the passenger side window.

"Park the car. Let's walk instead."

Walk? "It's raining."

She cocked an eyebrow and stared.

"I'll go park the car."

We continued the short distance to the west side parking lot where I removed my uniform shirt and laid it on the back seat. Then I hooked Meeka's leash to her harness, and we hurried back to the waiting drenched witch.

"I thought witches melted in the rain," I teased.

"Wrong kind of witch." She joined me beneath my oversized umbrella. "I enjoy walking in the rain. It's cleansing. What's troubling you, Jayne?"

I didn't even ask how she knew this time.

"No," she stopped me, changing her mind before I could say a word, "let's wait. I have a feeling this is something Mama should hear and there's no sense in you having to repeat yourself." Part green witch, part New Age guide, Morgan suggested we "be present in our walk" instead of talking.

The rain pattering on the umbrella sounded rhythmic at times, freestyle at others. I inhaled deeply. The air smelled amazing as the ground and plants soaked up the water and released petrichor, one of my favorite scents. Meeka, drinking from every puddle she came to, enjoyed it, too.

When we got to the bridge that crossed the creek, Morgan took the umbrella from me and closed it. She placed her fingers beneath my chin and tilted my face up to the sky, her fingernails, like tiny bayonets, poked my neck, giving me little choice but to obey. At first, the drops felt sharp as though they were stinging or burning me. I squirmed to free myself from her hold on me, but after a few seconds, a sensation that did feel cleansing took over. As more and more raindrops covered my face and the water ran along my neck and down the rest of my body, my stress started to recede.

Then, I started to laugh. No, not just laugh, I broke out in a fit of giggles. A memory of Rosalyn and I running outside in downpours to splash in puddles came to me. The word that memory brought with it was "free."

"See?" Morgan smiled, her voice gentle.

She hooked her arm with mine and we continued in silence along the single lane dirt path next to the stream. When we entered her cottage's front door, Briar called out, "Leave your muddy shoes at the door."

"Mama," Morgan called in return, "I brought a visitor."

Briar appeared from a doorway down the hall and smiled when she saw me. "Jayne. How lovely. Just in time for dinner."

"No," I objected, "you don't have to feed me."

"You're here," Briar said, "and we're about to eat. There's no sense in you sitting and watching us do so. End of discussion. I'd tell you to wash your hands, but it looks like you've already had a cleansing."

Easy to tell where Morgan learned her habits.

We took a moment to dry off and Morgan lent me a T-shirt dress, covered in broomsticks and pointy witch hats, to wear while my clothes dried. I took a seat at the small round table tucked into the corner of their cozy kitchen. All of it—from the wood floor inlaid with brick and scattered with multi-colored braided rugs, to the sage-green cupboards, to the four-foot tall and wide fireplace with a cauldron hanging from a hook—made me feel at home.

"I decided," Briar began, "that such a damp day calls for something comforting. The garden is rejoicing in all this nourishment. We should do the same."

She placed a large steaming bowl of homemade macaroni and cheese in front of me. I could tell just by peering into the bowl that the cheese would be gooey, the bits of diced pancetta salty and perfectly savory. Once again, I started to giggle.

"What's funny?" Briar asked, laughing with me.

"I'm not sure," I admitted. "I guess it's that this feels so perfect when not much else does right now."

Morgan held up a hand. "Eat now. Imperfections later."

After giving Meeka her own bowl of cooled mac and cheese, Morgan joined her mom and me at the table. I listened with happy contentment as they discussed their day with each other. Morgan had been grateful for the rainy day, not just for the gardens' sake, but because Shoppe Mystique wasn't quite so busy and she could catch up on restocking her inventory. It seemed that moonstones were in high demand this week. Briar had a simple day of enjoying her own cleansing—which I interpreted to mean she skipped naked around her garden—and preparing dinner.

Once we were done eating, I insisted on helping Morgan with the dishes while Briar and Meeka had a quiet conversation in the corner.

Finally, Morgan placed three mugs of tea around the table. "All right, tell us what's going on."

I told them about all I had learned in Gran's journals. I told them about my conversation with Effie and Cybil. And then about my visit with Flavia.

"I was so sure," I said. "Everything was leading up to the fact that Flavia was responsible for Priscilla's death. Do either of you remember preparing a brew on the night Gran died?"

"I did," Briar said immediately. "The girls from the healing center called me and said they needed something for a stomach flu. I gave them a concoction of mint, elderflower, and yarrow. My twist is to steep the mixture with a jasper stone, which is removed before consuming, of course. Why?"

"That brew was for Flavia."

"And why is that upsetting?" Morgan asked.

"Because it gives Flavia an alibi for the night Gran died." I felt my stress level rising again. Morgan pointed at the mug of tea in front of me. I took a sip and then another. I was calmer, but still frustrated. "Everything was leading to Flavia."

Briar took the mug from me and set it

to the side. Then she took my hands in her own garden-tough ones and just held them. Within seconds, the contact caused emotion to swell in me and the next thing I knew, tears were sliding down my cheeks.

"Look at me, Jayne." Briar's voice was gentle but firm. When I did, she said, "Is it that everything led to Flavia being the killer, or is it that you *wanted* Flavia to be the killer?"

I considered this for a moment. "I don't know."

"Yes, you do."

Using my own interrogation tactics against me, she said nothing, letting me sit in silence until I couldn't stand it anymore and had to respond.

"I wanted a quick resolution. I found out about Priscilla's death in Gran's journal and then spoke with Effie and Cybil. The three of them agreed on the circumstances and that's what led me to Flavia."

"But?" Briar prodded.

"But they weren't there the night Priscilla died. I have to talk to the people that were actually there."

"You skipped a step," Briar concluded. "Remember? I told you to gather all information before coming to me."

I laughed and pulled one of my hands from hers to wipe the tears from my face. "I guess I did. I went straight from secondhand information to accusation. That's not good police work."

"What are you going to do next?" Morgan asked. "What's your plan?"

"My plan is to speak with Laurel, Honey, Sugar, Reeva—" I looked pointedly at Briar—"and you. You were there. You know what happened to Priscilla."

"As I told you before," Briar said, "I can only give you my version of the events. After you have gathered information from everyone else, I will tell you what I remember and then help you put the pieces together."

"But I'm here now," I objected, my tone verging on whiny. "Help me out. Tell me what you remember."

Briar responded by pressing her lips together and giving me a mom look.

"There is one thing we can do to help her right away," Morgan said to Briar.

Oh no. Woo-woo time.

"Agreed." Briar seemed to read Morgan's thoughts. A common parlor trick with these two. "We can do that much."

They led me to the atrium at the back of the cottage. This room, with its floor-to-ceiling windows and glass ceiling, was where they gardened in the winter. It was truly amazing, and I wasn't at all surprised to find out that this was also their altar room. A Triple Moon Goddess symbol was etched into the top of the large wooden table at the center of the room. I hadn't noticed that the first time I was in here. I had noticed the tiles inlaid into the floor, but not that they created a circle around the table.

I stood patiently and watched as they prepared the table by smudging it with an herb bundle first then adding a cloth, a purple candle, and an incense holder. After a moment of silent meditation, Morgan presented me with two items.

"Amethyst to calm and soothe," she

said of the deep purple crystal she placed in my right palm and then a dark blue stone in my left. "Lapis lazuli for clarity. You need to cleanse them in the smoke of the incense now."

"*I* do? Why me?"

"Because if I did it, they would belong to me. By holding them in the smoke"— she lit the incense cone in the flame of the purple candle—"you infuse them with your intent."

"Let me guess. I need to be thinking something while I'm doing this?" I was getting used to Morgan's rituals.

"Very good," she grinned. "Our intent is to help you become calm and clear so that when the truth presents to you, you will see it. You weren't calm or clear when you spoke to Flavia. That has cost you time and unnecessary stress."

No matter how many times Morgan involved me with these rituals, I would never believe that anything unnatural or supernatural, or whatever, was taking place. But being with two people who believed so strongly, the way Morgan and Briar did, comforted me and put me in the proper mindset—calm and clear in this case. So, I played along.

Holding the amethyst between my thumb and index finger, I held the crystal in the smoke of the sandalwood incense. As I turned the crystal all directions in the smoke, I thought, *calm*. I did the same with the lapis lazuli and thought, *clarity*.

"Now what?" I whispered.

Briar took me by the elbow and moved me away from the table but still inside the circle on the floor. Then the two women held hands, encircling me with their arms as they did. While clutching my treasures, I looked between the two as they chanted what sounded like a prayer. When they were done, they simply released hands and stepped away. Somehow, that felt a bit anti-climactic.

"Who were you praying to?" I asked.

"Ma'at," Briar said. "She is the goddess of harmony."

"Ma'at presides over justice and truth." Morgan winked at her mother. "Sounds like someone we know." She gave me two small white cloths. "When you're not using the crystal and the stone, keep them wrapped in the cloths. That way no one but you can handle them."

"Using them," I repeated. "What am I supposed to do with them?"

"Place them beneath your pillow tonight," Briar instructed. "The truth will come to you by morning. Do this anytime you're seeking clarity."

"It will come to me. Like in a dream?"

"Not necessarily," Briar said, "but possibly."

"It's more like your intuition will be enhanced when you wake," Morgan added. "This will be powerful for you since your instincts are already strong. Trust them."

Before I left, Briar fed us one last time. Continuing with the "comfort food" theme of the evening, she had prepared a warm fudge cake which she topped with creamy vanilla ice cream.

"This," I said of the dessert, "is wonderful. It wouldn't fit with the breakfast aspect of our bed-and-breakfast, but it might be nice to have desserts available for our guests at night."

"If Tripp wants my recipe," Briar said,

"send him over."

"You don't think I could make it?" I smiled for the first time in hours.

"We all have our strengths, dear," she said and left it at that.

Chapter 23

I WOKE, WITH THE AMETHYST AND lapis lazuli beneath my pillow, to my alarm at six-thirty the next morning. The thought that immediately slammed into my head was that I had left the journals on my desk at work. I hadn't even shut them. I had placed the one I'd been reading face down on my desk at the spot where I had left off, which meant the morning after Priscilla died. The entry where Gran basically accused Flavia of murder.

"Are you kidding me?"

Meeka yelped and leapt off her cushion. The poor half-asleep dog tore around the apartment, searching for whatever the problem was. I caught her as she rushed from the living area back into the bedroom. Her little heart thumped hard inside her ribcage.

"Easy, girl. Everything's okay." I rubbed her ears and scratched her chest. "I'm sorry."

After another few seconds, she calmed down. Then, she glared at me.

"I said I was sorry." I opened the french doors so she could go out. As she left, she looked over her shoulder at me and snorted. I apologized again by placing one of Violet's biscuits on top of the kibble in her breakfast dish.

After a quick shower, I ran across the yard to grab breakfast and hopefully beat Reed into the station. Really though, at this point, there wasn't much I could do; he had either read them or he hadn't. Would he do that? Would he go into my office and read something that was obviously personal?

I opened the back door to the house and found two figures sitting at the breakfast bar. One I was familiar with.

The one sitting next to Tripp I didn't know.

Approximately five foot six, long wavy auburn hair, tiny waist.

"Good morning," I greeted with an elevated voice as neither of them seemed to have heard the firm closing of the door when I entered.

Tripp startled and jumped off the bar stool. "Jayne. Good morning. This is Alex."

The woman sitting next to Tripp turned around with a big smile full of gleaming white teeth. And rather large boobs held captive in a one-size-too-small tank top.

"Alex is the tiler I told you I was going to hire," Tripp explained like we had just talked about her.

I paused and thought. "You said you'd hire someone. I don't recall hearing a name." Turning on cop mode, because Sheriff Jayne could handle anything while Regular Jayne suffered from all kinds of insecurity, I held my hand out to Alex. "Jayne O'Shea. I own the property. Actually, I own all of the property

ORIGINAL SECRETS | 365

Whispering Pines sits on."

That was childish. And besides, my dad owned it. I didn't own anything. Yet.

A sunbeam blinded me when it reflected off her big white teeth. Alex shook my hand like she was one of the guys, giving me one of those sideward slap-shakes with a few enthusiastic arm pumps. She smelled fresh, like bedsheets dried in the sun.

"Nice to meet you. I've heard the O'Shea name. And Tripp has told me so much about you."

She had the sweetest little hint of a southern accent. Must've made her irresistible to the crew.

I forced my mouth into a tight smile then tugged my hand free of Alex's and continued to the counter to fill a travel mug. I had a feeling this would be a two or three extra-large coffee day. Then I went to the refrigerator. "Do we have any of those breakfast sandwiches left?"

"No. I ate them for lunch yesterday." Tripp gave me a pointed look. "Your dinner plate from last night is still in there, though."

Was that a dig? On the way home last night, first walking in the rain from Morgan's house to the parking lot and then driving the short distance from there, I thought about Tripp. I'd thought about him off and on all day. Jonah had hurt me, and I was taking it out on Tripp. I needed to let that go and move forward. As I'd planned while sitting on the patio yesterday morning, I was going to talk to Tripp, but both the house and his trailer were dark when I got here, so I decided not to disturb him.

"I got home late."

"Must've been really late." Tripp took his seat next to Alex again. "I didn't even hear your car."

Was he irritated with me? He was sitting next to the Goddess of Tile, and he was irritated with me?

"You know how my job is. Gotta catch those killers." I glanced between the two of them, shoulders practically touching. "What are you two working on so early in the morning?"

Oh god. Did she stay over? Flustered by this possibility, I reached into the refrigerator and blindly grabbed breakfast. I heard Tripp's voice but not the words he was saying. All I could think was that Alex had spent the night in Tripp's trailer. Guess that's what I got for being gone so much.

Like that was my fault. Working all hours of the day was the reality of the job.

Well, really it was kind of my fault. I didn't have to accept the position.

"Jayne." Tripp grabbed my arm and stopped me at the back door. "What's the matter?"

"What makes you think something's the matter?"

"Because you're holding a package of ground beef, an uncooked egg, and a cucumber." He glanced down at my hands. "Interesting breakfast choice, but if that works for you . . ."

And I left my coffee sitting on the counter. Next to Alex. I shoved everything into his hands. "Guess I'm distracted by this case. I'll grab something at the Bean Grinder. You should get back to whatever it is you're doing with Alex."

I was outside with the door halfway

closed when Tripp said something that sounded like "planning a fling." I pulled the door all the way shut, gave him a half-hearted wave, and rushed over to the Cherokee. Once there, I realized I didn't have Meeka's leash. Or Meeka.

~~~

Relieved to find that Reed wasn't at the station yet, I rushed inside, flicked on the lights in my office, and found the journals stacked in a neat little pile at the center of my desk. My shoulders dropped, like one of those giant balloon people deflating. Maybe he had just straightened up for me. Or maybe he'd read every word. Which he couldn't be mad at me about; I didn't write them.

Before I could deal with another thing, I needed coffee.

"Hey, Jayne," Violet chirped as I entered Ye Olde Bean Grinder.

"Planning the tiling," I blurted as I realized what Tripp had really said.

Confused, and probably a little concerned, Violet blinked and said,

"What?"

"Nothing. Just a frustrating start to the day."

She put the smile back on her face. "What can I make you this morning?"

The aroma that permeated the shop inside soothed me. Like the ghosts of a million coffee beans had just wrapped me in a hug. I needed that.

"My usual today, please." I calmed further at the thought of the extra-large mocha that would be in my hands in a minute.

Like any good barista/therapist, the ever-inquisitive Violet had already noted my demeanor. "Long night? No offense, but you look a little haggard this morning. What's going on?"

"Oh, you know." I shrugged, dismissing the question as I lifted the cover of the scone container on the counter in front of me. "What are my choices today?"

"Sugar's raspberry almond buttermilk have been so popular, we're keeping them stocked. The other is an orange scone with dark chocolate chips."

I took my time selecting one of each scone, hoping she'd move past me and my haggard appearance. That hope was dashed as she secured a lid on my coffee cup and, with an expectant look on her face, clutched the cup on the far side of the counter where I couldn't reach it. I could throw myself across and snatch it, but that would not be respectable sheriff behavior.

Giving in, I explained, "I reopened a case. There are a lot of pieces to this puzzle and it's got me a little stumped."

She nodded like she understood. And sure enough, she did. "Your grandma's case."

"How do you know that?"

"I was out for a walk last night and ended up over by The Triangle. I ran into Effie and she mentioned that she was a little worried about you." She paused until she had my full attention. "Does she have a reason to be worried about you?"

The greatest thing about this village was how everyone cared so much about each other. There were a couple of outliers that came to mind—instantly,

Flavia and Donovan—but overall it was one big family.

"No." I gave a grateful smile. "There's no reason to worry about me. Yes, I reopened Gran's case. There's a coverup of some kind going on, I'm sure of it." Damn. I didn't mean to say that much. "We'll keep that between us, right?"

Violet did her version of zipping and locking her lips, which was to wiggle her fingers in front of her mouth.

"Don't think you're alone with your concern, Jayne," she said. "You know how much we loved Lucy."

"Most of you," I amended. "Clearly, at least one person had a big problem with her."

"Just promise me you won't take all of this on yourself. If you need us, we'll help you in any way we can. Just say the word."

She slid my coffee across the counter to me but didn't release the cup until I agreed I'd ask for help.

"Thank you, Violet. I need to get to work." I held up my cup of coffee. "I'll probably be by for another one of these later."

Meeka and I hurried back to the station, where I was relieved to find that Reed still wasn't there. Was he coming in today? Or ever again? What if he was in cahoots with his mother and was involved with Gran's death? What if Flavia pushed me to rehire him so she could have someone on the inside? It wouldn't be the first time. She had Sheriff Brighton wrapped around her pinky finger.

I sat at my desk, slowly eating my scones and staring at the stack of journals while wondering what my deputy's mood would be if he came back to work. I had finished the raspberry-almond and was two bites into the orange with dark chocolate when the back door opened. Should I go out and confront him or wait for him to come to me? That decision was made when Reed immediately came into my office and sat in the chair across from me.

"My mother said you stopped by yesterday."

"I did." Regular Jayne squirmed inside while Sheriff Jayne reminded her that there was no reason to feel bad about investigating a case.

"She says you accused her of killing your grandmother."

I finished chewing and swallowed. "Martin, did you read the journals?"

He flushed bright red. "You've been so obsessed with those things for the last few days. Curiosity was killing me. I didn't read all of them, but I picked up the open one and saw my mother's name on the page. I backed up to the start of the entry you were reading. Kind of a shocker."

I didn't like him going through my stuff, but he did have the right to know what was going on in the station. I decided to bring him in on the case.

"Flavia tells me she didn't do it. She insists she didn't kill that girl, Priscilla, forty years ago."

"She didn't want to talk about it much, but she said the girl's death was an accident."

"It could have been. There was no investigation, so I have no proof either way. The thing is, I think that Priscilla's and my grandmother's deaths are linked somehow. That means someone from The Pack, the group that your mother and my father hung out with, could be a killer." I took a sip from my mocha. "I'll be out of the station today, interviewing people from that group."

Reed sat there and studied me for a long minute and finally said, "If Lucy's death wasn't an accident, you do need to figure out who did it. I don't think it was my mother, though." He glanced pointedly at the stack of books on my desk. "Maybe you should finish reading that journal."

I eyed him. "I thought you didn't read the whole thing."

He shrugged. "Might have finished that one." He stood to leave my office.

"I have a question for you. If my investigation does lead to your mother and I press charges, are you going to hold that against me?"

He glanced down at his hands folded in front of him and hesitated before answering. "If my mother killed someone, she needs to pay for it."

That helped more than I thought it

would. I finished my second scone and the remains of my now-cold coffee and returned to the journal.

This village means everything to me as do the families that live here. What am I supposed to do about this girl's death? I spoke to those who were at the Meditation Circle that night. They all, with the exception of Flavia, Karl, and Horace, said they didn't think Priscilla's death was intentional or planned. They said it started out innocently enough, with Flavia wanting to settle the conflict between Rae and Priscilla, but that she quickly became frenzied, pushing them to fight each other for the right to be with Gabe.

None of this makes any sense to me. Why exactly was Flavia so dead set on Gabe being the solution for Priscilla's situation?

Good question. I'd been wondering the same thing.

For the next few entries, Gran talked

about how Priscilla's death devastated the village. Convinced that not even tiny Whispering Pines was safe from society's evil influence, a couple of families packed up and left. The Originals stayed, but the closeness wasn't what it once had been. And then some new information regarding Priscilla's death came to light.

Rae showed up at my front door today, she was hysterical. I was terrified something had happened to Effie. It took a long time to calm her down enough for her to say it was her fault Priscilla was dead.

She insisted she didn't mean to do it, that Flavia pushed and pushed, egging on both she and Priscilla. The more they fought with each other, she said, the more Flavia's eyes gleamed with delight. Then Flavia whispered something in Priscilla's ear, and Priscilla charged at Rae. In an attempt to defend herself, Rae said she held out her arms to block the onslaught.

The next thing they knew, Priscilla

was lying on the ground "with blood oozing out of her ears."

Everyone agreed that Flavia wasn't responsible for Priscilla's death. She didn't strike the fatal blow, but it sounded like she initiated Priscilla's attack on Rae. If I could prove any of this, Flavia could be charged with aiding and abetting. But with no autopsy, not even a police report, I had little chance of even proving a girl had died.

The next entry:

I went to see Effie and Cybil today. Rae and Gabe were there as well. I asked Rae to tell them what she had told me. Poor Effie was a basket case by the end of Rae's statement, terrified that her daughter would go to prison.

I'm convinced it was an accident, and if the authorities ever do find out, most of the kids will come to Rae's defense. But Effie insists we can't know that for sure. Rae agreed and said she wants to confess, which upset

Effie even more.

I've decided that there's only one way out of this. Rae and Gabe have to leave Whispering Pines. I told them that once they're gone, I'll make sure that the situation is never discussed within the village again.

I felt numb. My grandmother had covered up a death. How could she have done that? Now that I knew, what was I supposed to do? If I had found all of this out six months earlier, when Gran was still alive, and was able to prove everything, I would have had to implicate her as well. Was I willing to tarnish her name now?

After Rae and Gabe had been gone for forty-eight hours, Flavia appeared at my door. She told me that, for Priscilla's sake, the truth needed to come out and demanded that I tell the villagers what really happened. I warned her to leave it alone, that the situation had been dealt with and we needed to move forward as a village.

She refused to let it go, pushing me to tell the truth as she must have pushed the girls to duke it out that night.

So, I summoned everyone to the pentacle garden and told them the truth as I understood it. I explained that after speaking with all the children present that night, I determined that Flavia was responsible for Priscilla's death, that I was handling her punishment, and that no one was to talk about this again. Then I told Flavia that if she wanted to stay in my village, she was to accept my decision without further question. She's well aware of her role in this incident. For now, she's quiet. For her own sake, I hope she stays that way.

Instigation. Seduction. Collusion. Intimidation. Bribery. Cover up. How many other crimes had my grandmother committed? I was so stunned, I could barely breathe.

Months later after no journal entries:

I feel horrible about what I had to do. But I couldn't let one girl take down what so many have built. More importantly, I couldn't let my best friend suffer for a simple mistake.

By "best friend" she meant Effie of course, but by "girl," had she meant Flavia or Rae?

I wanted to be angry at Gran. I wanted to be furious at all she had done, and I was for a few minutes, but then I read the final entry in the 1979 journal.

We did it. I can't believe we did it. The state of Wisconsin is letting us incorporate. After all the council's hard work, finally everyone can stay without worry. They can open businesses to support themselves and their families. More importantly, people will be able to stay in this place where they will be free of harassment and ostracism. This is what I wanted for them all along. This was why I opened my doors to those who didn't belong anywhere else.

And would that have happened if word had gotten out that a teenage girl, an unwed teenage mother, had died in a village with no law enforcement?

Chapter 24

I ATTACHED MEEKA'S LEASH TO HER harness with the "K-9" patch, and we headed for the front door. I stopped before stepping outside and turned back to Reed.

"I understand the conflict," I said. "Looks like your mother might have been the instigator, but my grandmother employed some strong-arm tactics."

"What are you planning to do about it?" Reed asked without looking at me.

"Not sure yet. I won't do anything without solid proof." I took a few steps closer to his desk. "Look, I like the teamwork we're forming here. What happened in the past isn't our fault and shouldn't affect us."

He stared, stone-faced, at me and just when I was sure I was going to have to search for a new deputy, he offered a weak smile. "Can't choose family, can we?"

"Wouldn't that be a blessing?" I pointed in the general direction of the village commons. "I'm going to do some interviews. I realize this has been an obsession for me this week, but I feel like I'm closing in on answers and want to finish this."

"Works for me. Go, be a Sheriff."

"Thanks, Martin."

Meeka and I power-walked down the Fairy Path and straight to Treat Me Sweetly. Sugar and Honey were the first interviewees on my list.

As usual, the shop was busy. From behind the ice cream counter, Honey gave us a little wave and called, "Good morning, ladies." Then she slapped a hand over her mouth. "That was disrespectful." She cleared her throat and tried again. "Good morning, Sheriff and

Deputy Meeka. We'll be right with you."

I cut through the crowd, leaned in, and in a hushed voice said, "We're here for official reasons. I need to speak with you and Sugar."

Honey paused, as though trying to guess at what that might mean, and then said, "Well then, let me make a few staffing tweaks. Go on through to the office in back and have a seat. We'll be right there. Can I bring you anything?"

I contemplated an ice cream cone. "Thanks, I'm fine."

"Coffee? We give Violet scones, and she provides us with a blend that goes perfectly with anything sweet."

"That sounds good. I'd love a cup of coffee."

"Go on and make yourself comfy."

I'd never been in the sweet shop's office. Giant cookie and candy stickers covered the walls. The telephone on the desk looked like a big banana split with the ice cream scoops as the receiver. I couldn't help but smile. I settled into a chair in front of the desk and a minute later, Sugar appeared with two steaming mugs in hand.

"Honey is getting the staff organized. She'll be right here." She sat on the other side of the desk and pushed a mug across to me. "Official business, hey? What's going on?"

Before starting, I took a sip; Honey was right, this blend was amazing. I turned on my voice recorder and set it on the desk. "That's so I don't have to take as many notes. Tell me everything you remember about the night Priscilla died."

She sat in silence for a moment. "Good Goddess, I haven't thought of that night in years. How did you uncover that?"

"I finished reading Gran's journals from 1979. Effie and Cybil corroborated what Gran wrote."

"Of course, they did," Sugar said. "Lucy and Effie were peas in a pod. There wasn't a thing one wouldn't have done for the other. When they realized what had happened to Priscilla and who did what, your grandma wouldn't consider any other option than to save Rae."

"What are we talking about?" Honey joined us then, sliding into the chair next

386 | SHAWN MCGUIRE

to her sister's.

"The night Priscilla died," Sugar informed.

Honey gazed down at the mug of coffee in her hands and remained silent for a moment. "We were just little then. I was ten, Sugar twelve."

"So, you were there?" I asked.

"For a while," Sugar said. "Your dad made us leave. He didn't want us getting in the middle of something that might turn ugly."

"But we didn't leave," Honey added with a grin. "Remember? We hid in the trees with Willie."

"Willie?" I asked, shocked. "You mean Blind Willie?"

"He wasn't there," Sugar said.

"He most certainly was," Honey insisted. "I remember very clearly. Dillon made us leave, Willie found us hiding in the trees."

Sugar squinted, thinking back, and then shook her head. "I don't remember that. She's the one you want to talk to, Jayne. She's got a memory like a beartrap."

Following their conversation was like watching a hummingbird flit about. "All right, Honey, tell me what you remember."

"I remember everyone gathering around the fire pit," she began. "The group split in two, like they always did at that point. Dillon, Briar, Laurel, and Gabe were on one side of the fire pit. Horace and Karl were on the other. Flavia, Priscilla, and Rae were in the middle."

"Hang on." I did a mental inventory of the group. "Where was Reeva?"

"She wasn't part of the group anymore," Sugar said. "After Rae and Gabe got together—and especially when Flavia set her sights on Horace and Karl, whichever was paying attention to her at the moment—Reeva basically disappeared."

"Reeva really liked Karl," Honey explained and then frowned. "She liked Gabe first."

Sugar swatted a dismissive hand. "All the girls liked Gabe."

"Of course they did." Honey placed her hand to her heart and batted her eyelashes. "He was so cute! Anyway, Reeva couldn't handle watching Flavia go after Karl, too, so she just stopped coming around."

Unfortunately, I understood sister issues. Rosalyn flirted with Jonah one New Year's Eve. She couldn't handle champagne; claimed the bubbles did weird things to her. That night, the bubbles made her ultra-flirty. I found her in the kitchen, backing Jonah into a corner, telling him, in this little sex-kitten voice, that she wanted "just one little New Year's kiss." Jonah still loved me then and pushed her away. To this day, I wasn't sure I could trust her.

I shook my head, realizing I'd let my mind wander and the interview get off track.

"Why, exactly, was everyone at the Meditation Circle? What did Flavia tell you to get you all there?"

Honey crossed her arms and pouted. "No one told us anything. We were the little kids so got left out of the big kid stuff." Her pout turned into a giggle and she glanced at Sugar. "We used to sneak around all the time. Remember that?"

"Our secret missions?" Sugar grinned back. "I remember."

I leaned across the desk. "What secret missions?"

"We knew for weeks that Flavia and Priscilla were up to something," Sugar began. "The whole group, I mean, not just Honey and me. The two would be off by themselves, talking behind their hands and looking over at the group. Finally, we decided to enact Operation Little Girl."

"Operation Little Girl?" I asked.

Sugar nodded, looking as pleased as her younger sister did. "Honey was only ten and she was a tiny little thing."

Honey stood, wiggled her backside at me, and said over her shoulder, "Two decades of making ice cream has taken care of that." Then she blushed at her own actions. "We're supposed to be professional, aren't we?" She sat back down with her hands clasped around the coffee mug in her lap.

"Because she was so little," Sugar continued, "no one noticed when she was around. We decided that Honey would join Team Flavia and I would stay on Team Dillon."

I looked up from my notebook at Honey. "You weren't really on Team Flavia, were you?".

"Good Goddess, no," she insisted. "I just hung out near them and acted like I was playing when they were having their little meetings." She pushed her shoulders back and held her head high. "I heard everything."

"What did you hear?" I asked.

"Flavia told Priscilla that she should be Gabe's girlfriend. Priscilla said she didn't like Gabe, she liked another boy." Honey glanced at Sugar. "The baby's father, we assumed. Whoever he was. She never did tell us." Sugar nodded her agreement with this. "Anyway, Flavia kept insisting and coached Priscilla on what she had to do. She said Priscilla needed to promise Gabe things. She needed to get him alone and then flirt and stuff."

Ten-year-old Honey was in front of me as surely as forty-something Honey was, and ten-year-old Honey was blushing a brilliant shade of berry at this memory.

"Why would Priscilla agree to this?" I wondered aloud. "If she liked someone else, why wouldn't she tell Flavia she didn't want to do that?"

"She was under Flavia's spell," Sugar said. "That's the only way to explain it."

That would be a figment of speech anywhere else. In Whispering Pines, being under someone's spell could be a literal thing.

"Are you saying that Flavia cast a spell that would make Priscilla obey her?" I couldn't believe I even asked that question.

"Guess that's possible," Sugar considered. "Not what I meant, though. It was more that Priscilla was so desperate she would have gone in any direction someone pointed her in if they guided her."

A scared teenage girl, possibly suffering from postpartum depression, does as she's told. Sad, but believable.

"Priscilla was desperate," I echoed, "that's why she did what Flavia said. What about the other side of this? Rae and Gabe were already tight. Why wouldn't Rae just walk away? Why fight that night?"

"The thing about Rae," Sugar recalled, "she was real prideful and real angry. The Wiccan kids acted like they ruled the village." She held up a hand. "Before you say it, yes, we're Wiccan, but we never teased anyone."

"Except in the pulling pranks way," Honey added with a mischievous grin.

Sugar glared at her for a second and then broke out in her own grin before turning serious again. "The others teased the fortune teller kids something awful."

"It wasn't pretty," Honey agreed. "The thing was, Rae didn't even want to be a fortune teller. She said she never had a vision in her life, but the older tellers insisted it would happen if she practiced, or whatever they do to turn it on."

That sounded a lot like Lily Grace's story.

"Rae couldn't just walk away," Sugar said. "She had people telling her from every direction what she was and who she was. I think that night was her chance to stand up for herself."

"All right," I said, "everyone is gathered at the Meditation Circle. Then what happened?"

"Willie made us leave." Sugar slapped a hand on the desk. "I remember now. When it became obvious this wasn't going to be a nice, calm discussion, he took us home."

Seriously? "Neither of you saw anything after the initial gathering?"

Honey shook her head. "Nothing. Willie said the big kids were about to get into trouble, and we didn't need to be around for it."

"I've got to be honest," I said, "this is kind of a letdown after all that buildup, but you did give me some good information. Bits here, bits there, and soon I'll have the whole story."

Honey rushed back to help with customers, and Sugar stayed in the office while I gathered my things.

"I warned you, didn't I?" she asked.

I tucked my notebook into a pocket and reached for my voice recorder. "About the muck and my beliefs being rocked? You did."

"Not much good comes from digging up the past. Maybe you should have left well enough alone."

Morgan's words about Sugar sounded in my ears. *Goddess bless her, she means well, but Sugar's words are often double sided.*

"Maybe. But first, nothing about this is 'well.' Second, if you didn't want me to go digging, you never would've said anything. Would you?"

Chapter 25

AFTER LEAVING TREAT ME SWEETLY, Meeka and I cut through the pentacle garden to go to The Inn to talk with Laurel next. I was almost to the negativity well, the garden's midpoint, when I heard someone call my name. I turned to find Morgan coming my way.

"You're in a hurry," she said when she caught up to me.

"I need to talk with Laurel about the night Priscilla died."

"Such a gloomy topic," Morgan said with a frown. "It's two o'clock and I still haven't had lunch. Care to join me for a bite at The Inn's restaurant?"

"I could eat."

Even two in the afternoon during the summer tourist season meant we had to wait for a table. Once seated, Meeka took her standard spot beneath the table, Sylvie took our order, and I asked if she had seen Laurel recently.

"Recently?" Sylvie tapped the toe of one knee-high boot that was part of her all black Oktoberfest beer girl/Wiccan high priestess uniform. "That's subjective. We've been super busy today. Got a big party of some kind coming in tonight that we're prepping for. Anyway, I saw Laurel an hour ago . . . or maybe it was three hours?" She shrugged. "I'll track her down and send her over."

"Are you closer to putting together the pieces of that night?" Morgan asked once Sylvie had walked away.

"Closer, but nowhere near the full picture." I gave her some of the details on what I'd learned so far.

"I knew Flavia had a dark side, but I never would have guessed she'd do something like that."

"I'm trying to only gather statements

and not draw conclusions yet, even about Flavia. Honey and Sugar only knew a portion of what happened that night, so a lot is missing."

Sylvie arrived with a house salad and cup of vegetable soup for Morgan, and a side salad and basket of deep-fried cheese curds for me.

"Laurel's just finishing up with something," Sylvie said while topping off our iced tea. "She'll be here in a jiff."

"Salad and cheese curds?" Morgan asked.

"What? That's balanced." I held my hands out like a scale. "Healthy and yummy."

We were halfway through lunch when Laurel pulled up a chair to our two-top table. "I can't tell you how grateful I am to sit for a few minutes. Whatever you want to talk to me about, take your time."

"That looks good," I said of the burger she'd brought with her. "What is it?"

She held up her plate and turned it side-to-side. "Burger topped with corned beef, swiss cheese, sauerkraut, and thousand island dressing."

"A Rueben burger." It sounded like something Tripp would make.

"You got it," Laurel said. "It's not on the menu, but it should be."

Since she wanted to sit, I gave her a few minutes to relax and eat. I finished my cheese curds, slipping a couple to my furry friend beneath the table.

"I wanted to ask," I began, "what do you remember about the night Priscilla died?"

She paused in mid-chew with her eyebrows arched. "Priscilla? You mean the girl who lived here a long time ago?"

"Right."

"Can't tell you anything. Well, I can tell you what happened after the fact, but I wasn't there that night."

"Sure, you were. I just talked with Honey and Sugar, they said you were there."

Laurel smiled, amused. "They were such troublemakers. I swear they were everywhere at once. You realize they were just little girls at the time. They probably think I was there because I usually was."

"You're positive?" I confirmed.

She leaned in a little bit and lowered her voice. "I knew Flavia was up to no good that night. She'd been causing trouble for weeks between Rae and Gabe. Then there was the drama going on in the group. I was sick of it all so didn't go that night." A far-off look shadowed her face as she shoved the last bite of her burger into her mouth. "The group used to be so much fun. We did everything together. Really. None of us were ever alone unless we wanted to be. And then Rae and Gabe hooked up."

"I understand that Flavia liked Horace and—"

"Just Horace," Laurel supplied.

"I heard she couldn't decide between Horace and Karl," I said.

"She wasn't interested in Karl." Laurel shook her head as she wiped burger residue from her fingers with a napkin. "She only paid attention to Karl because Reeva *really* liked him. Have to say, I'm glad Flavia and Horace got together; that settled her down for a while. It's heartbreaking how everything ended with him dying in that bear attack. The way

Reeva and Karl ended was devastating, too."

"Sounds like Flavia and Reeva were competitive," I said.

"Reeva wasn't at all competitive. She's one of those people who's naturally good at everything she does. Flavia struggles. That's why Reeva stepped away from the group. She decided to let The Pack be the thing Flavia had that was all her own."

"You sound sure of that," I noted.

"She and I were close. Not best friends; Reeva and Rae were best friends. We were close, though." Laurel's expression took on a faraway look. "Reeva's biggest flaw is self-sacrifice. She left the group not just for Flavia, but also to make things easier on Karl. Flavia went after him more when Reeva was around. She did the same thing for Rae." Laurel glanced at her watch. "Is that really the time? I've got to get back to work. Got a family reunion coming in tonight. They booked the entire inn." She spoke faster. "As for the night in question, Dillon and Briar stopped by to let me know there was a gathering that had something to do with

Priscilla, Rae, and Gabe. I told them I was done with it all and didn't even want to hear about anything else. Next thing I heard, Priscilla was dead. Wish I could tell you more, but I honestly can't."

"Every little bit helps." I tried to hide my disappointment but probably failed. "Whether it helps me understand that night or not, understanding what makes Flavia tick can only be a good thing."

Laurel gathered together her plate, napkin, and water glass. "If I think of anything, I'll let you know."

"I appreciate that," I said. "Thanks for talking."

She put a hand to her lower back with a pained expression. "Thanks for letting me sit."

She gave us a little wave and disappeared into the front lobby. I returned my attention to Morgan.

"I can't say that was a strikeout, but it was far from a home run."

"You may have more than you realize," Morgan said. "Maybe it's time to talk to Mama. What are you thinking about?"

"The statement Sugar and Honey gave

me. They were just little at the time; they can't possibly remember the events accurately. The only thing I can take from their interview was that the gathering happened."

"That's something."

Morgan, always ready to offer encouragement.

"Laurel gave insight to some of the other kids, but nothing helpful for that night. I already talked to Flavia. As for kids who were at the Meditation Circle that night, I'm down to Reeva and your mom. Reeva wasn't there so she wouldn't be any more helpful than Laurel."

"As I said, maybe it's time to talk to Mama."

I flipped absently through the pages of my pocket-sized notebook and a name caught my eye. "Maybe Honey and Sugar gave me more than I realized. They said Blind Willie was there that night. At least he was until he took them home. An adult who witnessed the goings-on would be far more likely to remember what had happened years later than teenagers. I feel like I should talk to him."

Morgan dabbed the corners of her mouth with her napkin, placed the napkin on top of her salad plate, and pushed her chair back. "Then let's go talk to Blind Willie."

Chapter 26

BLIND WILLIE LIVED AT THE
farthest north edge of the Whispering
Pines acreage. Morgan knew how to get
there, but it meant a hike through the
woods.

"You're sure you know where he
lives?" I asked after a half an hour of
walking.

"I know," Morgan assured in her calm
way.

She seemed to float through the
woods, the underbrush never once
tripping her up, branches never snapping
out and scraping her. I, on the other
hand, lumbered along, stumbling over a
tangle of tree roots, getting pine needles

from low hanging branches stuck in my hair, and acquiring enough scratches on my arms that I planned a stop at Sundry before going home because there was no way I had enough ointment to cover them all.

"I'll make you a poultice when we return to my cottage," Morgan promised.

"First, I don't know what you just said. Second, why aren't you having troubles?"

"A poultice is a paste made from herbs that you apply and wrap with a cloth to heal skin issues. For your scratches, I'll make a blend of chamomile, Irish moss, and Adder's tongue." She glanced over her shoulder at me. "Yes, Adder's tongue is an herb. As for why I don't have problems, I'm a green witch. Nature and I are never at odds with each other. Try being one with your surroundings rather than charging through like a bulldozer."

"I'm not—" At that moment, as I tried to force a pine sapling out of my way rather than stepping around it, I swear the big tree next to it, it's mother or some other overly-protective family member, poked me in the eye. "Fine, I'll stop charging. How much further to Willie's?"

"Not far. Perhaps five minutes."

Meeka loved our romp through the woods. I took her harness off to be sure she wouldn't get stuck in any of the tight spaces she insisted on squeezing through. Her white fur was closer to brown from the dirt, and it would take a good hour to get all the burrs out of her coat tonight, but she was having fun.

When we finally arrived at Willie's "shack," as Maeve had called it, my jaw dropped. Clearly, she had never been here. If she had been, she would have used a different label. While not large, Blind Willie's house was a log cabin any home magazine would be proud to have on the cover. A fieldstone chimney ran up one side. An eight-foot-wide covered deck wrapped around the other three sides. To the left of the house was a stack of firewood that would easily last until spring. To the right was an orderly garden big enough to supply Willie with all the vegetables he could want.

"This is impressive," I said.

"Wait until you see the inside,"

Morgan replied.

We climbed the four stairs that led to the front door and knocked. A few seconds later, Blind Willie appeared from around the garden side. For a moment, he seemed surprised to see people on his porch, then he lit up.

"Morgan Barlow." He approached her with arms wide and wrapped her in a hug. "Haven't seen you in years."

"Good to see you, Willie." She pushed away from him. "You could use an herbal bouquet, though."

"If I'da known you were comin', I woulda took a bath. Will you be here long?"

I held a hand out to him. "I'm Sheriff O'Shea. I need to talk to you about an event that happened years ago."

His head bobbed up and down like he had expected this. "Go on in then. Make yourselves at home. Got a jug of fresh sun tea on the counter. Pour yourself a glass while I go make myself less aromatic."

He disappeared around the back of the cabin again.

"Where's he going?" I asked.

"Willie bathes in the stream until it freezes over. I don't recommend looking out the back windows until after he returns."

Morgan was right about the cabin's interior. All the furniture was made from pine logs, handmade by Willie himself, I assumed. The kitchen had gourmet appliances, slab granite countertops, and hickory cabinets. His bedroom seemed to consist of the bed tucked into the far left corner. Most impressive of all was his computer set up.

"This is high-tech stuff," I mused.

"You know he's a multi-millionaire?" Morgan asked.

"I heard that."

"I believe he still runs his company from here via video conferencing."

"How does he run all this equipment?"

"He installed utilities—electric, gas, water, and sewer—but prefers greener sources. There are solar panels on the roof, along with a wind turbine, and a generator around back as backup. There's a satellite dish back there as well."

"So, his conspiracy theories . . .?"

"They're based on things he reads on the internet."

I was still ogling the setup when Willie came in the front door, went straight to the jug on the kitchen counter, and filled a beer stein to the top with sun tea. He offered us a fill-up and settled into a big log chair with wolf heads embroidered all over the cushion fabric. "What can I help you with, Sheriff?"

He seemed far less nutso than when I'd first seen him on Maeve's porch.

I took the matching wolf chair across from him. Morgan sat on the arm of my chair. "I understand you were—"

"Oh, hang on a sec."

Willie strode to his computer and covered it with a tinfoil blanket. Then he turned on a device that affected Meeka immediately. She barked, pawed at her ears, and then ran out the front door.

"Sorry 'bout your dog." Willie gestured at the device. "It emits a high-frequency tone to stop them from listening to our conversation."

"Them who?" I asked.

"The government, of course."

Just when I thought he wasn't nutso. I held up my voice recorder. "Will your device interfere with this?"

"Probably."

I put it away and took out my notebook. "I understand you were at the Meditation Circle the night a girl—"

"Priscilla." Willie looked down at his large, square hands which, despite his bath, still had dirt caked beneath the fingernails. "I was there. For part of the night, at least."

"Can you tell me what you remember about that night, Mr. Haggerty?"

He squinted at me and looked behind him as though expecting to see someone there. "Who's Haggerty?"

I glanced at Morgan who gave an encouraging nod. "You are. That's what I read in my grandmother's journals."

"Who's your granny?"

"Lucy O'Shea."

"Oh!" Willie slapped his hand on the arm of his chair and lit up like he did when he saw Morgan on his porch. "You must be Jayne. Or are you Rosalyn?"

I smiled, surprised by his reaction.

"You got it the first time. I'm Jayne."

"That Lucy was such a doll. She had me over for dinner every few months."

"She did?" Morgan pouted playfully. "You came to the village and never stopped in to say hi?"

"Wasn't in the village. I came down to have dinner with Lucy." He gave her a wink, that I didn't allow myself to interpret, and then turned toward me. "I haven't been Haggerty in fifty years. Call me Willie."

"Yes, sir. What do you remember about that night, Willie?"

He started out saying almost exactly what Honey and Sugar had, that there was basically a face-off between Rae and Priscilla with Flavia leading the show.

"I took those little girls back to their parents when I realized something bad was about to happen with the bigger kids, so I was gone for a bit." He shook his head, a sad expression creasing his brow. "Those little ones didn't need to see all that."

"How long were you gone?"

"Ruth and Jonathan lived, oh, a

quarter mile west of the Meditation Circle. I waited until I was sure the girls were in the house and not likely to squirt out again. I was gone probably twenty minutes." He chuckled and scratched his beard. "Those two were little scoundrels. Nosing in on everyone's business. Only one I ever met that's nosier is the little one at the coffee shop."

I had to laugh at that. "You mean Violet?"

Willie pointed at me. "That's her name. That one could pry the Queen's secrets out of the Royal Guard at Buckingham."

"I don't doubt that. So, you dropped the girls off and went back to the group?"

"I did. I was worried something bad was about to go down."

"Tell me what happened when you got back there."

"They were all circled around the fire pit." He looked up at the pine-paneled ceiling and pointed as though counting something. "Eight in all. Those three girls still in the middle. One of them"—he touched his nose—"she had the pointiest nose I ever seen. She was angry, too. Talking real loud and telling the other two that they had to fight for what they wanted. 'If you really want him, Reeva, fight for him!'"

Morgan and I looked at each other.

"Reeva?" I asked.

Willie nodded big, like he understood the question I hadn't asked yet. "That's what she called the girl with the short red hair. I don't know what her real name was, but I know she wasn't Reeva. Me and Reeva used to run into each other in the woods all the time. We'd have long talks. She was always worried about what it took to have a good life."

"You'd be the one to answer that," Morgan stated. "Wouldn't you, Willie?"

"I'm a content guy. Not a thing in life I need or want."

"Not even a woman?" Morgan asked with a wink.

A momentary look of pain etched itself into his weathered face.

"You know full well I already had the greatest love a man could ask for," he growled. "Gone too soon. Couldn't handle a loss like that again."

Morgan placed her hands palms together. "Forgive me. I didn't mean to offend you."

He glowered for another second, then gave a dismissive sigh and swatted a big hand at her. "That Reeva was quite a case. She liked one boy and let her sister take him. I guess she liked this Gabe boy, too, and let the little redhead take him. I told her if she'd quit letting other girls take the boys she liked that would be a good first step toward a good life."

"Reeva liked Gabe?" I glanced at Morgan again. "I vaguely remember Honey or Sugar saying that."

Morgan arched a dramatic black eyebrow. "Interesting twist. Did you note Laurel's comment that Reeva had sacrificed something for Rae?"

"I did." Laurel left in such a hurry, I didn't get to follow up on it. She must have meant that Reeva stepped aside so her best friend could have the boy she liked. I turned back to Willie and got us back on topic.

"What did the other girl look like? The

other one who was fighting."

"The other one had long blonde hair and a little bit of a belly." Willie held his hands in front of his own generous midsection.

"Priscilla. She had a baby not too long before that night." To Morgan, I said, "Flavia called Rae 'Reeva.'"

"Flavia. That's her." Willie said mostly to himself. Then to us, "She said it twice. Wasn't a minute later, Flavia says, 'You don't get to just have everything, Reeva.' The other kids got mighty freaked out by those slips. I have to admit, she was one scary little girl."

This coming from a man the size of a VW Beetle.

"I don't know what happened between the girls while I was gone, but when I got back . . ." Willie frowned. "The rage on that Flavia girl's face, I'll never forget it. It was right toward the end."

A chill skittered through me. "The end?"

"Flavia had been pushing the redhead. You say her name was Rae?"

Morgan and I nodded in unison.

"Flavia was like the ref in a title fight. If one backed off, she'd go to the other and whisper in her ear." He patted both of his ears with the palms of his hands. "I couldn't hear what she said, but suddenly that Priscilla girl charged over and chest-bumped Rae. She did it a couple times. Finally, Rae exploded and shoved her off. Priscilla fell hard." He looked past us like he was watching it all happen. "Hit her head on that rock."

"No one tried to break this up?" I asked.

"Oh, they said stuff. They tried to get Flavia to back off. Told the girls that the whole thing was stupid and that they didn't need to fight. They looked in shock, like they couldn't quite believe what they were seeing. No one tried to physically break it up until that chest bump. Then Lucy's boy stepped in."

The air left my lungs. "Dillon?"

"Yep. Poor kid. Like I said, all the others just stood there. I don't think they really believed anything bad was going to happen. But when things got physical between the girls, it's like they all woke up. Dillon stepped up, but he was maybe a half-second too late. After Priscilla bumped her, Rae pulled her arms back like she was about to shove Priscilla." Willie demonstrated by holding his splayed-open hands by his shoulders, elbows pointing down at the ground. "Dillon just missed grabbing her arm. I mean *just missed*. If he would have reacted a blink sooner—"

"Priscilla wouldn't have died that night," I concluded, numb.

I had no clue my dad had been through something like that. The guilt he must have felt, knowing he could have saved a girl's life but didn't. I knew that guilt. If I would have reacted "a blink sooner" when my partner, Randy, pulled his service weapon on our informant, Frisky would still be alive.

I stared at my notebook, waiting for the threatening tears to pass, and cleared my throat. "Thank you, for your statement, Willie."

He cocked his head. "You okay, Sheriff?"

"Dillon is Jayne's father," Morgan

explained softly.

Willie considered that for a second and then thumped his own forehead with his big fingers. "Course he is. That's quite a burden he carries."

I looked at Morgan, her sad smile said she knew I was thinking about Frisky.

"A heavy burden indeed." I gathered my things together, needing to get out of the suddenly claustrophobic cabin. "I can't think of anything else for you right now. If I have any other questions, is it all right for me to come back?"

Willie stood in front of me and placed a gentle bear paw of a hand on my cheek. "Lucy's granddaughter is welcome in my home any day, any time."

Forty-five minutes later, I was leaning against the driver's door of the Cherokee in front of Morgan's cottage. She came out through the front door with a muslin-wrapped package the size of a nice T-bone steak.

"Soak the herb mixture in just enough hot water to form a paste. When it's cool to the touch, smooth it over the scrapes, and wrap it with the muslin strips." She patted the package, indicating both the herbs and the muslin were inside.

"Thanks, Morgan. I appreciate you taking me up to Willie's."

"Are you okay?"

I took a deep breath. "It was a shock to learn my dad and I lived through such similar circumstances, but I'm fine. Tell Briar that I'll come by in the morning. It's getting late."

Dusk was settling in, and it would be dark within the hour. Since her stroke seven months ago, in January, Briar tired easily, and I knew she wouldn't be up for a talk tonight.

"She'll be happy you're to this point. I think she's been wanting to talk about this for a long time." Morgan reached up and gave my shoulder a comforting rub. "Go home and try to rest well tonight."

Ten minutes later, I pulled up to the garage to find a crew member's truck still there. All I wanted was to sit on the deck with Tripp and relax. Maybe whoever it was would be leaving soon. Since lights were on in the great room, I went to the back patio and looked inside.

Chapter 27

TRIPP AND ALEX WERE SITTING AT the kitchen bar, beer and cheese-and-crackers spread out in front of them. Whatever they were discussing, it must have been hilarious, because Alex threw her head back, rested her hand on Tripp's arm, and laughed hard.

"Come on Meeka," I whispered. "Let's go upstairs."

It wouldn't matter if Alex left in the next ten seconds, I couldn't be the pal Tripp came to after a date.

Meeka looked at me, inside at Tripp, and back at me with a whine.

"I can't deal with that tonight. Let's go."

I pulled on an oversized T-shirt and a pair of boxers. Once I'd applied Morgan's poultice, I turned off the lights and climbed into bed. I lay there, listening to the sounds of the lake and the distant loons, but even the *shushing* sound of the trees through the screen door couldn't soothe me. At one point, something was moving around outside on the deck. Since Meeka's only reaction was to sit up and acknowledge the sound, it had to be Tripp, but he left right away without knocking or calling for me. I lay awake for hours after that, my thoughts rotating through the events that had happened at the Meditation Circle the night Priscilla died, especially my dad trying to stop Rae from shoving her. As soon as I pushed those thoughts away, new ones moved in. Images of Tripp and Alex alone together in my grandparents' house . . . in *my* house bombarded me.

I couldn't say when I fell asleep, but once I did, I dreamt of Tripp in the house with a faceless woman and not letting me inside. I woke with a start when my alarm announced that it was six-thirty. Unsure which scenario would be worse—Tripp making breakfast as usual, Tripp making breakfast for Alex and offering me whatever was left over, or Tripp not bothering with breakfast at all—I waited until the crew showed up before crossing the yard to grab coffee and something to eat. The bonus for that plan was that if Alex's truck was out there, I wouldn't know if she had just arrived or if she'd been here all night.

As I was filling my travel mug with coffee, Tripp walked in.

"Late night?" His tone was conversational, like he didn't really care one way or another.

"Not as late as yours." The bratty tone in my voice made me cringe internally.

He narrowed his eyes, trying to understand what I meant, then said, "Alex stopped by to show me—"

"I've got to get to work."

"Jayne." He grabbed my arm as I walked past and spun me to face him. "What's wrong?"

I jerked free of his grasp. "Nothing you need to worry about. See you later."

When I got to the spot where the driveway met up with the campground, I put the Cherokee into park and burst into tears. I wasn't even sure why I was crying, but the release of pent-up emotions felt good. I was immensely sad about what Dad went through that night so many years ago. I was angry that Alex was so damn pretty. I was angry that Tripp hired someone who was so damn pretty. I was devastated that Tripp seemed to have moved on already. It was my fault. I knew I was waiting too long and didn't expect him to hang around forever, but I thought he'd give me a little more time.

When my tears finally stopped, I lowered the visor and looked at the puffy, dark-circled eyes staring back at me.

"This is exactly what you were afraid of," I told the Jayne in the mirror. "You know you can't trust guys. This is why you waited, to see what he'd do to break your heart. Good thing you didn't let this go anywhere."

Excuses, excuses, Jayne in the mirror

replied. *You're justifying not taking a chance with him. You don't know that he'd break your heart. And you don't know why Alex was there last night. Tripp said she stopped by to—*

A flip of the visor silenced Jayne in the mirror. I didn't want to hear reason right now. I just wanted to be mad. Or sad. Or whatever it was I was feeling.

~~~

Halfway to the Barlow cottage, I came upon Morgan walking alongside the road. Checking first to be sure there were no cars behind me, I pulled to a stop and lowered my window.

"Blessed be, Jayne." She took one look at me and frowned. "You didn't rest last night, did you?"

"Trust me, I tried, but no. If I got an hour of sleep, I'd be surprised."

"Mama is ready for you. She was up very early in anticipation. I probably should have waited until this morning to let her know you were coming. I don't think she got much sleep either. You'll stop by to see me later and tell me how it goes."

It was more a command than a question. I promised I would, and then she continued on to Shoppe Mystique. I pulled to a stop in the cottage's short driveway and let Meeka out of her crate in the back. She immediately ran over and squeezed between the plants that made up the hedge surrounding Morgan and Briar's garden. She'd want to play with Pitch, Morgan's all-black rooster.

From behind the hedge, Briar exclaimed, "Well, Meeka. I assume your presence means that Jayne is here as well."

"I'm here, Briar," I called.

"The front door is open. Come on around."

Beneath the wisteria-covered pergola in the backyard was a small round patio table where Briar had set up a tea service for us. There was also a bowl with cut-up fruit and a plate with a dozen miniature poppy seed muffins. It was so charming, so thoughtful, I almost started crying again.

426 | SHAWN MCGUIRE

"Sit," Briar beckoned. "I'll run inside and grab the tea. I waited on that until you got here so it would be good and hot."

As with the other night when she insisted on giving me dinner, Briar wouldn't let me tell my tale until I had eaten first. Considering I hadn't had dinner last night, or gotten the chance to grab anything for breakfast before Tripp interrupted me, I was okay with this plan.

"All right," she said when I'd finished eating all but four of the little muffins. "Tell me what you've learned."

I wasn't sure how long I spoke, but I started by reminding her about how Effie and Cybil had agreed with what Gran had written in her journal. I recounted my conversation with Honey and Sugar. Then I explained how Laurel had given me insight into Flavia but couldn't give details about Priscilla's death since she hadn't been there that night. Finally, I told her about the conversation Morgan and I had with Blind Willie the night before.

"Good Goddess." Briar sat back in her chair. "That's a lot to take in."

"What can you add to that? You told me once I had all the pieces, you'd help me arrange them into a whole story."

"Let's do that, then." She added more tea to our cups. "You already know that we can mostly disregard what Effie and Cybil told you. Those three—your grandmother and Effie in particular—were inseparable back then."

"What about your mother? I thought Gran and Dulcie were so close."

"Oh, they were, but you know how things go. New people come into your life and hierarchies shift."

"Did something happen between Gran and Dulcie?"

Briar picked apart the mini-muffin on her plate, stalling. "Nothing *happened*. It's just . . . you understand that people can behave differently depending on who they're with?"

"Of course."

"Lucy and my mother had a history together. My mom taught your grandmother about Wicca and gardening. Your grandmother offered Mama and me a new life. Theirs was a more practical relationship. When Effie came, the friendship between she and your grandmother was instant."

That explanation didn't sit right with me. "Briar? What aren't you saying?"

She released a heavy exhale. "My mother felt that Lucy's attitude changed with every person who came to live here. Lucy had every right to be in charge, the land was hers and your grandfather's, after all. They didn't have to let any of us stay here, but they did, and Lucy seemed to become more of a ruler."

Whispering Pines is my kingdom and I am the queen here.

"I think Lucy regretted some of her decisions," Briar continued, "but once they were made, she didn't feel she could change them."

"You mean like telling the villagers that Flavia killed Priscilla?"

She paused for a sip of tea. "That was a big one. So was forcing Rae and Gabe to leave town. Priscilla's death was an accident, but just so Rae could forgive herself instead of running away, it would have been better for the villagers to know the truth. Hiding it just led to more conflict." She took another sip. "As for Honey and Sugar, they saw some things but nothing important. And, they were just little girls at the time. It doesn't matter how good they claim Honey's memory is, she was only ten, Sugar twelve. What do you remember from when you were ten or twelve years old?"

Good point. "Bits and pieces but not much. What about you? What do you remember from that night?"

She finished her tea and placed the cup back on the saucer. "I agree with everything Blind Willie told you. Flavia was determined to get the girls to fight that night."

"This is where it seems something is still missing. I can understand wanting to help Priscilla get a guy, but Gabe was already with Rae. Horace and Karl were spoken for. My dad, well, I don't really know what his situation was. He supposedly liked a girl but wouldn't tell Gran who she was. There had to be other eligible boys in the village. Why did she target Gabe? And why didn't he do anything about it? Why didn't he put a stop to things that night and take Rae home?"

"He tried," Briar promised. "You should've seen him. Once he realized what was going on, he tried to stop it, but every word he said was shot down by either Flavia or Rae. Priscilla had been after him for weeks, and Rae saw this as her chance to stand up and finally end it."

"Willie didn't tell me any of that. He must've been taking Honey and Sugar home at that point." I pictured the scene in my mind. The three girls in the center, Gabe helpless on the side. "I still come back to, why Gabe?"

"You tell me. What possible reason could a girl have for putting a boy in such an uncomfortable position?"

I sat back, linked my fingers behind my head, and stared up into the wisteria canopy, my tight neck popping when I did.

"Flavia had to be really angry about something," I began. "Of course she was angry; Flavia is always angry. Maybe Gabe did something to Priscilla and

Flavia wanted him to pay for it?" I lowered my eyes to Briar. "Was he the father?"

"No, he was not the father. I honestly don't know who was, but I'd stake my life that it wasn't Gabe." Briar's eyes gleamed. "Keep talking it out, you're on the right path. Flavia was angry . . ."

I stood and paced around the small patio, hands on my hips. "Was she angry at Rae for some reason? Did Rae do something to Priscilla?"

Briar shook her head, so I continued pacing.

"Okay, she was mad at someone, but not Rae. Not Priscilla, they were best friends." We'd be there all day if Briar didn't give me a clue. Wait, I was ignoring someone from that triangle. "She was mad at Gabe. Why?"

"This is the reason I wanted you to understand everything else first, so all these moving pieces"— she threaded her fingers together—"would merge for you at the end."

I returned to my chair. "Is Flavia lesbian? Was she mad at Gabe because she wanted to be with Rae?"

"Now that would be a twist." Briar had a good laugh at that. "No. Flavia wanted Gabe."

Who was this guy? "Did every girl in the village want him?"

Briar chuckled at this. "Pretty much. He was good looking, had a great future ahead of him, and oh my Goddess, could he make us laugh. We loved being around him because he was so funny."

"So Flavia wanted him, too? I thought she liked Horace. Or Karl."

"Flavia's wanting to be with Gabe had nothing to do with liking him. There was one girl in particular who did like him, quite a lot, and Flavia decided she wouldn't let her have him."

Reeva liked Gabe.

I sank back in my chair. "Reeva? Flavia has Horace, hits on Karl, and won't let Reeva have Gabe either?"

"This was still a little before Reeva became interested in Karl."

I was becoming increasingly frustrated with this. Every answer twisted around and created another question. I covered my face with my hands. "Briar, I just want to know what happened. I did the work. I understand all the pieces now, I think. Please, will you just tell me what happened?"

She patted my knee. "Very well. Gabe really was a great guy, but he made one very large mistake."

"What did he do?"

"He slept with Flavia."

I felt a little nauseous at that revelation. "Wow. Huge mistake. Why would he do that?"

"You'd never guess from the way she presents herself now, but Flavia was a real beauty. When we were teenagers, she took great pride in her appearance. She did her hair and makeup every day. She wore miniskirts that showed off a pair of very nice legs. The reason Priscilla was able to tempt Gabe the way she did—"

"Was because Flavia taught her how."

Gran's words from the 1979 journal echoed in my ears: *Dillon thinks she offered them sex. I wish I could say this comment surprised me, but it doesn't.*

I sat on the edge of the chair, vibrating

with anticipation for the punchline. "All right. He sleeps with Flavia and instantly regrets it?"

Briar smiled. "You're being mean, but yes, he did. This unfortunate event happened shortly before he and Rae got together."

"So he'd already been thinking about Rae?"

"As far as I know, yes."

I bit back a smile. "Flavia sleeps with him to keep him away from Reeva, but didn't realize Reeva had already passed him off to Rae?"

"Basically."

"Why does Flavia hate Reeva so much?"

"That," Briar said with a frown, "I can't answer."

"Did Flavia expect that Gabe would want to be with her?"

"Honestly, I think she did. She'd already lured Horace and Karl. Your dad, well, he was kind of untouchable because of who he was. By that time, your grandmother was ruling the village with a firm fist. None of us girls wanted to have to deal with her wrath, so we stayed away from Dillon."

Poor Dad. No wonder he wanted to get out of here so badly.

"I'm sure Flavia had been expecting Gabe to follow like the other boys had."

"And it backfired. Is that when Flavia went to the dark side and caused the rift in the group?"

"That's when."

"The fight that night," I reasoned, "really had nothing to do with Priscilla getting together with Gabe."

"Nothing whatsoever. Priscilla was feeling very vulnerable right then. She had this baby and no idea what her life was going to become. Flavia was, and is, very persuasive. She convinced Priscilla that she could get Gabe, but, as you now know, it wasn't to help make Priscilla's life better."

"It was all to mess with Reeva's life."

"Exactly."

I shook my head, once again blown away by human behavior. "The irrational wrath of a teenage girl."

"You know that for Flavia, not being in

control of her public persona is the worst possible punishment."

"Which is probably why Gran sentenced her to just that in the end." I blew out a breath, exhausted by this puzzle. "Because Flavia had to have her way, a girl died. And none of you did anything about it. Except my dad."

Briar stared past me into her garden. "I can't explain our lack of action that night, Jayne. People tend to not want to get involved with other people's conflicts. As teenagers, we were used to adults stepping in to stop our fights."

"That's exactly what Blind Willie was about to do when my dad made his move."

"Perhaps it was morbid curiosity," Briar continued. "Maybe it was because we'd been summoned and told we had to be witnesses. Perhaps we simply wanted to find out how far things would go. Regardless of what happened, I assure you we all suffered greatly for our choices that night."

I couldn't argue with her about that. I'd witnessed street fights with tons of spectators during my time as a patrol officer, and honestly, if I hadn't been a cop I can't say that I would have done anything. Of course, those weren't fights between my lifelong friends. I'd like to think that would have made a difference.

"I want to bring everyone from The Pack together. Including you. I want to go through this one last time to make sure there are no other twists needing to be uncovered. Somehow, this all ties to my grandmother's death and that's the piece that's still missing."

"When and where?"

"The conference room at The Inn just as quickly as everyone can get there."

~~~

It took nearly an hour, even with the help of the walkie-talkies, to get the remaining members of The Pack—Briar, Sugar, Laurel, Honey, Flavia, and Reeva—together in the conference room. It was interesting to watch Flavia and Reeva together. The tension between them was silent but palpable, especially when Reeva took Flavia's preferred chair.

"Why are we here?" Laurel wanted to know.

"I know you have that reunion group taking over The Inn," I acknowledged. "I'll be as fast as I can with this."

I'd had an hour to go over everything in my mind, so it didn't take me long to rehash the how's and whys of the night Priscilla died. Sugar, Honey, Laurel, and Reeva listened raptly, since they hadn't been there to witness the events. Briar nodded in silence, agreeing with me. Flavia sat with a pained expression on her pale face and didn't argue with even a single point.

"There's something that occurred to me as I was putting all the pieces together," I said. "There's one person I keep forgetting in all of this. I was so focused on what happened to Priscilla, I kept forgetting to ask about the baby. What happened to the baby?"

"Velma sent him away," Reeva said.

"How do you know this?" I asked.

"I offered to help her with him," she

explained. "Velma was an older lady, in her sixties at that point, and not able to get around very well. There was no way she could have cared for an infant. I had graduated from high school and was looking for a job, so I asked if she was interested in hiring me as a nanny. She decided it would be too painful to have the child here in the village. He'd be a constant reminder of Priscilla, so she asked her niece to take him."

At least he stayed in the family. "None of you have any idea who the father was?"

For the first time since entering the room Flavia spoke. "You've forgotten one other Pack member. Perhaps you should talk with your father."

Chapter 28

I SPRINTED TO THE STATION AND sent an instant message to my dad. Hope you got the email I sent a few days ago. If a video call is possible, I need to talk to you. It's urgent but not an emergency. It took multiple tries, and when it finally went through, he said he was busy at that moment but could do a video call in two hours.

Those were quite possibly the longest two hours of my life. To pass the time, I wandered the commons and spoke with some tourists, although what we talked about, I couldn't say. I stopped in at Grapes, Grains, and Grub to get lunch to go and brought it back to the station.

"Wasn't sure what you'd want," I told Reed, "but since you're all health nut now, I got you a veggie burger and side salad."

"Why are you buying me lunch?"

Because his mother was a horrible person. "Just felt like paying it forward today."

He gave me a wary glance but let it go at that. "Did you get the answers to all your questions?"

"There are two left, and I'm hoping those will be answered in about a half-hour."

I explained that I would be speaking with my father shortly and while I would be in the station, the only reason I should be disturbed was if the building caught fire. Reed gave me a salute and promised to be on alert for flames.

I sat at my desk, picking at my mushroom and swiss burger and continually checking that the Internet connection was still good. When it was finally time to make the call, the connection wouldn't go through. My heart fell to my feet as I tried again and again. Persistence paid off, and suddenly I was staring at my dad's face. Just that fast, my throat clenched, tears stung my eyes, and every ounce of missing him slammed into me.

Weathered, deeply tanned skin with happy crinkles around his ice-blue eyes . . . my ice-blue eyes. Equal amounts of black and gray in his short hair.

He looked healthy and happy, and I couldn't help but wish he could look that way when he was here.

"Look at my girl." His deep voice was slightly dusty. "Look at how beautiful you are. I like the new haircut."

The chin-length bob wasn't new. I changed it a month or two before coming here, but it was new to him.

"Thanks, Dad. You're looking good, too. Desert life clearly agrees with you."

He flinched the slightest bit, and even though I hadn't meant it as a dig, I felt like a shmuck.

"Where's my grand-dog?"

I pushed the chair back from the desk and patted my lap. Meeka jumped up and inspected the face on the screen. Flat faces confused her, but the wagging of her tail said she recognized the voice.

"I don't know how good the connection is here," he cautioned. "As much as I would love to sit and talk with you all night, let's get right to whatever is bothering you."

I was about to object that there was nothing bothering me, but I had said this was an urgent call. There was no time for candy coating.

As simply and efficiently as I could, for what felt like the hundredth time, I revisited the night that Priscilla died.

"It was ultimately an accident," I concluded, "but Flavia instigated everything. If this was an open case, I'd accuse her of something. Aiding and abetting . . . or, better still, a higher-class felony."

"And I'm sure you would enjoy every moment of it."

"Won't argue that." I smiled at him, and my nerves kicked in. Time to answer one of those two questions. I gripped Meeka's silky coat for comfort. "Look,

444 | SHAWN MCGUIRE

Dad, there are a couple things missing in all of this, and I feel like if I can answer them, I'll be able to figure out who killed Gran."

"Killed her?" He sat straight. "Why do you think someone killed her?"

The further into the contents of Gran's autopsy report I went, the more he slumped back into his chair.

"It wasn't an accident, Dad. Someone killed her. I don't know why, but I'm sure these two deaths are related."

He squared his shoulders as though preparing for battle. "What are your missing pieces?"

"Flavia told me I should ask you who the father of Priscilla's baby was."

From almost 7000 miles away, I watched the tan drain from my father's face.

"Priscilla was going to reveal the truth that night." He looked to the side as his voice broke. He cleared his throat and looked back at me. "We had talked about it the day before the gathering, and I was prepared to stand by her side."

Already knowing the answer to the

question I hadn't yet asked, I pulled Meeka in closer to my chest. "What are you saying?"

"I'm saying that I am the baby's father." He said this evenly, his voice solid now. "I liked Priscilla, but I can't say that I loved her. I had plans to go off to school, maybe see the world, and she didn't want to leave Whispering Pines. I would have done what I could to support the baby. But *she* didn't want me involved."

Meeka squirmed and broke free from my grasp. Guess I held on too tightly. "*Who* didn't want you involved? Priscilla? Her mother?"

"No, your grandmother. She was obsessively concerned with status and appearances then. Everyone treated her like royalty, and it went to her head. Priscilla and I told our parents what had happened and what we wanted to do. Velma was more forgiving and willing to help us come up with a plan. My mother forbade us from telling the truth."

"Does Mom know?"

Deep sorrow joined the weathered

lines on his face. "Do you remember the last time we were in Whispering Pines as a family? You were twelve, I believe, and Rosalyn was eight."

I couldn't help but laughing at the irony of that question. Since I'd arrived here, few days had passed that I hadn't thought of that visit.

"I remember, very well. That was the weekend Rosalyn and I figured out that Gran was Wiccan, although we didn't realize that was the right label at the time. We walked in on her doing a ritual in the room over the garage. Rosalyn told Mom about Gran in her beautiful robe the next morning. Then we left so fast we didn't get to finish eating our waffles. I figured that was what sparked the feud but never understood exactly why."

Dad's head bobbed up and down in a nod. "Your Gran had an awakening of sorts by that time. I think it was age and the fact that Gramps wasn't doing very well. She realized she had fewer years ahead of her than behind. Basically, the guilt of everything she had done surrounding that incident—accusing

Flavia, forcing Rae and Gabe to leave, denying me my son—all caught up with her. She told your mother, against my wishes, what had happened."

The twists just kept coming. "Gran told Mom about the baby? Without your permission?"

"If I would've told your mom from the start, that might have made a difference. By that point, it didn't matter that it was Gran who told her and not me. Georgia couldn't get past the fact that I'd kept that secret from her all those years. I never could forgive your grandmother for what she'd done." He grew quiet and stared into the distance. "If I had to guess, Gran was doing a healing ritual that night. Probably asking the moon to protect her children."

"The Goddess Hecate," I mumbled, recalling some of Gran's words from that night. "Is that why you're always overseas? Because things got too stressful between you and Mom?"

"I suppose that's part of it."

"And because you didn't save Priscilla?"

449 | SHAWN MCGUIRE

He rubbed his hands over his face. "To this day, I have nightmares about that moment. I vividly remember standing there telling myself to do something, to move. Guess it was because I never for one second thought anything like that was going to happen to her."

"That's how I felt in the moments before Frisky died. I could have saved her, but I didn't believe Randy would really pull the trigger."

This time, fatherly concern showed on his face. "Sounds like the next time I'm stateside, you and I need to have a heart-to-heart discussion."

"I'd like that. A lot."

"Did I answer your question?"

"You did. I still don't know who murdered Gran."

"I'm sure you'll keep digging."

"Did you ever have any contact with your son?" I stumbled over the word, hardly believing that I had a brother. That kind of blew my mind.

"My understanding was that he grew up with Velma's niece. I never met him, but I heard that he got to spend time in

Whispering Pines with his grandmother as a child."

In that instant, the last piece presented itself. It hovered in front of me, ready to fall into place. In my mind, I held my hand beneath that spinning piece, keeping it from completing the puzzle. I had one more question to ask, and the last thing I wanted was to hear the answer. I set daughter Jayne aside and summoned cop Jayne; she could handle this.

"Dad, do you know the baby's name?"

"I do. Priscilla named him Donovan."

Chapter 29

ON MY WAY OVER TO QUIN'S clothing shop, Lily Grace's vision became clear to me. *A porcelain baby doll. The old-fashioned kind with those dead-looking eyes that open and close.* If I blended all the facts in that vision together—that Donovan made porcelain dolls, that he was the baby I'd been wondering about, and that his mother was dead—Lily Grace was spot on again.

I entered the shop, took one look at Donovan behind the counter, and almost threw up my mushroom swiss. Honestly? He was my brother? If I had to have a secret sibling, couldn't I get a cool one? I mean, I'd already suffered twenty-two years with Rosalyn.

He saw me from across the shop and gave me his typical bored eye roll. He must have sensed a different vibe coming off me this time because he looked again and straightened a little. I waited patiently while he finished with his customer and then went over to him.

"We need to have a little talk, Donovan."

"No time. I'm busy as you can clearly see."

"This is official business," I said evenly. "I need you to come with me."

"And I told you to go away."

"I'll give you one more chance."

He turned his back on me, so I removed the handcuffs from the cargo pocket on my right thigh, grabbed his right arm, and pulled it behind him. Gasps and expressions of shock rose from his customers. It had been a while since I'd cuffed anyone, so the application wasn't as smooth as I would have liked, but after a momentary fumbling, I had both cuffs on him. For a split second, I realized his hands looked like Dad's and my stomach roiled again.

"Don't make me pull out my Glock," I demanded. "I really don't want to do that with all these people around, so just come with me now."

At my feet, Meeka growled. If he was smart, Donovan wouldn't put the sharpness of her tiny teeth to the test.

He walked in silence as I led him out of the shop and the quarter mile to the station where Reed was on guard in case Donovan caused any problems. I directed Donovan through the station to the interview room and to a simple metal chair.

"If I take the cuffs off, will there be a problem?" I asked as I set my voice recorder on the table pushed up against the outside wall. "Because I can leave you cuffed."

He said, "No problem," and nothing else.

Reed motioned me over to the doorway. "Are you sure you can do this?"

I was too close, I knew that, but Reed didn't know how to interview. There was no way I could risk letting this part get messed up.

"Yeah, I'm good." Before he walked away, I added, "Stand in the doorway here and observe, would you?"

He paused, analyzing my motive. "You need a witness?"

"Best to cover all the bases on this one."

The details of Donovan's mother's death weren't pertinent, so I didn't rehash the events at the Meditation Circle again. I did tell him about the conversation I'd just had with Dad.

"How long have you known that he was your father?" I asked.

"About seven months," Donovan replied.

"Who told you?"

"My grandmother. She obviously knew from the start. Wait"—he held up a hand—"I should specify, my grandma Velma told me. Grandma Lucy never once made contact with me."

Just when I thought I couldn't get sicker, he reminded me that Gran was his grandmother. It was hard enough to share her with Rosalyn.

"Seven months ago? That's when you moved here. Is that why you moved here? To connect with the O'Shea branch?"

He scowled and shook his head in tiny, crisp movements. "Good Goddess, no. I moved here because my grandmother had died and left the store and her house to me." He paused and gave me a sinister smile. "As you well know, when you go through someone's house, you can come across interesting items. One of the things I came across was a letter addressed to me."

He must've known this day would come because he didn't fight telling his story at all. In fact, he seemed to revel in doing so. Or, more likely, he was simply eager to rub it all in my face.

"What the letter said, in a nutshell, was that it was time for me to know the truth about my lineage. Lucy had forced Grandma to remain silent for years. She threatened her with kicking her out of the village if she ever said a word about Dillon being my father."

"Weren't you worried about her doing

the same to you?"

"I had a home which I've held on to. I had a job which I took a leave of absence from. I could easily go back to both should the need arise. When I got here, though, I quickly became friends with Flavia and shared the letter with her."

"Amazing how scum attracts more scum." I paused for a nanosecond, remembering that Reed was standing in the doorway. Just that fast, I dismissed the concern; Reed seemed to understand the truth about his mother. "Did Flavia know? Did Priscilla ever tell her the truth about who the baby's daddy was?"

"Turns out my mother loved my grandmother dearly and would've done anything to protect her. The only person Priscilla told was Velma."

He was basking in this moment. Screw that. Time to get right to the important part.

"You killed Lucy O'Shea, didn't you?"

While inspecting his fingernails, he said, "Yes, I was responsible for Grandma Lucy's death. Want to know how?"

The fact that he didn't hesitate to

spout the truth astounded me. I crossed the room to double check that my recorder was recording, and to quash the fury rising in my chest, before saying, "I already know how she died. I just didn't know who did it or why. You hit her on the head, specifically the left side of her forehead. There were no other marks on her body, so the impact was hard enough to kill her. Then you placed her in the bathtub to make it look like she drowned, but you hadn't anticipated Dr. Bundy. Actually, not to knock Dr. Bundy's skills, but a first-year student could have figured this one out. There was no water in her lungs, she couldn't have drowned."

"And still, no one caught me."

"Wrong. I caught you. Underestimated your little sis, didn't you?"

This time, his smug smile faltered for a beat.

"Okay, we know how," I said. "Why did you do it?"

"You're close but off just a bit on your theory, *Sis*." Donovan held his thumb and forefinger a half inch apart. "Let's back up a little so you fully understand. This all started because I wanted Lucy to finally claim me."

"Oh!" I placed one hand over my heart and wiped away a nonexistent tear with the other. "Poor little Donovan. Just wanted someone to love you?"

He arched an eyebrow and stared blankly at me, making me feel like a bratty little sister. Regular Jayne poked Cop Jayne and told her to get back to work.

"I admit it," he said without apology, "I was a wounded little boy. I grew up knowing that my father's family wouldn't claim me and that my mother's family had passed me off like a box of hand-me-down outfits. I wanted the satisfaction of hearing the O'Sheas admit I was blood."

I knew what it was like to grow up with my father being absent. Still, I knew he loved me even though he wasn't around much. I couldn't imagine the pain of feeling unloved.

"I figured Grandma Lucy would insist on proof of paternity," Donovan continued, "so I entered the house one time when I knew she wasn't there. No, I didn't break in, she never locked her doors."

I hated that he knew that about her.

"I searched the house until I found the room that was obviously dear old Dad's, found an old hat with strands of his hair stuck inside, and sent it off for DNA testing." He leaned back, appearing totally at ease. "Did you know that you can get results from a paternity test in as little as twelve hours? I didn't pay for the express results. It's not like I was going anywhere, and I didn't expect Lucy was either. Five days later, I had proof that Dillon O'Shea was my father."

"Then what?" I asked. "You went over to the house with your paternity claim check in hand? What did you expect Gran would do? Fall to her knees or wrap you in a hug, proclaim the error of her ways, and welcome her long-lost grandson into the family fold?"

"Don't be dramatic, Jayne." Donovan rolled his eyes, bored with me again. "I fully expected that she'd kick me out of the house. Quite possibly, she'd call the sheriff to have me arrested. I told her, all

ORIGINAL SECRETS | 459

I wanted was for her to admit the truth, and I'd leave."

"And then what? You'd sue the family for rights to the village?"

His face brightened. "What a great idea. Believe it or not, I'd never thought of that. Two thousand acres divided by three would be"—he glanced up at the ceiling, calculating—"666 acres per heir. Unless there are more of us out there, of course."

I glared at him and refused to acknowledge the crass statement. "You had your DNA results, you had your truth. Why kill her?"

He leaned forward and said, "Here's where your theory goes off-track. You see, I didn't hit her." He sat back again. "I have to say, Lucy was one feisty little lady. Those little blue fingernails of hers were mighty sharp. She got me right here."

He indicated three faint scar lines on his left cheek. I'd noticed them before but thought nothing of them. Now, I loved them.

"You say you didn't hit her, so what happened? You knocked a seventy-some-

460 | SHAWN MCGUIRE

year-old woman to the ground?"

"I'm not a heathen, Jayne. She charged at me, and I defended myself. She'd already gotten my left cheek, I wasn't going to let her get the right as well. For all I knew, she'd try to gouge my eyes out next. All I did was hold up an arm to keep her from attacking me again. The impact of running into me caused her to fall and hit her head against that gorgeous antique tub."

The irony of Gran dying in basically the same way Priscilla had didn't escape me. I wouldn't give him the satisfaction of telling him that, though.

I needed a moment before asking my next question. "Did she die instantly?"

"No, but I thought she had. Turned out she'd only lost consciousness for a few minutes. When she came to, she had an awful headache. She threw up a number of times." He tapped the base of his nose. "Liquid of some kind was draining from her nose."

The autopsy indicated one of her pupils was dilated, indicating a traumatic brain injury.

"At one point, she had a seizure." Donovan frowned and shook his head. "I knew it wasn't good."

My throat constricted and I couldn't speak for a few seconds. "Did you even try to help her?"

"Sure, but you know how impossible it is to get medical attention here. Maybe with Effie's granddaughter at the healing center now, things will be better, but at that time there wasn't much that could be done for dear Gran."

I clenched my fists hard, pressing my nails into my palms. I focused on that pain rather than my anger. I wouldn't hit this guy; I wouldn't do anything that would risk him getting off on a technicality.

"Why put her in the bathtub?"

"She laid down on her bed. That's where she died, if you're curious. Guess we could've left her there, but considering that lump on her head, a slip and fall into the tub seemed logical. Hadn't thought of the water in the lungs snafu."

I stared at him, mute, until he looked me in the eye. "What do you mean *we*?

Who was there with you?"

He paled as he realized what he'd said. "No one. I was there alone."

I could almost hear Flavia telling him that he was never to mention her involvement in this.

"New topic," I said before I completely lost it on this guy. I pulled out the picture of the full stop mark from Gran's file.

"You were the last one to see Gran alive. How did this mark end up on her?"

He thought for a while, absolutely silent while the gears of his brain spun for an answer. Finally, he let out a heavy sigh. "That was Flavia. Like the harlequins I make are my thing, that mark is her personal send off to the next life. I have no idea what it means."

"Flavia was at the house with you then."

He refused to agree or disagree with the statement. I mentally added desecration of a corpse to the list of things I could have her charged with.

"Did Flavia trash my house?" I asked.

"I don't know."

"Did she draw sigils all over my

walls?"

"I don't know. I'm not a hitman, Jayne, or a thug for hire. If she was involved with any of that, I have no knowledge of it." He leaned forward then with an eager look on his face. "New topic. Tell me about our sister. What's Rosalyn like?"

I'd had enough. I couldn't stand being in the same room with the man for a second longer. I read him his rights, locked him in a jail cell, and called the County Sheriff's Office to have someone come and take him away.

Chapter 30

HALF AN HOUR AFTER DEPUTY EVAN Atkins took Donovan away, my phone rang.

"Jayne, it's Evan."

"You don't sound happy. Why don't you sound happy?" Even as I asked the question, I knew I was going to hate the answer.

"He escaped."

"What? Who escaped? Donovan? Are you kidding me? What happened?"

"He was in the booking room. We took off the zip cuffs and used a standard set to cuff him to a table. I left him locked in the room and while I was gone, he was able to break the chain on the cuffs. Twisted it or something. I have no idea how he did it. I knew I should've left the zip cuffs on him. Anyway, I went to get him to move him to a cell. He was waiting by the door, ambushed me as I re-entered, and locked me inside the room." He paused, sounding pained to have to tell me this. "By the time I got someone to let me out of the room, Donovan had walked out of the building."

"Walked out. No one tried to stop him?"

"You know how small our station is."

I did. The pentacle garden was bigger.

Atkins released a heavy sigh. "It was the front desk clerk's first day, and he wasn't prepared for this kind of situation. None of us were. We put out an APB, and everyone is looking for him. He still has that one cuff on and is an easy guy to identify. I can't imagine he'll be free for long. I just wanted to warn you because—"

"Because he might return to Whispering Pines and come after me. I get it."

"Or he might not," Evan tried to

soothe my concerns. "I don't think he's out to hurt you or anyone else. He had plenty of opportunity to do that if that was his intent."

"True." This only minimally eased my mind. "He told me he kept his old home. I don't know if it's a house or an apartment and I don't know where it is. It's a long shot, but you may want to check there."

"On it. We'll locate it and send someone over there."

"I should contact Madison PD and let them know to keep an eye on my mom and sister. Guess I should contact my mom as well."

"Better to err on the side of caution."

"Evan, are you okay? Did he hurt you?"

"Got a few good shots to my ribs and gut. I've got a lump on my head where it hit the wall, but no concussion. I can feel a headache coming on, and I'll be sore tomorrow, but for now, I'm good."

"Sorry to hear you were attacked."

He made a sound that meant, *no big deal.* "I'm going to follow up with everyone and see where we are with this.

I'll be in contact later. Don't hesitate to call if you need help."

I hung up with Evan and then called my captain in Madison. He said he'd already seen the APB but hadn't realized it was associated with me. He assured me he'd give it special attention. Then, I called my mother.

"This is the second time in a week you've called me at work."

Before she could hang up, I blurted, "Mom, there's a killer on the loose. You and Rosalyn need to take precautions." She remained mute the entire time I explained to her what had happened and what she needed to do. "Are you still there? Do you have any questions?"

"I'm here. I'm trying to decide if your being in that profession makes things better or worse."

"There's a little more to this. I spoke to Dad on a video call earlier today." I told her who the escapee was. "I wasn't looking to get secrets from Dad. It was a cop thing that turned into a personal thing."

After a short hesitation, "That's the

excuse you pull out whenever you have to tell me something I won't like. That it's a cop thing." This time, she remained quiet longer. "I knew this would come out at some point. It's part of the reason I wanted to just be rid of that house. Part of the reason that if I never return to that village again, I'll be fine with it."

"This happened way before you and Dad even met."

"I realize that," she snapped. "By never telling me about it, he effectively lied to me for almost two decades. And now, all these years later, because he and his mother decided to keep this secret rather than deal with the truth, my daughters and I are in danger." She inhaled a shaky breath. "He should have told me. I shouldn't have learned this from his mother." Then more quietly, "She had no right."

"I'm really sorry, Mom."

"I need to get back to work."

This was the most intimate conversation we'd had in years. Maybe ever. I wanted to keep talking. I wanted her to explain to me that this was why she'd been so cold, so distant, so shut off for all these years. Right now, though, that wasn't fair of me to expect. This thing that shook her world sixteen years ago was out, and she needed time to process how to handle that.

"Promise me," I said, "that you'll be aware of your surroundings. Don't take any foolish risks. I don't think they have the manpower to station anyone near the house at this point, but if you suspect anything, if you have any reason to believe Donovan is near you, call Captain Grier directly."

"You told me this already."

"I felt like it was worth repeating. Do you want me to call Rosalyn?"

"I'll call her," she answered immediately. "It's bad enough that you know this, I don't want her knowing it as well. Not yet. I'll come up with something to tell her." She exhaled. "Don't worry, you girls are the most important things in my life. As I have been since you were little, I will protect both of you no matter what. That means not letting anything happen to myself so I can be here for you."

I was too stunned to reply. Rosalyn and I were the most important things in her life? I'd never felt that, she'd never given me a reason to feel it, but I believed her.

"I've got to get back to work . . . and call your sister." She hesitated before adding, "Be careful, Jayne."

I was able to croak out goodbye before hanging up. My mother had never been one to express feelings and despite the discussion we'd just had, I didn't expect that to change. I was okay with that for now. I had all the change I could handle for the moment.

To satisfy my own curiosity, I checked the status of the APB. And then again ten minutes later. And ten minutes after that. Maybe it was best that I just go home and try to think about something else. I still had more than twenty years' worth of journals I could read. Or maybe I'd just veg in front of the television and watch a stupid movie.

"Mother," Reed said from the main room. "What are you doing here?"

"I need to speak with Sheriff O'Shea. Please leave."

"Sorry, Flavia," I said as I stepped out of my office. "I make the rules in this building. Reed is welcome to stay and hear whatever it is you have to say."

Reed closed the gap between us and spoke in a low tone. "Actually, it's after five and I'm supposed to meet Lupe for dinner. Do you mind?" He tilted his head at the backdoor, indicating he'd like to leave.

"Not at all," I said, matching his tone. "One thing, Lupe wanted to help with this investigation, but I kind of shut her out. Is she mad at me?"

Reed flushed slightly. "You say that like I would know. How would I know?"

I grinned at him. "Right. Go, have fun on your date. Or whatever it is. Would you do one thing for me? Swing past Quin's first and let Ivy know that her boss won't be coming in anymore?"

He gave me a little salute and left the building.

I turned to face Flavia and gestured at the chair next to Reed's desk. "Would you like to sit?"

"No. This won't take long," Flavia informed. "I came here for two things. First, I expect that you will keep everything you have learned to yourself. None of what you have dug up is anyone else's business. Things happened forty years ago that I am not proud of.

"Second, I expect you will leave me alone now. I told you I was not responsible for Yasmine's death. I told you I was not responsible for Lucy's death. Now you have your truth."

I stared at her long enough to make her squirm. "You must have been absolutely giddy the day my grandmother died. To carry around all that hate for so long, I can't imagine how free you must have felt."

Flavia didn't respond.

"I know you didn't cause Gran's death. Sounds like it was an accident. Just like Priscilla's. You were involved with both, though. Donovan told me that you were there to help him figure out what to do with Gran's body after she died."

He hadn't, but he practically did.

Besides, I wanted to see her reaction. Maybe she'd confess.

"A complete and total lie. I told you, I was sick that night."

"Right, your alibi. Look, you may not be a murderer, but at the very least you assisted in covering up Gran's death. And according to witnesses, you instigated and encouraged the fight between Priscilla and Rae, which makes you partially responsible for that outcome."

Her pursed lips twitched, like she was dying to comment but wouldn't let herself.

"When Donovan arrived in Whispering Pines," I continued, "and told you what he'd learned about his mother, I'm willing to bet you instigated his revenge plot."

"A bet you would lose," she hissed.

"I also think that you instigated the vandalism of my house. Donovan told me that you drew the full stop marks on both Yasmine and my grandmother. The same marks I found on my walls. I may not be able to prove any of that right now," I shrugged, "I may not ever be able to prove it, but trust me, for as long as we both are in this village, the last thing I'll do is leave you alone. On the contrary, I'll have an eagle eye on you, and if the opportunity for me to take you down ever presents, I promise you I will. Remember, the O'Sheas still own the land you live on."

Flavia stood and tried to stare me down but got no satisfaction from me. With a sniff, she spun on her heel and left the building.

Meeka sat across the room, staring at me.

"I know, that was a little childish. But it felt really good!"

Before going home, we stopped by the businesses along the Fairy Path and made a loop around the commons to let everyone know what had happened with Donovan. If he dared to step a toe back in this village, I wanted everyone to be prepared to act.

I timed it so my last stop would be Shoppe Mystique as it closed. I needed a few minutes of Morgan time before heading home. We settled into the reading room with mugs of "Chill Out" tea, and I caught her up on the Donovan drama.

"I never know what to expect when you stop in," Morgan said.

"I promise, one day I'll come in as a customer."

"Or just visit as my friend." We sat there drinking tea and enjoying the silence for a while, and then Morgan asked, "Shouldn't you be getting home to Tripp?"

"It may be too late for that." I told her what I had witnessed yesterday morning and last night.

"You think the man who is obviously crazy about you has moved on after only a few weeks? I don't buy it. I think you're scared of your feelings for him and are looking for any reason to avoid risking your heart again."

She sounded like Jayne in the mirror.

"I've been sleeping with those crystals under my pillow. You told me they would help me see the truth. Maybe that's what I saw between him and Alex."

"Sometimes, like secrets in this village,

the truth is buried deep. I know that becoming sheriff and fixing that house are only part of the reason you want to stay in Whispering Pines. Dig deeper, Jayne. Don't be afraid to take a chance."

Chapter 31

ALMOST AS THOUGH HE KNEW I wanted to talk, Tripp was waiting on the sundeck for me when I got home. I told him I needed to change clothes and would be right out. Two minutes later, I sat in the chair closest to him. I handed him a fresh beer, and he handed me a plate of barbecued ribs, grilled corn on the cob, and seasoned fries. Knowing that once I started talking I wouldn't likely be able to stop, I ate my dinner while it was hot. Besides, I was nervous and not sure how to say what I needed to say.

Once I'd taken my last bite and before

any other topic could come up, I wiped my fingers, sticky with barbecue sauce, on a wet wipe he had set on a side table and told him what had happened with Donovan.

"Are you okay?" he asked, concern heavy on his face.

"I'm shocked to learn that I have a brother, especially a scummy one like Donovan. I'm relieved to know the truth about what happened to Gran. I'm devastated that she suffered like she did at the end. I'm disappointed to learn that she wasn't the person I thought she was."

"It's always hard when we learn our parents are actual, fallible humans, isn't it?"

Tripp had recently learned that his mother, after abandoning him when he was thirteen, had died two years ago from a drug overdose. If anyone understood the shock of learning the truth about a family member, it was Tripp.

"Maybe she was just going through a bad patch at that time."

"She might not have been the woman you thought she was, but that doesn't mean she wasn't the grandmother you believed her to be. Everyone wears a different persona depending on who they're with."

That's almost exactly what Briar had told me.

"Are we done with that topic? Can I bring up something else?" As soon as I nodded, he said, "You're angry at me. What did I do?"

My heart was pounding. Did I really want to open this up? I didn't, but I had to know the truth.

"Is there something going on between you and Alex?"

"She works on the crew, so there's that." He looked closer at me. "Wait, you mean *between* us? You think I'm interested in her in some way other than being her boss? Are you serious?"

"I came down for breakfast yesterday and the two of you were shoulder-to-shoulder."

"We were discussing tiling options for the bathrooms." He looked confused, shocked, and a little offended. "I promise, all I was thinking about was bathrooms.

There was nothing remotely romantic going on."

"She's beautiful."

"Is she?" He moved a little closer, his left knee bumping against my right, and looked me dead in the eye. "I hadn't noticed."

My mouth went dry. "Don't lie to me."

"I'm not lying to you. I never have, never will. Not sure how to convince you, but it's the truth." He gave me a look that made my heart stutter. "All I can see is you, Jayne. Since that first night when we went to dinner together at The Inn, remember?"

I smiled. "I remember."

"We were waiting for our food and you started talking about the possible ways Yasmine Long had died, and I knew there was something different about you. You became indignant when I told you that the council wouldn't approve a job for me, and I thought, there's a woman who cares about others. You explained how the negativity well works, and I thought, there's a woman with a playful side. You looked me in the eye, and I thought, there's the most beautiful woman I've ever seen."

My voice wouldn't rise above a whisper and I could barely breathe as I said, "I'm a little bit afraid."

He took my hands in his. "Now *that* is a lie. I know for a fact that you're a lot afraid. But you know that I—"

I moved to the edge of my seat. "I know that you would never purposely hurt me."

"Never."

I stood, and he stood with me, my hands still in his. "Morgan told me that if I wanted to know the truth, I needed to dig deep."

"Did you? Did you dig deep enough?"

"Almost."

I pulled my hands from his, wrapped my arms around his neck, and kissed him long and deep. His lips were soft, his mouth urgent. I grabbed handfuls of his blonde curls and held on so he couldn't pull away. I pressed my body against his. Electric tingles coursed through me as his hands slid from my shoulders, down my back, over my hips, and back up again.

When we were both breathless and reaching the point of being unable to stop, I held one last long kiss to his mouth and pulled away.

He rested his forehead against mine, his breathing heavy. "I like it when you go digging."

I laughed. "I know this is going to sound insane after that kiss, but I need to take this slow."

He parted his lips, surely about to say something about how we had been taking it slow, so I placed a finger to his mouth and locked eyes with his light hazel ones.

"One thing I know I can trust," I began, "are my instincts, and my instincts are telling me that we could be really good together. I want to go slow and take in every minute of us. I want to explore us without rushing. I want us to keep slowly unfolding to each other the way we have been. I want to be with you without missing anything." A feeling of extreme vulnerability hit me. "Is that okay?"

He pushed my finger away, placed his hands on either side of my face, and kissed me long and slow again. "I'm along on this ride, every step of the way. If you want a slow, winding journey, you've got it."

There was something in his tone. "But?"

"But I have no intention of taking it easy on you. Fair warning: the next time you're around when I'm coming out of the shower, I may not bother with a towel."

At that moment, a single blast of wind blew in off the lake. It made the pines lean back-and-forth, side-to-side, their branches and needles whispering together. Almost like they were cheering in agreement.

Dear Reader,

Thank you for reading ORIGINAL SECRETS, book three in the Whispering Pines series. Word of mouth is the very best promotion. Please consider leaving an honest review. It doesn't have to be long, a sentence or two is great! Not only will you help other readers find my work, you'll help me to be able to continue writing more books!

Best wishes,
Shawn

Suspense and fantasy author Shawn McGuire started writing after seeing the first Star Wars movie (that's episode IV) as a kid. She couldn't wait for the next installment to come out so wrote her own. Sadly, those notebooks are long lost, but her desire to tell a tale is as strong now as it was then. She grew up in the beautiful Mississippi River town of Winona, Minnesota, called the Milwaukee area of Wisconsin (Go Pack Go!) home for many years, and now lives in Colorado where she is a total homebody. She loves to read, craft, cook and bake, and spend time in the spectacular Rocky Mountains. You can learn more about Shawn's work on her website www.Shawn-McGuire.com

Made in the USA
Columbia, SC
07 May 2022

60096091R00293